Way of Life

BY A. HAMILTON GIBBS

After the First World War, A. Hamilton Gibbs spoke out for the loyalty and decency of the younger generation. The book was SOUNDINGS, a leading best seller in the year of its publication. It was followed by other novels notable for their sincerity, their idealism. Many readers remember with warm pleasure LABELS, HARNESS, CHANCES, and the rest. Now Major Gibbs speaks again and with equal power for the generation that fought World War II.

Of this generation, Bill Thatcher was an American who fell in love with an English girl, Minchen, daughter of a wounded and decorated veteran of World War I. And Minchen fell completely in love with Bill. These were talented, sensitive and intelligent young people who, unmolested, would surely work out their way of life to the satisfaction of themselves and others. Their lives should have had no more connection with slaughter than the old English village where Minchen lived, in which the thatched cottages slept peacefully apart from the routes of the bombers. But war is in the background of their love, its harsh discord echoes through their days, their hopes and plans.

Will Minchen and Bill, deprived of the right freely to choose their way of life, rebelling bitterly against the intrusions of war, be able to work out their future in spite of it? In this timely and compelling novel the hope and optimism of youth are contrasted with the disillusionment of the older generation, represented by Minchen's father, who although ostensibly withdrawn from the world has acquired the long-range view of the world's problems and needs.

Way of Life

Way of Life

by

A. HAMILTON GIBBS

Boston

LITTLE, BROWN AND COMPANY

1947

FIRST EDITION

Published September 1947

Published simultaneously
in Canada by McClelland and Stewart Limited

PRINTED IN THE UNITED STATES OF AMERICA

Way of Life

Part One

THE city lay black and dormant in the moonless night.

A voice spoke over a telephone.

Thousands of men staggered out, cursing, torn from a snatch of sleep, to man searchlights and guns.

The silence was broken by the wail of sirens.

The sky became filled with a vast permeating drone, a million beams of light, bursting shells; the city a trembling chaos of gunfire, punctured by colossal explosions as racks of bombs tore into its vitals, spewing up bodies, buildings, streets, in sheets of flame. . . .

The droning dwindled and presently the gunfire slackened off . . . ceased.

The All Clear sounded.

In the moonless night the city was a blazing torch.

CHAPTER ONE

THE VILLAGE WAS CALLED LITTLE MINCHEN.

An American paratrooper, amused by the name, had wandered up from the camp down the hill, some five-foot-ten of him, lean, hard and straight. He walked as a panther in new country, collected, instantaneous; eyes and ears, every sense, receiving, weighing, rejecting, accepting. His hair — service caps don't hide it all — was dark and short above good cheekbones and a firm mouth. Ordinary enough? All right, but what is it about a face in the subway that calls one's eyes back for a second look? Some quality, some possibility, some gift of God. This boy had it.

He stood still now in the middle of the village street, looking, listening too, marveling, letting it soak in, his thought idling . . . the corners of his eyes and mouth relaxing from their tightness. . . . Older than time, and neat, and the quiet of it! God, it gives you a catch in the throat! Apart from those damn planes all you can hear is bees, and birds, and once in a while the voices of children that you can't see, and the beech leaves rustling, and will you get an eyeful of the flowers everywhere?

He let out a trickle of cigarette smoke, flicked off the ash. . . . The hush to it is as though you'd stepped into an open-air cathedral, the trees the pillars, so that you want to take off your hat and walk on tiptoe, only you'd feel like a dope doing it. . . .

For all that, the feeling was right, sound, and he went on softly, knowing himself a trespasser, and glad of it, for he was stepping back through quiet centuries and half thought he might see a shadow of some Elizabethan yeoman through any one of the open doors of the bulging cottages, their thatched roofs dripping with flowers and their outside crossbeams blackened by weather.

And it isn't dead either, he thought on. You can hear the kids still, and there's a cat on that doorstep, curled up, sleeping, safe . . . and an old dog, good and old, with his head on his paws but one eye looking at me; and the wisps of smoke mean cooking, and women — lucky women — whose men will come back from the fields at sundown, unwounded . . . and they will sit out on their doorsteps in shirt sleeves, smoking, and not talking much. . . . You don't have to, here. It's it . . . the magic mountain . . . the sort of place some men might have been looking for all their lives, perhaps without knowing it, and of course never finding it; the place they dreamed of when life had been pushing them too hard and they wanted to duck, to cover up for a while until they could get back enough guts to go on with it . . . or even, if they were pushed beyond the limits, to say to themselves: "The hell with guts! If they'd let me in here, I'd stay and never come out!"

Perhaps that was all tripe. Perhaps it was just what he was bringing to it, having found his way there just a hair under par. But as he went on, his eyes drawn right and left, he told himself that it was like balm pouring over him and not letting up at any step. He could feel things inside him melting and being washed away; and from the outside there came flowing in an unexpected great kindliness for his fellow man. He knew, with conviction, that here there could be neither murder nor even meanness; that behind those open doors no man would ever round on his wife, nor any woman nag her husband; that the children they bred — the ones he could hear — would never pull the wings off butterflies, had never tied tin cans to the tails of those cats. . . .

He smiled at himself at that. Kids are hellpups anywhere, but all the same it's the feeling I had, and it's good, and I'll hang on to it against everything I know. . . .

The cottages were on either side and the street curled along between them. At the left the ground went on up sharply, dense with beeches; but on his right he saw that the ridge, which was the village, dropped steeply. Down there was the ribbon of road up which he had climbed. It spilled between hedged fields, ended abruptly at the main highway that went like a thin white bar across miles and miles of rolling country spread out like an infinite series of different-sized rugs.

It dawned upon him gradually that he had seen no church, no chapel, and not a single shop. . . . Of course not. What for? They would spoil it. When these people needed anything, they went down the hill, probably on bikes if they were young. Certainly they wouldn't tolerate cars roaring about, honking! There was no hurry here, not the least feel of it. It told you that the earth took its time and the four seasons came and went. And for all the jeeps down below and the planes overhead — damn them — it still took nine months to bring a child into the world, didn't it? — or a calf for that matter. These people knew that. They were holding on to it. Let the people down in Friar's Dene have their roaring traffic, and their church and their chapel, and school and bank, and their choice of "pubs" and movies and all the shops, and now, of course, by the nature of things, their army camp . . . the army camp . . . my army camp!

At the thought his eyebrows drew together again. For a brief moment, by the magic of Little Minchen, he had mercifully forgotten it. Now it was all at once back again, like a gyrating maggot in the otherwise sweet apple of his mind — the thing that had been pushing him, the steady pressure, the day-and-night hum of the engines of his trade, the engines of death, now the essential accompaniment of life. . . . As he glanced down at his uniform, he gave a short odd laugh. Wasn't it probably his shroud? Not that it was of the slightest importance in the long run . . . not any more so, that is, than the venereal they'd have to go to work on when the troops marched out of Friar's Dene, or the crop of bastard children that would come later. . . .

The click of an opening latch came sharply, cut like a merciful knife into his thought.

There was a tall man, a six-footer, coming out from behind a hedge of ramblers, a good-looking guy with a swell tan . . . but those lines in his face were not put there by the mere passing of time. And that cane in his left hand . . . why his left? Ah, I see. The limp . . . and his right hand, for God's sake, is one of those elaborately manufactured things that work on wires, or springs, or however they do work — the kind they stuck on a man after the last war, the kind they've vastly improved on for this war! Yeah!

And the paratrooper, young and unbroken, tempered like steel, was moved. "A leftover, poor lug!" he muttered. And then a thought laid itself like a cold hand on his stomach. "God! Suppose I should . . ."

But once again gloom inside him was interrupted; for the big man, shirt open at the neck and sleeves rolled up on at least one magnificent forearm, came to a slightly limping stop at he reached the soldier, nodded at him and smiled.

Marvelous things happened to those lines in his face, so that the soldier found confirmation. . . . Guess I was right if this is the kind they breed up here! . . .

The man spoke. "Lovely day, isn't it? . . . Your first time in the village?"

The soldier's eyes were on the other man's, boring in . . . liking what he found. He nodded eagerly, grinned. "And I've fallen in love with it!" he said. "I've never seen anything like it in my life, but in an odd sort of way that I can't explain it's like . . . well . . . like coming home."

The older man nodded also, quietly, in perfect understanding. "I rather thought it had got hold of you," he said. "I was watching you as you came along. It hit me just like that twenty-five years ago."

"And of course you've been here ever since!"

"Of course!"

Young man and older man smiled at each other — a bridge between the two of them.

The older man crossed it first. "Look here," he said, "my wife and I were just about to sit down to a cup of tea. I wonder if you'd care to join us?"

A second's withdrawal. . . . It was the uniform of course — or was it? Surely it was more than that! . . . He wanted it to be more than that! . . . "Thank you, sir!" he said. "I certainly would."

"Splendid!" said the big man. "By the way, my name's Wainwright." He shifted the cane to his cork hand and held out his left.

H'mh'm! Awkward ass, taking his left with your right! Ought to have known! It was like calling attention to it, damn it! . . . Pretty swell of him to pretend not to notice. . . . "My name's Thatcher, Willard Thatcher — generally Bill."

Wainwright's eyebrows went up slightly. "Ah!" he said. "Perhaps that explains something. There have been Thatchers in these parts for a hundred years or so. . . . Come along in, Bill." He held the gate for the American to pass.

"You don't say!" said Bill. "Thanks!" As he entered the gate his eyes reached out to the cottage. The thatch was a foot thick and climbing roses went leaping up between the windows as though they were trying to see in, and on the flagged path was a large yellow cat licking himself, with swallows flashing and weaving a foot above his head. . . . The whole thing was like music! . . . He turned to the older man. "You know," he said, "I don't really believe it. I shall probably wake up in a minute."

The big man smiled. "Does it look so very different?"

"It's not that!" said Bill. "It's—everything. The place—the day. It's you—your asking me in." He smiled. Odd how easy it was to open up to him. "For another thing, this is the first home I'll have been into since I left mine a year and a half ago. That's one hell of a long time, as you know!"

The big man looked at him quietly. "I do know. It's long enough to mark a man!" he said. "Suppose I go first and show you the way?"

He passed in at the open door.

Bill Thatcher followed.

THERE was no sound in the village. It was wrapped in sleep.

No sound . . . until grumbling, sleepy machine gunners flopped down on the hard cobbles at either end of the road through and set up their weapons, like terriers waiting at a rat-hole.

Then a tank came clattering and rattling into position. From armored slits projected the nozzles of flame throwers, one facing right, the other left.

At a command, the flame throwers roared into action while the tank advanced slowly down the village street.

Some bedroom windows were open; the rest might just as well have been. The white-hot flame was as all-devouring as divine vengeance, the screams as impotent as those of the damned. The smell of burning houses became tainted with the smell of roasted flesh. Here and there, from doorways, like rats smoked out, men and women, children in their arms, dashed blindly . . . to be dropped on the cobbles by the gaily chattering machine guns. . . .

Soon there would be no sound again in the rubble of that village. It would be wrapped in eternal sleep.

CHAPTER TWO

LONG ENOUGH TO MARK A MAN. . . . WHO SHOULD KNOW BETTER than this man with the limp and the cork hand?

John Gordon Wainwright, known in Little Minchen as "cockeyed" Wainwright, was all the correct things — Eton, Oxford, a Blue, an officer in the First World War, twice wounded, twice decorated . . . and at that point in the list it unfortunately went all wrong.

According to family traditions, he should have gone into the Diplomatic, or have stayed in the Army, or at the very least have stood for a seat in the House — God knows they could do with men like Jack Wainwright to help raise the tone of the place a trifle! But to chuck it all, and go and grow vegetables! And buried in that God-forsaken hole! Really, you know, 'straordinary, what? Must be a touch of shell shock, don't you think? And frightfully rough on Muriel, poor old gel! She'd never swing a leg over a saddle again!

Perhaps they were right about its being shell shock. If it wasn't that, it must have been a form of insanity, or just plain cockeyed. What else could their crowd think of a man who openly laid down such blasphemy as: "These bloody politicians! These bastards! Their brainless blundering gets us into this shambles; and now when the guns have barely stopped, this filthy, so-called statesman gets on his feet at a public banquet and says, 'Gentlemen, there are bargains to be had in Germany!' Bargains . . . with a million unburied corpses out there in the mud! What did we die for, a whole bloody generation of us? For this honorable gentleman to dishonor us all, to make the great agony a shame and a cheat, a dirty scramble for pounds sterling? The war to end war . . . God Almighty, how they must have chuckled with glee when they handed us that one! We went for nothing! The whole damned cycle has begun again! I tell you, Muriel, that if we are fools enough to have a son, we'll live to see him trampled into the mud of Flanders for pounds, shillings and pence!"

It was of course scandalous, blasphemously unpatriotic, for an officer to utter these things in 1919. *A dirty scramble for pounds sterling* . . . Didn't he know that the cost of victory was terrific? Hadn't he brains enough to realize that the strain on the national economy must be relieved at all costs? . . . The fellow was a whiner, an "idealist," a mental case!

Or what could his neighbor, the banker, do when Jack Wainwright stormed in after dinner one night and said: "Write me a check for a hundred, Bill! That idiot Tom Higgins's kid got tossed off the haying machine today, and his leg's mangled. Be months before he's out of hospital. They'll probably have to amputate. You won't miss the hundred as much as the kid'll miss his leg! Thanks. . . . I'll let you know if I need any more."

And then there was the episode of young Harry Higgins, brother of Tom, who had taken to beating up his wife on Saturday nights when he came home drunk with barely a shilling left out of his week's pay. "These poor bloody animals!" said cockeyed Wainwright. "What the hell are you to do with them?" He promptly walked down the hill to the field where Harry was spreading manure. "Get down off that wagon!" he said. "I want to talk to you."

After a slight pause Harry did so.

"Is it true," asked Jack, "that the last three Saturdays you've knocked your wife about?"

Harry Higgins spat, scratching the back of his head. "Maybe

'tis. Maybe 'tain't. Anyhow 'tain't nobody's business but mine."

"That's what *you* think!" said Jack. "Now listen, you! I've seen you grow up in this village and you're nothing but a pub-crawler. The sooner you drink yourself to death the better. But you're not going to hit your wife again, see! Why not? In the first place she can't hit back, and more importantly, I don't happen to like it. You'd better try and remember that. I warn you that if I ever hear of your doing it again, I'll give you the damnedest licking you've ever had! Think it over!"

Wainwright's wife could have given a clue to him, but she would rather have died first. Muriel was small and quiet and did things, and had a tiny secret smile always, as though there were something awfully funny going on all the time just round the corner, and it wasn't any good telling you because you wouldn't have grasped it. She hunted, cross-saddle always, and you only had to see her in action to know that the horse loved it, would rather have her up than any of the rest of her crowd. But the Master had never succeeded in making her accept either mask or brush — odd little devil! . . . And all through the show from '14 to '18, when they were all sounding off about Ypres, Bapaume, Loos, you became aware, eventually, that sometime or other she had slipped out of the room. . . . And then, in early '19, the undead came straggling back. One of them was Jack Wainwright.

He came to her, in a hurry. "Is there anybody else?" he asked. The tiny smile and shake of the head answered him. "Then look here," he went on, "I've got to tell you something. . . ."

She looked up quietly at the large man with the two ribbons which they had given him in exchange for a cork hand and a permanent limp and a distraught face. "I believe I know, Jack!" she said.

"You can't possibly!" said Jack. "And until you do, I can't ask you to marry me."

"Yes, you can!" said Muriel.

"Christ, I knew you were like that! It's the thing I've been hanging on to!" He reached out and took one of her hands—that could handle anything on four legs. "You've got to know this! I'm . . . out! They've licked me. I just want to crawl away into a hole and hide. There isn't a bloody thing left . . . God, man, myself, anything! I'm . . . empty, and scared! It would have been better if I'd stopped a shell! So it's the damnedest thing I ever did to ask you to marry me, but . . . will you?"

"Would tomorrow be all right, Jack?" she said.

There was no big wedding, with the hunting crowd—what was left of them—guzzling champagne and making throaty speeches. They went off together in a prewar two-seater, paused for the necessary time at the Justice of the Peace, and kept on going down the road. It was not an easy road for Muriel. Her war job had just begun. She was to learn that it takes more than time to bring a man back from No Man's Land.

As though fate occasionally had a conscience, they found Little Minchen at a moment when there was a vacant cottage, and in that haven their first and only child was born. For reasons that were private to both of them—though perfectly obvious if you thought it over for a fleeting moment—they named the child Minchen.

"Sentimental? Whose child is it, for God's sake? . . . *Minchen Wainwright* . . . It scans! . . . Hi there, little Minchen! Have I got nerve enough to take you in my arms, or will that head of yours drop off? . . . Better take her back, Muriel! I'm sweating with funk. . . . And worse than that, I'm scared again. To think that you and I have been guilty of bringing so lovely a thing as she is into this stinking hopeless world! It's the damnedest piece of helplessness! And one day we'll get socked for doing it. She'll be just ripe for the next shambles, you mark my words!"

* * *

He was right. The child was born in 1920, and this was the spring of 1944. And a quarter of a century is slightly longer, for marking purposes, than eighteen months.

Nevertheless, it was not merely eighteen months away from home that was behind the young American. Sicily was behind him too — that paradoxical island of infinite beauty, of international hermaphrodites, of charming Lesbians and prosperous pimps. But Bill Thatcher had not been privileged to know that normal peacetime aspect of it.

His knowledge was sharper, won at the landing at Gela and enriched by months of crawling, rock by rock, up and down the relentless mountains which echoed ceaselessly to the roar of gunfire and bombs, snaking forward on his belly between buddies with their guts hanging out, some with only a bloody stump where a leg had been, others without faces and still alive. . . . Salerno had underlined it. Anzio had nailed it down . . . and as yet it was only the spring of 1944, hardly a beginning.

As he followed the Englishman into his castle, his eyes were alight. Gloom had dropped from him like an unwanted raincoat in a burst of sunshine. Just inside the door was a small table with a tall vase full of roses on it. Bill laid his cap beside the vase, bent down and took a deep sniff. There were always flowers in the hall at home. . . . In two quick strides he was behind his host again, and then through a doorway and into the living room. . . . It was like the village. It got you by the throat, took you right in, was quiet, enfolding. And it wasn't just the effect of light and the flowers. It must be what they had done to it, this man and his wife. . . . He heard Wainwright say, "My dear, let me introduce Corporal Bill Thatcher. Bill, my wife."

Bill pulled himself together. He must have been standing there gaping like a complete idiot. "I beg your pardon," he said, "this . . . took hold of me. It sings, doesn't it?" He smiled as he went over to the dark-eyed small woman who was looking at him across the teacups. "How do you do, Mrs. Wainwright? Do you and your husband always invite stray dogs in?"

"Good heavens! You weren't feeling like one out there, were you? I do hope not!" Muriel gave him her hand.

"Well . . . just a touch maybe!" said Bill with a grin. "But not now, thanks to you both. You know, this is the sort of thing that doesn't happen except in fairy tales. Do you mind if I'm awfully rude and stare at you and the pictures and the flowers and everything?" He was still holding her very small hand, but shaking it with the care he would have used if it had been of the thinnest china. . . . What a little thing she was! And those eyes of hers . . . so damned friendly and understanding. You felt you could tell her anything. . . .

With a smile Muriel took back her hand, undamaged. "I think," she said, "I'm going to follow my husband's example. How do you like your tea — Bill?"

Bill nodded. "That's swell of you!" he said. And then, after a second, "My tea? Oh, any way you care to fix it, thanks."

"That doesn't help me at all!" said Muriel. "I like mine with milk and sugar. Jack likes his plain. Now, how do you have it at home?"

Bill laughed. "You're like my mother. She always has cream and sugar too, and kids me because I prefer it straight and strong." He turned to his host. "Have you been to the U.S.A., sir?"

Jack Wainwright was over the fireplace tapping out his pipe. He smiled approvingly at his wife's neat lead. "Unfortunately, no," he said. "I did think of going after the last war, but . . . well, you know how it is. One gets bogged down, entangled in a million little things, and, before you know it, the opportunity's gone! I've many times regretted it. What part of it do you come from, Bill?"

"If you gave that opening," said Bill, "to some of the boys in my outfit, they wouldn't stop talking all night. You're pretty safe with me though, because I was born and brought up in Boston. We don't talk about it much. We think it speaks for itself." He laughed.

Wainwright smiled. "Good wine needs no bush, eh? I suppose it makes you Harvard?"

"Yes, and no!" said Bill. "You see, my father was Dartmouth and it naturally meant a great deal to him to have me follow in his footsteps. I'm glad I did. My sons — if ever I have any — will go there too . . . although their chances look pretty slim these days!" He moved quickly to the tea table to save his host a limp. "May I pass these for you?"

"Thank you," said Muriel. "That one's yours and the other one's for Jack."

Bill took the right cup and a plate of crackers over to the mantelpiece.

"Oh!" said Jack. "Thanks. . . . Over here, as you probably know, every Oxford man considers Cambridge with polite tolerance. Would you say that Dartmouth has something that Harvard hasn't?"

"That's another opening, isn't it?" said Bill. He handed the crackers to Mrs. Wainwright, took his tea and sat down in one of the big armchairs. "I suppose the real answer is the same in every college — just the idea, the sentiment, the roots you put down in your four particular years. Harvard's all right. As a matter of fact I'd been doing postgraduate work there for a couple of years when the draft caught up with me."

"What kind of work were you doing?" asked Jack.

"Music," said Bill. "Composition, harmony and so on. And who do you think they had in composition? Stravinsky!"

Muriel took up the ball. "Stravinsky? How marvelous! We have quite a number of his records. You must have got a great deal from him."

"As far as I'm concerned," said Bill, "that little man has just about everything. I wouldn't have missed working under him for anything in the world! Why, he . . ."

Was there an army camp down below? Had he been a lonely soldier a few minutes ago? Bill Thatcher didn't remember. In his enthusiastic description of Stravinsky he was back home again, reliving it, incidentally sharing it with the big Englishman and his wife, who, for no good reason — except that it was the place, the mood, the moment — seemed to have got under his skin. In the course of the next hour and a half, which seemed like a minute to Bill, Jack Wainwright and Muriel ceased to be hosts and became guests. They had met Bill's father and mother, his kid sister; had been to the old farmhouse under the elms in the Berkshires; had skied at Hanover; had listened to the carols in Louisburg Square on Christmas Eve; had been to a symphony concert with Stravinsky conducting his own music; had heard of the pastorale that some day Bill was going to write, a pastorale (laughingly) that was going to end all pastorales . . . just as a beginning.

The host-guests were charmed. It was young enthusiasm, intelligent, likable, and clean and bursting with energy and ambition; and with it all a crisp, slangy way of putting it that gave them many laughs.

And then, suddenly, as though some floating antenna of his mind had picked up an order, Bill looked at his wrist watch and jumped to his feet. "Judas!" he said. "I've got just ten minutes to get back to camp!"

Jack Wainwright rose to his feet promptly. "There's only one way you can do it," he said. "Ride down on my bike."

"Oh, but really, I —"

"Don't argue! Come along and I'll get it for you!"

"Very good, sir!" Bill turned to Mrs. Wainwright. "You've been perfectly swell! I ought to apologize for having talked you to death, but you must admit it was really your fault. . . . And may I use the bike as an excuse to come again?"

"You don't need any excuse," said Muriel. "We'd both like you to come whenever you can."

"Thanks a million!" said Bill. "I'll take you up on that. Good-by now!" He hurried out after Jack Wainwright, caught him up at a shed where the bicycles were kept.

"There you are!" said Jack. "You'll be on time without having to break your neck. . . . Oh, and by the way, if you're not on duty tonight, why don't you drop in at the recreation hut in Friar's Dene and introduce yourself to my daughter? She lends a hand entertaining, playing the piano."

Across the bicycle Bill held out his hand. "Sure thing! I'll do that. Good-by, sir. I can't thank you enough, but I'll keep on trying!"

Jack Wainwright smiled, shook him by the hand. "We have to thank you for coming!" he said. "So long, Bill, and don't forget the house is yours, any time. . . . Take it easy now!"

He watched the boy wheel the machine out of the gate, vault into the saddle; answered the wave of his hand and the cheerful grin. But when Bill was out of sight and Jack Wainwright turned to limp back into the cottage, his face had set in deep lines again.

Muriel was clearing away the tea things. At the sight of her husband she paused. "What is it, dear?"

Jack's hands were clenched behind his back. "It's this stinking blasted war! What chance has that boy — a paratrooper, an expendable! And millions of other good lads like him have to die, God forgive us, so that a lot of blind men can sit around another so-called 'peace table' and haggle and bargain and play politics again! . . . My God!"

SPRING comes early in the south.

The mimosa was in bloom, the perfume of it an intoxication.

But the men of the long column, riding at ease on tanks, trucks, mobile guns, were laughing and joking, singing in chorus, decorating their helmets with sprigs of the yellow flowers, soft as swansdown, every time they halted.

It was good to be alive on a day like this, full of good food, warmed by the good sun, with no foot-slogging to do, rolling swiftly along with your buddies through a countryside that kings had paid to see. . . .

And then, thousands of feet above, a man spoke into a microphone. . . .

One by one, the planes of the formation peeled off in a roaring power-dive, presently leveled out. Sticks of bombs turned lazily in the blue sky. The earth rocked. Vehicles disintegrated into bits of twisted metal, twisted men. Sheets of flame bloomed more yellow than the mimosa, exploded gasoline tanks, blasted trees. . . .

Like hunted rabbits, the unhurt plunged for the cover of a blade of grass, the nearest ditch, the slightest depression in mother earth that would take pity on their human bodies.

But the planes came back . . . and back again . . . strafing, spraying with bullets, as though the perfume of death were an intoxication.

The good task performed, the aviators laughed together through their microphones. It was good to be alive on a day like this!

Spring comes early in the south.

CHAPTER THREE

THE SWING-DOORS OF THE MONK AND PAUNCH SPILLED FIVE cat-footed paratroopers onto the sidewalk.

"Jees! Wouldn't these lousy pennies and shillings knock you for a loop?"

"You said it! But the beer's all right!"

"Listen! We got to find out what sort of dames they got around here!"

"Aw, c'mon! Let's give the dump the once-over first!"

It was evening and darkish, but the shops still functioned. Ever since the coming of soldiery, the shopkeepers of Friar's Dene had revolutionized their hours. In order to do their bit, they abandoned the peacetime closing hour of five o'clock and, behind carefully shaded lights, stayed open until nine. Even with the poorly paid English troops their reward for patriotic willingness had been stimulating, but now that the Americans had moved in surely it would prove to be the God-sent tide which taken at the flood leads on to fortune.

With the lingering sting of good beer in the backs of their throats, the five swung right down the High Street—a slow, purposeful progress from window to window, with now and again an entrance in unison, all filled with childlike eagerness to see, to touch, to smell, to taste, to compare, now that they were behind the looking glass.

"Hi-ya toots!"

"Boy, has she got what it takes!"

"I'll say!"

The words might be in a strange idiom, and therefore only vaguely comprehensible, but five pairs of male eyes need no interpreter. And the uncomplex English maiden's blush behind the counter was an admission of total understanding of that ocular blitz. Her answer was meant to be in kind. "Hullo! You're the American boys, aren't you?"

For three seconds there was a deep silence in which eye strenuously avoided eye. Then somebody smothered a laugh.

"H'm-h'm! Look's like we've landed on a virgin island . . . or something!"

"And how!"

" 'Sall right! She's doin' fine!"

"I'll stay with it!"

"Listen, sister! How's about one of them tobacco pouches?" A pointing finger. "How much in money that I can understand?"

From the glass case beneath her hand the girl brought one up. "Three and eleven three!" she said.

This time the laugh was not smothered.

"Do tell!"

"That ain't money! That's a call for a fake kick."

"Holycrise! Why don't they talk the language?"

"Did you catch that one on the fly, Wise Guy?"

Bill Thatcher, alias Wise Guy, merely laughed.

The other one produced a crinkling pound note. "All right, beautiful, you win! Wrap her up, and if there's anything left over out of this after you've done the figuring, does a jar of face cream for yourself say anything to you about a date with me sometime?"

"Jees, you sap! You don't think you can make 'em that easy, do you?"

"Watch out, sister! He's been to all the movies. He's a big bad one!"

And so, out into the cobbled streets again, beady-eyed, wisecracking, easy, masterful, with pungent comment at such shop signs as "apothecary," "haberdasher," "sweet shop"—the small change of difference that makes an odd rattle at first acquaintance.

A little farther on Bill Thatcher caught sight of a structure marked RECREATION CENTER. WELCOME! It was his ears rather than his eyes that led him to it; for the door had been left open and the music of a piano came calling to him, so that he stood still pushing away the street noises.

"Aw, c'mon, bud! Just another lousy juke box!"

"You don't want to plant your fanny this early, do you?"

"Hell, we ain't seen nuthin' yet!"

Bill laughed. "You're all deaf! That's playing! I'm going to drop over and take a look. Meet you back at that saloon in half an hour. O.K.?"

"O.K., sucker!"

Bill's rubber feet squished as he crossed the street. He went up three wooden steps and into the large roughly finished hall specially rigged up for the soldiers' benefit. His eyes went at once to the piano in the far corner. It was a girl playing. Two or three of his outfit were leaning on the back of the instrument. . . . What in hell did they know about Borodin? There were others at a coffee and tea counter, talking their heads off. . . . Of course! They'd have preferred the juke box! Some more were sitting in straw chairs with evening papers. The painted wooden walls were plastered with posters—King and Country, Winnie and the V, a new American flag alongside the British. . . . The girl at the piano had her back to him . . . dark hair, a lot of it, and curly, bent over the keyboard . . . What they called an "entertainer.". . . Entertainer? Why, of course! That must be the daughter that Wainwright had sprung so casually! What do you know! . . . And did she know those guys were giving her the eye? . . . She did not. She was a thousand miles away, keyed to the camel bells and the squeak of their harness, the sour smell of them, the wild procession in the blazing sun. . . . Bill Thatcher nodded to himself. That was playing all right! She hadn't learned that in Little Minchen, or Friar's Dene either! . . . He went over, silently, as intent as she was; and at the final notes which he knew so well he slid quickly onto the piano bench beside her. "You must be Miss Wainwright!" he said.

The curly head came up quickly, her eyes surprised . . . brown ones.

Bill smiled. "Right!" he said. "I recognize you. You've got a lot of your father, but the mouth and chin are your mother's."

Minchen Wainwright laughed. "Then you simply have to be Corporal Thatcher—*the* Corporal Thatcher!"

"H'm!" said Bill, "I'm not quite sure what I ought to do about that one!"

"Well, Mother and Dad have been singing your praises all through supper. Your ears must have been red-hot, Corporal!"

They smiled at each other.

And then came a voice from the top of the piano. "The Wise Guy with red-hot ears! Whadda you know!"

Bill said quietly, "Excuse me a moment while I shoot a little G.I. stuff. We don't seem to be as much alone as I should like!" He turned and looked up at the others grinning over the back of the piano. "Listen! Will you bums scram, for Pete's sake? I was the first to establish this road-block and it gripes me to work with an audience! I'm holding down all the priorities, so beat it, see! You'll find the beer at the corner saloon fit to drink, in case you don't know!"

Reluctantly they began to melt away.

Bill said, "Thanks! Be seeing you!" Then he turned to the girl again. "Now," he said, "I can really take a look at you!" He did so, holding out a packet of cigarettes to her. . . . Those brown eyes of hers met yours without a flicker of self-consciousness or loose sex. You didn't have to snatch a furtive slightly glandular glance at her when she wasn't looking. You could take in the details of her quietly and unperturbed . . . and not without considerable approval! . . . He struck a match for them both. "Thanks!" he said. "That's done me good! You know . . . your father didn't have time this afternoon to tell me your name. Is it all right with you to cut out the William the Conqueror stuff? I answer to the name of Bill."

She laughed — and again it was like her father. "They told me that!" she said. "My name's Minchen."

"Nice idea!" said Bill. "I'll bet it was 'little Minchen' when you were a kid in pigtails. And I'll make another bet that it was your father who picked the name. He's quite something, that father of yours! And so's your mother! They probably don't realize what they did for me this afternoon. Was I feeling low up there!"

"What was the matter?" asked Minchen.

Bill dragged at his cigarette, shrugged a shoulder. "Oh . . . I don't know. A little of everything — no mail from home, no pay day, no nothing. . . . You know . . . or do you?"

Minchen nodded. "Perhaps I can guess," she said. "I used to howl sometimes when I was at school abroad and hadn't had any letters. Of course that was nothing really, compared to you in uniform."

"You're wrong there!" said Bill. "Believe me, I'm learning fast! If ever I have kids away from home, I'm going to write them every single day . . . and air mail!"

Minchen laughed. "What a lovely picture that makes!"

Bill laughed with her — at something else. It was she who made the lovely picture. . . . What was it about all three of them that made you feel sorry you hadn't known them years ago, made you feel you wanted to make up for lost time? They sort of . . . did things to you. Minchen too. She had it, that quality of . . . of what? Maybe it was just quality. . . . "Tell me," he said, "was it while you were in Europe that you learned your music? I don't have to tell you that you're good. The way you handled that Borodin would have pleased the old master himself!"

Minchen said, "Do you really think so? I'm awfully glad! I love him! . . . Yes, I did learn in France. But Mother told me that you had studied under Stravinsky. What extraordinary luck! You must have got an awful lot out of it! . . . I want to hear you. Please, Bill!"

"It was luck," said Bill, "but you're the lucky one now. They haven't interrupted you. You can work every day. The last time I had my hands on a piano was in a bombed-out house in Taormina . . . but at that, the piano was in tune!" He laughed. "How about seeing if I can still make the Rachmaninov Prelude sound like anything?"

As his hands came up on the keyboard, Minchen slid away from him along the bench to give him room.

For a while he ran up and down the notes, feeling out the piano, to say nothing of his G.I. fingers.

Suddenly he turned to her. "By the way . . . I'm coming up tomorrow afternoon with your father's bike. Will you be there?"

Minchen nodded. "Yes."

Bill smiled at her. "O.K.!" he said, and began to play.

THEY were old people, stumbling, crowding, bewildered, like cattle in the stockyards. The men wore curls, beards, skull caps. They held tightly to their wives' hands to give them comfort, strength, courage . . . or to get it.

Men with rifles urged them on.

Dusk was falling and the evening chow would be ready if only these old bastards would hurry!

From the treetops birds were singing their evening song above the long open coach in the freight yard. A broad ramp led up into it.

Someone shouted: "All aboard for the Promised Land!"

There were laughs from the men with rifles.

Stumbling, crowding, bewildered, the old people helped each other up the unaccustomed incline of the ramp. The long-curled men began chanting in unison. . . . By the time the last one was inside they were squeezed body to body.

Then the doors slid shut—airtight doors.

The men with rifles lit cigarettes.

An officer blew a whistle.

A man on top of the coach turned a nozzle. . . .

Presently there was no more sound of chanting, only the birds singing their evening song.

CHAPTER FOUR

THERE WAS A MOON WHEN MINCHEN MOUNTED HER BICYCLE to ride home.

The main road was an endless chain of military trucks of extraordinary shapes and sizes—American trucks, the drivers of which whistled shrilly at her and made kissing noises in the full flush of their cloistered youth.

She waved a hand—a brief pennant of recognition—turned up the gravel road to Little Minchen pedaling hard; presently, as usual, had to dismount because of the steepness of the hill. There was a tiny smile curling her lips.

She didn't know that anything had happened. She thought that she was just biking home on a lovely spring night, as she had done now for almost two years, after thumping out sloppy sentimental songs for numberless shadows who had flickered in and out of Friar's Dene. Shadows make no impact, leave no trace. None had ever touched her. She had gone home always alone, alone in the sense that her mind, her thoughts, her self, remained her own, unoccupied by any other personality.

Tonight she found that she was not alone. Bill Thatcher was with her, even though he was not with her. He was the cause of the smile. He was still sitting on the piano bench of her thoughts. . . . It was rather extraordinary to have a man coming up the hill with you, even if you couldn't talk to him, not out loud, even if you could only smile remembering the things he said and the way he said them, and the music that was in him. He had a way of going about things, of being, of taking, of looking at you with those clear unruffled eyes that seemed to weigh you, to know you, to go right through you . . . curious eyes, cool as a brook, just looking, without impertinence, but all the same you knew they were taking you in, all of you, perfectly calmly, as though he had a right . . . which of course he had! But he established it differently, without doing a thing, just by being himself. . . . None of the others had been like that when they all came up at the end and Bill had introduced her to a lot of them, quite in his own way though — as if she had been behind barbed wire and he was on guard duty! They had all had the personal smirk of self-consciousness, or self-evaluation, that most men seemed to have when they met a girl — and the other way round too. But from the very beginning there hadn't been a sign of it in Bill. . . .

He was coming tomorrow. It would be fascinating to find out more about him, to see how he liked the cottage, to hear him play on her own piano. . . . But was he coming? Yes, he was. He had said so, and you instinctively believed him. . . . Why? What was it about a man you'd never seen before that made you sure you could believe him . . . about almost anything?

She found herself puffing as she reached the top of the hill. She had plugged up it, pushing her bicycle, faster than usual. For a moment she stood, breathing hard, before getting on the machine again. . . . Somehow at night when Little Minchen was asleep it took on an added loveliness, especially in moonlight, more especially in peacetime. But now the whole valley was vibrating with the rumble of trains lugging enormous weights, and those incessant army trucks whined shrilly on their tight tires, and as usual the sky was tainted with the far-off drone of bombers going out or coming back. . . . The sleeping village was like a sounding board, trembling with the throb of distant war — distant but ever-present, enveloping, nerve-racking, like a disease from which everybody was suffering . . . and you had to listen to them all describing their daily symptoms . . . even though you hated it, despised it, even though you knew that terror and brutality and wholesale killing were somehow not real at all, but senseless things that you had to listen to, and refused to read about, and couldn't possibly believe, much less imagine happening in Little Minchen. That was absurd, out of the question! . . .

She mounted again. The steady crunch of her tires made its usual cheerful accompaniment, until in a minute or so she dropped off at the garden gate. A series of purry mews greeted her. Tail erect, with his white boots and white bib gleaming, the yellow cat came stalking down the path. The girl answered him in his own language, wishing, as always, that she could translate. Then she said, "Hullo Frankie!" and reached down. He stood up on his hind legs and nuzzled his head hard into her hand, purring raucously, eyes tight shut. Minchen propped her bicycle against the picket fence, bent down and slipped a hand under the cat's chest, picked him up and held him so that his front paws were across her shoulder, his head under her chin. "There!" she said. "Now you can ride in with me!"

She went along the flags with him, pushed down the thumb latch, ducked through the blackout curtain, and was home again.

Her mother's voice said quietly, "Hullo darling!"

Her father cocked an eye at her over the top of his book. "Picture of girl with cat," he said. "Damned attractive picture too, if, as a humble parent, I may be allowed to say so. . . . Well old thing, how did it go tonight? Tell us about the Yanks. Many of them show up?"

Just for a second Minchen stood there, looking. . . . It was all so perfect. Dad on one side, Mother opposite; books, pictures, the piano; everything she had grown up with . . . how lucky they were . . . their three lives packed into that room like a precious roll of film in a box padded thickly with memories of all the lovely things that had ever happened. . . . There weren't any unlovely things. There couldn't be. There mustn't be. . . .

She bent down, spilled the cat to the carpet and went and perched on the arm of her mother's chair. "Hullo darlings!" she said, and smiled at her father. "Did they show up! . . . Heavens, I feel as though I'd spent at least two years in America! It was perfectly wonderful! They're all so intensely alive! I haven't had such an exciting evening since I began going down there!"

"Excellent!" said Jack Wainwright. "Isn't that good? I suppose they were all keen to chew the rag with you. I bet a lot of them had never met an English girl before."

"Really, I don't believe they had," said Minchen. "Just before closing time about a dozen of them gathered round the piano and they didn't want me to play any more. I was introduced to them all, but I'll never be able to remember their names. There were Greeks and Czechs and Italians, all talking at once!"

Her father smiled. "Introduced? Don't tell me they've started chaperons down there!"

Minchen laughed. "Well, I had one tonight, let me tell you. Can't you guess who it was? Bill Thatcher!"

"Ah," said Jack. "So he did drop in! I mentioned it so casually, just as he was hurrying off. I hardly thought he'd heard me."

Muriel looked up at her daughter. "And didn't you think he was nice?"

Minchen didn't answer the question directly. She said, "You should have heard him play! He hadn't touched a piano for goodness knows how long, but it didn't seem to make any difference. He's wonderful! And then afterwards we tried one or two things together, but of course we didn't have the music for four hands. I'm going to dig it up so that we can go to work on them here when he comes."

"Good idea!" said Jack. "That'll give him a real touch of home. Have you any idea when he's likely to come?"

"Of course!" said Minchen. "He's coming tomorrow afternoon."

"Tomorrow afternoon . . . But I thought you told me that you Land Girls were having some sort of meeting in Friar's Dene tomorrow afternoon. Had you forgotten, my dear?"

Minchen shook her head at her father. "Not at all!" she said. "But as it happens, it's going to be the first meeting at which Miss Minchen Wainwright will be marked absent!"

TWO men snaked up the grassy embankment on their bellies. One glanced at the illuminated dial of his wrist watch . . . Twenty minutes yet. He smiled. They lugged their box of dynamite to the railroad track and went to work with quiet, quick hands.

Five miles away the troop train chugged along. Young soldiers were sprawled snoring, reading letters, drinking wine, belching, telling dirty stories, singing, of home, of Mother, of the girl they'd left behind. . . . Home? It wouldn't be long now. They'd got 'em on the run!

The two men finished their job. The one with the watch whispered: "This'll make the fifteenth!" He laughed.

Like two furtive night animals, they snaked back down the grassy embankment on their bellies, rose when they reached the cover of the woods, and hurried away, ears turned backwards, listening. . . .

CHAPTER FIVE

IT HAD BEEN LAID DOWN BY WINSTON CHURCHILL THAT THE TOTAL use of England for defense and food was essential in a total war.

Angry peers, whose sacred lawns had lain undisturbed through the centuries, witnessed the vulgar plow in action right up to the mullioned windows; bomb craters, dangerously near St. Paul's Cathedral, were made to sprout carrots and onions where the previous crop had been ledgers and account books; stands of oak, prized since Alfred the Great, came crashing down at the bite of the two-handed saw; greens and fairways of championship courses disappeared beneath hutments, munition sheds, hangars. . . .

In anticipation of the paratroopers, Friar's Dene found itself sharing this spring plowing with the rest of England. These expendables were going to need elbow room during their brief spell of living. Infinitesimal parks, the back yards of dolls' houses, might become their fighting objective for training purposes, but first they must be able to hurtle up into the limitless blue. So, strangely shaped trucks, like the ones Minchen had dodged on her bicycle, were duly unloaded and the full fury of their content unloosed upon the countryside.

Like a regimented plague of giant locusts, bulldozers in echelon fell upon the green slopes and devoured them, leaving in their wake a brown gash hundreds of yards in width. They were followed in their turn by rock crushers, sprinklers, cement mixers and spreaders, machine upon machine — an ordered chaos, a precise confusion, a ceaseless kaleidoscope of men and instruments, of dust and clamor, of sweat and guts, of drive and willingness, of knowledge and pride, of awe and ruthlessness. . . . And then, metaphorically, upon the seventh day they rested and looked upon their handiwork, and saw that it was good. . . .

The amazed citizenry, appalled but fascinated, hardly knew what had hit them. Although only some seventy miles from London, the blitzed and ravaged capital, they knew nothing of war. How should they? It had never touched them, till now. They had only read, with angry comment, descriptions of it; they had only listened, a mug of beer in hand, to the polite narrative of broadcasters; their only eyewitness view, and synthetic, was at the local movie; they had even received a quota of cockney children — nasty little brats — during the first hurried evacuation, secretly thanking God when the last of them eventually went away again; some of their young men had not come back in the days after Dunkerque. . . . But it was all impersonal, remote, a constant aggravation rather than an overwhelming calamity. "If they'd 'a' been Londoners they'd 'a' taken it just like the rest of 'em!" they muttered. And they would. But meanwhile there was every reason and cause for the proper emotions of anger, distrust, suspicion, at the rationing of food and supplies, at the government regulations and pronouncements in the matter of their crops, their soil, their cattle, their increased production. . . . Strangers a-comin' in to tell them!

An unimportant pin point on any map, they were off the bomb route and therefore, now that a German invasion was impossible, as safe and almost as comfortable in their habits as though peace had been declared. It was accordingly an unparalleled outrage to have a horde of machines rooting up their past, concreting their present, and jeopardizing their future. "Weren't there any other piece of land they could go and dig up? Some of them dukes' private parks fer instance? Wi' the one breath they tell you to increase your crops, and then wi' t'other they rip out your fields! And for what? To have a lot of men come droppin' out of the skies in their parryshoots! 'Twere an invention of the devil anyway!"

It was indeed as though someone had rubbed Aladdin's lamp, had uncorked the genie from the bottle of brass . . . Squire Oaks's place and Three Finger Hill and Mile Bottom had gone forever, and along with them Tuppens, Chimney Woods and Druid's Ladder. "Man and boy for nigh on five hundred years they'd a-known them landmarks, been laid to rest under 'em, friendly-like, when their time came, and now . . ."

Now the ancient landmarks had indeed disappeared, but new ones had sprung up in their place—collapsible and sliding, utterly immoral, that threw the proper shadows at the proper time of day, that had the outward seeming of familiar things, haycocks, cottages, hedges, barns, hillocks, spinneys—and most important of all, photographed as such. And when you saw how it all worked, and had watched the great troop-carrying planes take off, with a fleet of gliders in tow, to return at the end of their flight and be whisked away into complete disappearance, you said to yourself in a rapture of admiration that if only Mahomet had known the present-day trick the mountain would have accepted his invitation; that Canute, if not born at the wrong time, would have been Chief of Naval Camouflage. . . . And then the seriousness of it all might have hit you and, perhaps, with a twinge in the intestines that you wouldn't for the world admit was fear, you might have remembered that the only way out for Sindbad the Sailor was to order the genie back into the bottle, seal it again hermetically and hurl it once more into the depths of the sea. . . .

Even the men who slept now on what had been Three Finger Hill in camouflaged hutments knew no dreams woven of the fabric of Old England—of a highwayman, for instance, whose three fingers had been shot off before he was caught and hanged and gave the place its name. Their dreams were of Texas and New York, of Abilene and Sioux City, of Winnetka and Poughkeepsie . . . and sometimes now of Salerno and Taormina so that they would wake, sweating, with strangled yells, only to be told to "pipe down for crisake!"

On this first night in the new camp, lying there half awake in the unquiet dark, made up as always of savage snores, of grinding teeth, of Gargantuan burping, Bill Thatcher tossed restlessly. At dawn the tough training would begin again, but tonight sleep eluded him. . . . The thing to do was to float out of it all in your mind, think yourself somewhere else. So he closed his eyes and kept them shut and went back . . . and was standing on the grass under the elm trees, looking in at the window of the old house. It was there that he had said good-by, at the foot of the broad steps, the car's engine already turning over . . . and he remembered that the sun had glinted on the brook that gurgled at the foot of the garden . . . and all Dad said was "Good luck, son! Take care of yourself!" But Mother hadn't said a thing. She had sort of . . . hung on to him, just for a moment, and kept on smiling. . . . Pretty tough on women, when you came to think of it! Why, even the kid sister had cried, funny little devil that she was! . . . Had women always done that when their men went off to war, the Greeks and Romans? You never read about that in the textbooks . . . and the poor damned G.I.'s of those days, scattered all over the map, they must have been just as homesick, once they'd had a bellyful of killing. . . . A lot of hooey those lousy classics, written by the guys who were never there, who played safe at home. . . . Imagine some Harvard professor, puffing at his little cigarette, and writing up the Sicilian show. . . . Judas! . . . And at that, it was a picnic to what was coming! This business of invasion . . .

He turned uneasily on his cot, as though the small physical gesture would help him to duck the issue. And then a couple of loud belches broke loose in the dark. . . . Those canned beans, thought Bill. Somebody ought to compose a tone-poem on a sleeping-hut at night with twenty G.I.'s in it . . . a chance for the bassoon . . . but, all the same, if you could ever get the conscious and subconscious woven in together it'd be the human animal as he really is. Must try and think that one out sometime. . . . Boy, it's going to take a long time to get back when this is all over! When I think of the lousy job I did this evening on that prelude . . . but the girl was good . . . and I don't mean just at the piano either. She's got what it takes all right! They've all got it, all three of them. . . . And that village of theirs . . . it's another world. Queer, that the name Thatcher should belong up there. Must write Dad and tell him. . . . Little Minchen . . . big Minchen too. Swell kid. Glad I'm going up there tomorrow . . . or is it today? She . . .

Sleep came.

LOVERS in lilactime, sweet fever pulsing in their veins. . . .

Soldier and girl in leisurely step, each with an arm about the other's waist. Mars and Venus from all time.

What was he whispering? The words were foreign, but what girl would not have understood on a spring night? Wasn't youth calling, while war dragged on and on?

From the country lane, a grassy alley wandered off into the friendly cover of the woods whose sticky buds had at last burst into green. There would be bluebells for a carpet . . .

Urgently he wheeled her towards it. Her feet resisted . . . a little . . . just enough. Then she broke away and ran ahead among the eager bluebells, where, soon, he caught her, with a laugh. . . .

Lovers in lilactime!

. . . She came out alone from the friendly cover of the woods, not running, now the task was done. There was no need. He couldn't follow her now. . . .

But she must be careful, more careful this time. . . . Her eyes went up the lane and down. She crouched and wiped her bloody weapon on a tuft of grass, the strong steel hatpin that left no telltale marks. . . .

CHAPTER SIX

ON THE STROKE OF FIVE-THIRTY NEXT AFTERNOON, MINCHEN was at the end of the village looking down the hill. He had said five-thirty . . . and there he was, a speck at the bottom, trying to take the hill at a rush on her father's bike. Would he be able to do it? She never could. . . . He couldn't either! She smiled, not unpleased that he couldn't. He was getting slower and slower. . . . He was off! She laughed, waved a hand.

He waved back, trudging, but quickly, hard as a steel spring. Soon she called out "Hullo, Bill!" and he called back "Hi!" And then—it was amazing how fast he came—he halted in front of her, grinned, took a couple of deep breaths.

"On the dot?" he said. "Bet you haven't been here more than a minute!" His eyes made a quick pleasant trip up and down her. "Different skirt, different blouse, different shoes. Effect perfect!"

Minchen laughed. "Good heavens! You certainly have a beady eye!"

"There's a little more to it than that!" said Bill. "In the first place, I haven't had a chance to talk to a girl like you in a dog's age. And second, you've been in my mind—not as a girl like you, but you yourself, the individual. For instance, do you know where you were at dawn this morning?"

"What on earth do you mean?" asked Minchen.

"Let me tell you!" said Bill. "You weren't on earth at all. You were up twelve thousand feet in a glider . . . with me.

We've been practising take-offs and landings in battle dress, and while we were circling around I found that I had you along, and did we talk! . . . You know, it's a funny thing what happens up there. Your mind seems to break loose and works awful fast. I suppose it's because in spite of nineteen other guys sitting there, you're all alone with a pretty immediate future that may be your past five minutes after you've landed!" He laughed. "I suppose you were really sleeping like a babe while that was going on?"

Minchen shook her head. "Far from it!" she said. "Do you happen to believe in telepathy?"

"I might!" said Bill. "Why?"

"Well," said Minchen, "you see . . . you weren't really up there at all. You were working with me in the vegetable garden. And you were also a small boy marching off to have your music lesson every afternoon . . . and the other boys made fun of you. But you didn't care. Sometimes you stopped to have a fight with one of them. And you licked him too! . . . And then all of a sudden, you grew up and went to college, and there was a piano in your room and a growing pile of music on top of it. And you were a sort of Pied Piper, because everybody wanted you to take them off into your world . . . just as they do now . . . and always will. . . . What were we saying to each other at twelve thousand feet?"

Bill's eyes were on the girl's—those nice brown ones without any flimflam. "Thanks for the 'always will'!" he said. "That'll be something to aim at all my life, won't it?" He propped the bicycle against the bank and produced cigarettes. They each took one, and he lit up for them both.

"Apparently you don't want to answer my question!" said Minchen.

"I don't remember exactly what we said in the plane," said Bill, "but, believe it or not, we landed in the Berkshires and you and

I had an early breakfast with my family. They were surprised to see us, naturally, but my mother and father thought you were swell, and you liked them a lot too . . . Think it might have been a sort of mirage, a reflection of some future moment? Who knows? It was all as plain as day. . . . I begin to believe that anything can happen up there."

"Who knows?" echoed Minchen. "I hope it was a mirage. I should like to think that someday I may be there giving a series of recitals. If Beecham and Barbirolli can go over all the time, why can't I . . . someday?" She laughed.

"There's nothing to stop you," said Bill. "You know, I always feel sorry for the poor devil who doesn't have 'someday' in his mind — to be a musician, a writer, a lawyer, a farmer. It doesn't make any difference what, but you have to have it there in front of you — don't you think so? — the yen, the urge, almost the knowledge that someday you're going to get there, knock the world for a loop! You've had the feeling sometimes that you absolutely know you can do it?"

"Tremendous, isn't it!" said Minchen. "And if only it would last! But the current gets switched off and you're left fumbling and stumbling. . . . Are you going to compose, or play, or do both?"

The side of the road was built up into a grassy bank. She sat down on it. Bill sat himself near her, half turned to face her. At their feet the road ran downhill, and there were miles and miles of quiet countryside before the eye was stopped by the horizon, that kindly line that cut them off from what lay beyond.

The lowering sun was in their faces, gently warm; and nearish noises of farm wagons and horses, a barking dog, voices, the immediate rustle of beech leaves, were like a protecting screen around them, as though, perhaps only for a moment, this tiny oasis were granting them sanctuary . . . respite. . . .

But it was the good moment, and place, in which to yield to

the urge of life, to the subtle ever-mysterious delight of sharing a sympathetic emotion with someone of the opposite sex.

Bill said, "I'm going to do both. Just think of playing your own stuff with the Boston Symphony, Minch! That would be the peak, wouldn't it? You know, when I was telling your mother about the evening I heard Stravinsky conduct his new symphony, I tried to imagine myself in his shoes. . . . Colossal conceit, if you like, but then again . . . someday! All the same, I don't know. That is, I don't seem to be so dead sure any more. I wish I still was." He broke off frowning. "Remember what I said about anything happening up at twelve thousand?"

"Yes," said Minchen. "But why should that touch your music?"

"I don't know," said Bill. "I don't know whether I can even explain it. . . . But I've been getting the feeling that there's something a hell of a lot bigger, that the world isn't so simple as it used to seem. There's something awful wrong with it. It doesn't seem right any more just to make good yourself and have a swell time doing it and bringing up your kids to do the same thing. I used to think that was all it was. But those buddies of mine have taught me a lot, and up there at twelve thousand making music's begun to look pretty small. The whole earth looks pretty small, and there are too many dead Yanks lying around, and concentration camps, and draftees. Something's got to be done about it . . . afterwards. See what I mean? It reduces the symphony and oneself to about the size of a pin point, so damn small you can't see either of them any more!"

Minchen dropped her cigarette, ground it out with her shoe. "That's more or less my father's point of view," she said. "The whole thing's perfectly ghastly! . . . But what are you going to do, Bill? What can you do?"

Bill twisted his shoulders. "You're asking me! I haven't found the answer yet. I don't know that I ever shall . . . And in some ways I'm sorry the thing ever crept up on me! It's damned uncomfortable, rather like an earthquake cracking up your foundations!" He made a noise like a laugh. "I suppose your father picked up that limp and the hand in the last war? Nice couple of souvenirs!"

"Not to mention his point of view!" said Minchen. "When one thinks of all that he might have done! And all he has is a couple of silly decorations that he hides away in a drawer!"

"Yeah, I know!" said Bill. "My father was over there too, but in all these years he's never peeped a peep. I'm beginning to get the idea myself! . . . What's your job, Minch? I suppose, like all the rest, you were drafted for something or other. I hope to God you don't make shells all day. It gripes me to see photos of women doing that!"

"And writing their names on with messages for Hitler! No thank you!" Minchen shook her head in emphatic agreement. "No. I'm a Land Girl. You see, at the end of the last war Dad chucked London and everything that went with it. He just dug in here and began to grow vegetables. He said it was all he was fit for. Can you imagine! . . . Then when this war began, the government told him he'd have to produce three times as much. So I joined the Land Army and was allotted to helping him, after a little local wangling! They had to give him somebody, so why not me?"

"You're darned right!" said Bill. "All the same I wonder they didn't send you a couple of hundred miles north or west, and send a total stranger to your father! . . . And so that's why you were out working at dawn this morning. I get it now. And then in the evening you do your bit again by going down and playing to the troops. Been doing that long?"

"Two years," said Minchen. "You see, there have been

troops in Friar's Dene ever since Dunkerque — British troops."

"British, eh?" said Bill. "For Pete's sake, what was the matter with them?"

Minchen raised one perplexed eyebrow. "The matter with them?"

Bill laughed. "Your left hand looks awful bare to me!"

For a second she looked at her left hand, then tumbled, and laughed too. "Oh, that!" she said. "Well . . . there were two or three who tried to fill the gap, but I'm still foot-loose and fancy-free! . . . What about you? How many girls are crying their eyes out for you in Boston?"

"Just two!" said Bill. "My mother and my kid sister."

Minchen jumped up quickly. "Dad's going to be as mad as a hornet if we don't show up pretty soon! We're all going to have an early supper, and he's wangled something to drink in your honor."

"Judas!" said Bill. "Was it a break for me to discover . . . Little Minchen!" He grinned as he jumped up, reached for the bicycle, and they fell in step together along the village street.

It looked as though the sun had splashed it with a patina of red-gold and patches of blue shadow. Here and there a drift of smoke, almost amethyst, twisted from a chimney. Just a little way along, a group of clamorous urchins was playing hop-scotch in and out of chalk marks in the middle of the street. One of them, too small to be welcome in the game, was sitting under the hedge, watching, an unhappy cat clutched tightly to her stomach. Flights of swallows were shrill above their heads. Here and there a man, or a woman, from a cottage door called out "Evening, Miss Minchen!" And Minchen answered their smile and their greeting.

Bill said, "You know, I've only read about all this. It's the old feudal stuff. It gets you, doesn't it?"

And then they came to the gate of the cottage, and the yellow cat was duly picked up into Minchen's arms and rubbed knowledgeably under the chin by Bill.

"He was on exactly the same spot yesterday, laying for you!" said Bill. "Shall I run the bike into the shed? You see, I already know where it lives!"

"Oh, don't bother!" said Minchen. "Put it beside mine. Nobody ever steals anything here."

"Of course not," said Bill. "They wouldn't want to, here." He leaned it against the side of the cottage, next to Minchen's.

And then Jack Wainwright appeared in the doorway. "Hullo there, you two! . . . How are you, Bill? Glad to see you!" He patted his daughter's shoulder, shook hands with Bill.

"Awfully glad to see you, sir!" said Bill. "The bike saved my life last night, and it's back in good shape. . . . I hope I didn't keep Minchen talking too long?"

Jack Wainwright smiled. "Your timing's perfect! We're going to celebrate tonight by having a spot before feeding. In honor of the U.S.A., I managed to commandeer a bottle of Scotch from my neighbor — one of those rich fellows who always has a great deal more of everything than is good for his soul perhaps, but I think he'll get to heaven for all that!"

"He will on this night's work, all right!" laughed Bill.

Jack Wainwright waved a hand towards the door. Minchen and the cat went in first. Bill followed into the hallway.

"Lupines tonight instead of roses!" he said as he put down his cap. "Did you fix those, Minch?"

Minchen laughed. "You really don't miss much, do you? . . . No, it's Mother's job to do the flowers." She led the way into the living room. "Hullo, Mother!"

"Hullo, darling!" said Muriel, and then, to Bill, approvingly, "So you noticed the lupines!" She gave him her hand.

Bill took it carefully. "You'd be surprised how many things

I took away with me from this house yesterday, Mrs. Wainwright!"

"And you don't know how much you left behind!" said Muriel.

Over in the corner, the unaccustomed tinkle of ice, the glug-glug of a newly-opened bottle, the hiss of bubbly water, each had its brief moment of importance. And then Jack came over, tray in hand.

"I feel," he said, "that tonight a toast is in order and it deserves to be drunk standing!" When each one had taken a glass, he put the tray down, faced them with his own glass raised. "Here's to peace this year . . . and may your generation build a better world than ours did, Bill!"

Bill touched Jack Wainwright's glass with his own. "Peace this year . . . please God!" Then he turned to Minchen. "It's up to you and me to drink to the rest of that prayer together. It's what we were talking about . . . remember? And is it going to be a tough assignment! Are you scared?"

Minchen's eyes met his. "No. I'm not afraid!" she said quietly. Their glasses touched and they drank.

B*ASEL*, SWITZERLAND, DEC. 8.—*In the peace and quiet of this neutral city, Arthur P. Templeton, American president and general manager of the Bank of International Settlements, sits down daily with his fellow directors, all bankers, some German, some Italian, others English, French and Dutch.*

When asked how he was able to do business with enemy nationals, Templeton said: "It naturally requires a considerable amount of tact, but up to now we have been doing fairly well, and expect to do so in the future."

After the last annual meeting of the Bank of International Settlements the board declared a four per cent dividend.

The presence of Templeton in Basel was not known to Secretary of the Treasury Morgenthau, who stated that the Treasury had had no contact or communication with any American of that name. Mr. Templeton is traveling on an American passport and received his Swiss visa from the Swiss Consulate General in Washington. The Swiss Consulate General said that his credentials came from the highest sources.

The Norwegian Legation recently protested against the operations of the Bank of International Settlements, basing its protest on a report that the Bank of International Settlements handed over to the Nazis thirty million dollars in gold bullion which had been deposited with the Bank of International Settlements for safekeeping by the Czechoslovaks.

This rumor was said by the British and Dutch Legations to have been without foundation.

"*. . . Up to now we have been doing fairly well . . .*"

CHAPTER SEVEN

YOU WOULD HAVE BEEN PLEASED WITH THE PICTURE THEY made, sitting there, after supper. You might well have found yourself saying that it stood for the highest thing civilization had produced — a happy family group gathered together at the end of the day's work; the flame of a wood fire dancing in the fireplace; the young girl curled up in an armchair with a big yellow cat asleep in her lap, the girl's eyes on the boy's face as he sat, rapt, at the piano; the Mother busy with her needle, a tiny smile at the corners of her mouth as she glanced from time to time at her daughter; the Father in a big armchair, his feet outstretched on a footstool, a curl of tobacco smoke coming from his nostrils. . . .

Symbolic of the Good Life, you would have said, content, culture, the art of gentle living, a little money put by; the older ones basking in the supreme satisfaction of seeing the youngsters coming along nicely, not wild harum-scarums, whooping it up in night clubs, restless, dissatisfied, lost, but truly happy in themselves, their thinking, their music, their future. . . .

Beautiful indeed . . . but what about the uniform? And had you been blind enough not to notice, or remember, that the gay chintz at the windows hid things called "blackout curtains"? And if you had taken off your colored glasses, you might have caught another detail, not unimportant — that the feet of the older man were not very still on their footstool.

The boy stopped playing. For some moments the final chord hung on the air. Then he closed the piano and rose. He said to

Minchen, "It's like being home again to get your hands on a piano like that! Thanks a lot!"

Mrs. Wainwright smiled at him over her embroidery. "It's for us to thank you, Bill! That was perfectly beautiful. . . . What are you going to do with your music after the war?"

The question was harmless enough — the perfectly normal assumption of life's going on to its allotted span.

But the boy thought differently. He came over to the fire and sat down in the armchair that was waiting for him in the circle. "I wish I knew!" he said. "Minchen raised that question before supper. There's nothing else in the world I want to do, composition and playing too . . . but maybe there's something else for me to do. . . . What do you think, sir?"

It was not Jack Wainwright sitting there with restless feet. It was Major John Gordon Wainwright, D.S.O., M.C., seeing again face after face of all the English Bill Thatchers, young, cheerful, assured, trampled deep in the mud of Ypres, the Somme, Loos. . . . Some of them had played the piano too. And now, God forgive him, it had to be this boy, this most likable American . . . motionless in an oozy shellhole, a clump of blasted trees off to the right up a slope alive with machine guns . . . it was raining like hell too. . . . "What was that?" he jerked out. He sat up abruptly in his chair, looked round with strained eyes that changed as he saw where he was. . . . Muriel, thank God . . . Minchen, thank God again . . . this boy looking at him with a query in his eyes. . . . "I beg your pardon!" he said. "I — I was a thousand miles away. Your music, Bill! Did you ask me something?"

Bill lit himself a cigarette. Perhaps it was a compliment to his playing, perhaps it wasn't! It didn't matter anyway. There was something in the older man's eyes and voice that was an invitation. Like his own father, this man might have gone gray at the temples, but the six feet of him stood up straight and strong.

He still packed a wallop in at least one fist. And for all his cork hand, he was the kind you'd like to have with you when you'd shed your parachute and were ready for big trouble with that tight feeling at the pit of your stomach. . . . "As a matter of fact, I did," he said. "Mrs. Wainwright wanted to know what I was going to do with my music after the war. I've begun to find it a hard question. Do you think music, as a career, would be living up to that toast of yours — building a better world? I somehow don't!"

Major Wainwright passed a hand over his chin. It rasped. . . . After the war! After the war! . . . God Almighty! They had all said that, those lads who were dead. . . . He got up, frowning, went to the fireplace, began tapping out his pipe, odd questions sprouting in his mind. . . . Do I fob him off? Play the idiot boy as usual? Smirk and agree? . . . Or don't I? He's a good lad. He's seen enough to ask himself questions. And more than that, he's American! . . . He turned round and looked at him for a moment. Then — "Tell me first," he said, "why don't you, Bill?"

Bill took a deep drag at his cigarette. "It's not easy to put into words," he said. "I guess the Salerno show started it. Anyhow, since then, I find that the answers have all become mixed up. I used to think I knew it all. . . . Now I know I don't! At least that's something!" He gave a laugh, at himself, and plunged on. "But there's an uncomfortable feeling that winning the war isn't the whole answer. That if we all lick it for home when it's over, and go get a job and forget it, we'll be in exactly the same position as we were before Hitler got going! And that doesn't make sense! And that's why I'm bothered about going back to music. . . . I suppose I'm crazy, but . . . well . . . I find myself cursed with a budding sense of personal responsibility, as though there ought to be something I could do about it . . . help to nail it somehow! What do you think, sir? Is that all haywire? Am I just sticking my neck out?"

It almost seemed that Major Wainwright had been holding his breath. His exclamation was like an explosion. "Good God! . . . If only there were millions more with the same craziness! If only I had felt like that in 1918! If we all had! . . . But we didn't! I didn't! We are the generation that failed. We sat on our backsides and left it to our noble leaders, and that's why you are all in uniform again today! We ought to be down on our knees apologizing to you!"

Bill's eyes were quite steady on the older man's. He said, "You're the first man I've heard say that. . . . Thanks! . . . You see, at night in the barrack rooms we all sound off, and there's a pretty general feeling that something sour has been going on since the last war, and that we're the ones who are paying for it. You can blame it on Salerno. . . . Of course, I know that that was only a picnic to anything you went through, or to what's coming when the invasion gets going; but you'd be surprised at what it did to some of us!"

Major Wainwright shook his head. "Perhaps I can tell you what it did to some of you," he said quietly. "The Roman conquest, the Somme, Salerno . . . the payment's the same! You've made the first installment. But you only had to stick it for a few months, and then you had the luck to be taken out of the fighting and sent here for further special training. On the surface you're all quiet again now, and damn pleased with yourselves at having done a hell of a good job on the Jerries, and you're about ready to go out and do another; and meanwhile you feel that you own the world and all the beer and women in it. . . . Quite right too. Haven't you earned it? But . . . there's another small item, isn't there? Sometimes, just before going to sleep, you can see and hear Italy again, smell it, feel the rocks under your feet, and the dead under the rocks . . . and it makes you sweat a little. There's . . . something not quite right about it all. And then too, although at the back of your mind you know that the other fellows are dying like flies all the way up Italy at this moment, in a queer, sneaky, ashamed way, you don't give a damn! It's not your show at the moment. It's just their bad luck . . . and there's something not quite right about that either! As it happens it's the thing that makes you convinced that you personally are coming through, that there isn't a bullet with your name on it . . . and it's the same thing, curiously enough, that makes me gloat every day that this village remains untouched, the thing that makes most war-workers and civilians more interested in meat and butter and a raise in pay than in D-Day!"

Bill's shoulders were twisting. "Judas!" he said. "That's hitting it on the nose!"

"A mere beginning of what we're making you pay for!" said Major Wainwright. "You might call it the first psychological stage. How do you like the idea of three more years of it, Bill? Three more birthdays and Christmases?"

"Three more years!" said Bill. "For Pete's sake!"

"We took it," said Major Wainwright. "Odd things begin to happen inside you by that time. The second inevitable stage . . . Not only your nostrils, but your mind and soul will be tainted with rotting dead and blasted earth. You'll find yourself a thousand years old. You'll find that you can't hear music any more. It'll have been drowned out by the guns. It'll have lost its meaning, become an echo of something you once thought you loved, something you meant to devote your life to. . . . Another small payment. . . . And you'll have made the discovery that all sorts of things, good things, aren't what you used to think they were. It may give you a shock, for instance, to find that you can't talk about anything to your father and mother, that there's a wall of something between you. . . . You may be asking yourself reluctantly whether God is not a myth, a luxury that only fat and comfortable civilians like myself can afford. It's possible that you may have arrived at a glimmer of understanding of what Dr.

Johnson meant when he defined patriotism as the last refuge of a scoundrel. . . . And on the great day when they've unconditionally surrendered, and every right-minded civilian and soldier goes out and gets hysterically and patriotically plastered, you may find yourself on that day shaken, bewildered, groping, not very sure either of victory or peace . . . or a future, because all the people at home will be wondering what the hell's got into you! And even that isn't the final payment that my generation demands of you. The final payment comes when your own son is drafted for World War Three!"

"Ah, no, not on your life!" Bill was on his feet, beginning a march up and down in front of the fireplace. "We're not going to let it go sour again like that! World War Three is out! I tell you we're not going to stand for it! I don't see myself apologizing to my son!"

"No?" The query was very quiet. "What are you going to do?"

"Do?" Bill repeated it angrily, then uncertainly. "Do? . . . Judas!" Finally he swung round on Major Wainwright. "Listen, you've been thinking about these things for twenty years. Let me ask you. What would *you* do, if you had your time over again?"

Minchen nodded violently. "Oh, I'm glad you asked that! That's exactly what I've always wanted to know! What would you do, Dad?"

Major Wainwright looked from the girl to the boy. Weren't they equally important, or impotent, as the case might be? "I'll tell you what we ought to have done," he said. "We ought to have organized every man and officer left alive on every front, every woman who had lost a husband or son. We ought to have chucked out every prewar politician with his constipated prewar thinking. We should have made every Cabinet Minister the secretary of a golf club, every Ambassador the doorman of a swagger hotel. We should have rounded up all the international bankers and dumped them on the island of St. Helena for life. Then with a clean slate we should have formed not a League of Nations, but a World League of All Nations, with World Law and World Police and World Courts, and World money, and with a single World sovereignty — all the economic and political problems in one vast pool of world interest. All our tuppenny-ha'penny nationalism is as dead as a doornail, now that the airplane has made the world the size of a duckpond. To all intents and purposes your country has done it, Bill. There may still be states' rights and jealousies, but none of them want to make war on their neighbors any more, now that they are under one sovereignty. The Swiss have done it. There are three races who gave up their nationalism and live in perfect harmony under one flag. . . . It could have been done in 1918, and, if I believe in anything any more, I believe that our one chance of salvation depends on those things being done after this war."

Bill nodded thoughtfully. "The size of a duckpond's right! That's all it is. But a single World Government in all this mess of fascists? Aren't you jumping the gun? Isn't that a dream?"

Major Wainwright shrugged his shoulders. "In all probability!" he said. "But isn't it worth working for? The only excuse I can offer for my generation's not doing it, is that there hadn't been a World War before. We didn't realize that the moment had come to begin again. We still had faith in our leaders, God help us — Baldwin, MacDonald, Chamberlain. We sat down and licked our wounds, and found ourselves bilked. We listened to them mouthing the old, old rigmarole in the usual noble phraseology — balance of power, security, blocs, mandates, trade concessions . . . and, by God, they've already begun to do it today, before the killing is half over! They're already doing their damnedest to wangle future 'spheres of influence' with expatriate governments. They're whispering about a 'Western bloc' against our greatest ally, Russia! If you let that happen, it means World War Three, and Four, and

Five! . . . So you see, your going back to music — both of you — is as hopeless as my growing vegetables or Anthony Eden's succeeding Churchill at 10 Downing Street!"

Bill looked at Minchen. "You hear that! Swell chance we've got!" He swung round again on the older man. "But listen, we've said that we're going to take care of that. Roosevelt says, and everybody in the U.S. from the White House down agrees, that the peace is going to be made to stick!"

Major Wainwright held a match to his refilled pipe. Through a cloud of smoke he said, "The White House practically gave birth to the League of Nations. But it died there too, didn't it?"

"Meaning," said Bill, "that we'd be damned fools to rely on Congress to back us up?"

"My dear man, one postwar congress is painfully like another!" said Major Wainwright. "I find it difficult to imagine Churchill's becoming a political idealist. He has already laid it down that he is not fighting this war to see the liquidation of the British Empire. Somehow that smells of oil and tungsten. It smells of the Greek king being hoisted back on his throne at the point of a bayonet, and be damned to democracy!"

"In other words," said Bill, "if Congress doesn't stand behind Roosevelt and the Charter, we'll find ourselves roped in to European power politics. Is that the idea?"

"Politely, gently, but inevitably!" said Jack Wainwright. "And you will find yourselves bilked in the same old way. . . . I happen to think that Roosevelt's 'Four Freedoms' will eventually be recognized as one of the great human utterances of all time. For that matter, unfortunately, so was the Bible. But while the King James version is still held to be great literature, it is hard to see that its precepts have much effect upon human conduct. We may all have a copy by our bedside, but we cheat, lie, steal, lust and make war to our heart's content . . . don't we?"

Neither Minchen nor Bill found anything to say. Major Wainwright gave an odd laugh. Then he leaned forward, tapping the arm of his chair with his pipestem.

"Listen, Bill!" he said. "If there hadn't been a doubt in your mind that drove you to ask me things, I wouldn't have opened my mouth this evening. But before I shut up and we all have a drink, I want to say something to you — and to you also Minchen — because you're both young and believe in life, and especially because you, Bill, are American, and keen and full of immense energy and faith in yourself — and the future. . . . I want to lay this down as God's truth: that it will be equally your fault if your children have to go to war! Learn by our failure, Bill! Get it through your heads, both of you, that on V-Day your job, instead of ending, begins. You've got to be at the peace table working like hell to defeat the patriotism, the statesmanship, and, above all, the nationalism, of the world's leaders. Their primary object, always and forever, is to see that their own individual country is taken care of in the division of the spoils by hook or by crook. And if one thing has now become self-evident, it is that the waging of peace is a million times more important than the waging of war. It's up to all of you who have the luck to come back from hell to wage peace, sweat for it, watch over it, nurse it, day in, day out, with everything you have left of brains and guts! You'll have to initiate the most drastic changes. You've got to see that honor is put before interest, that the only divine mission of any nation is to help every other nation to enjoy the right to life, liberty and the pursuit of happiness, that real patriotism is not a local shot-in-the-arm but as universal as air, rain, sunshine! . . . What do you say, Bill — and Minchen too? Are you going to sit and play the piano, as I hoed my vegetables, and watch the patriots make slaves of every little man in Germany who was machine-gunned into slavery by the Nazi gang, or, which is just as immoral, build them up again into a strong Germany because one day, soon, we may need Germans as allies against Russia?

Are you prepared to see them throw the word 'honor' into the international muck-heap? This war is supposed to be for freedom, isn't it?—not for the protection of oil interests, or munition makers, or international cartels! That's why your place must be at the peace table, to safeguard the world from that kind of thinking. There's work there for Minchen, for all women, but for you especially, Bill, because you're American. We may not be willing to admit it yet, but Europe is on its knees to America. You're the world leader. You've sanity and idealism. You've been out of the international mess. You've held out to us ideals that the little man everywhere craves, a way of life that draws him like a magnet—the Four Freedoms ideal which we'd like to believe in, but hardly dare to. . . . If you and your generation can make them world-wide, it's the only task that matters when this war is won! It's the only thing that will let all the Unknown Soldiers of both wars sleep easy at last in their graves! It's life instead of death!"

Major Wainwright stopped.

For a moment no one spoke.

And then out of the evening sky came again the drone of bombers. . . .

Major Wainwright gave another of those odd laughs. "Forgive me!" he said. "I'm nothing but a decrepit Job bellyaching from my dunghill. . . . Let's all have that drink!"

"AND now for news of the home front we take you to Washington, Chris Leifer reporting." . . .

"Good evening, ladies and gentlemen. The strike in the ammunition plants is assuming serious proportions. Twenty thousand men are idle tonight; and Union officials, standing firm in their demand for extra wages, are reported unwilling to compromise with the War Labor Board. It is believed the President will give the order for the army to take over the plants tomorrow morning. . . . The truck drivers of Massachusetts are also out. In twenty-four hours the city of Boston will be foodless. Governor Saltonstall has called on the State Guard to operate the trucks. . . . Meanwhile the gasoline shortage is acute. Over two million gallons a day are being sold in the Black Market, and coupons representing several billion gallons have been stolen from local Ration Boards. The OPA expects to make some important arrests in the near future . . . In anticipation of Italian casualties, which are expected to be heavy, every effort is being made to secure more nurses for the army. In the opinion of many observers on Capitol Hill, women may have to be actually drafted for this important service if the President's appeal to their loyalty remains unanswered. . . . During recent weeks the financial pages of our press have reported a sharp rise in the stock market when Allied reverses have foreshadowed a longer war; and an equally sharp drop when Russian advances have promised an earlier peace than expected. This stock market reaction shows that American business is worried over its peacetime future. . . . And now a word from my sponsors, the makers of cute, crunchy, crumbly, Marshmallow Biskies . . ."

CHAPTER EIGHT

FRIAR'S DENE WAS A PLEASANT PLACE OF OLD HOUSES WITH gardens, tree-shaded shops, full of leisurely bustle, an air of half-speed. All roads led to the market place, the keynote of which was a Roman fountain in the center. At some later date a drinking trough for cattle and horses had been added. Cobbles surrounded it, winding streets radiated from it, shops bordered it. Among these, on the south side, catching the sun whenever it deigned to shine, was the inn, the Monk and Paunch, once a coaching stop, with an Elizabethan overhang in front. Its swinging sign was of the same vintage—a thick wooden panel, framed in iron, a faded painting on each side revealing dimly a Hogarthian monk with a pewter tankard in his hand. On either side were movie palaces, flashy with neon lights. Farther along were a church, imitation Gothic; a chapel, considerably more severe; and the Recreation Center. Banks, antique shops, bookshops, men's outfitters, were interspersed along both sides of the High Street.

You might, if you were driving in peacetime, be tempted to stop there for lunch on cold beef and old ale, or to look over the antique shops, or to pick up a jar of the local honey which was not without reputation . . . and then you'd have had enough and be on your way.

But if you were a G.I. planted in the local camp, and had seen both movies over and over, and lost your last nickel at craps on the pub's billiard table, and had written your letters home in the Recreation Center, and thumbed through all the old magazines, and had plugged up one side and down the other of every goddam street in the dump . . .

Perhaps you think you can take a normal man suddenly away from his normal life, his family life, however humdrum, put him in a costume, isolate him with thousands of other men, teach him all the unrefined ways of killing, plug him with solid food, and expect him to remain a model of faith, hope and chastity.

Perhaps you think that a cheery army chaplain, with little games and group singing and ready words of encouragement, can hold the floodgates; or that a cup of coffee at the hands of a clean, sweet-smelling, pretty Red Cross girl doesn't drive him half crazy; or that the nakedness of the pin-up girls merely stimulates his mental appreciation.

Furthermore, by nature every animal is secretive, in simple self-protection. His lair is his home, whether it be a one-room rear in a tenement or a whole palace; and whether he wants to beat up his woman, or make love to her, he seeks the privacy of closed doors.

When you put him in uniform, privacy is the first thing he loses. He must wash, eat, snore, burp, grind his teeth, sleep, evacuate, under the eyes of twenty other animals, washing, eating, burping, all together. His most secret habits, physical idiosyncrasies, emotional disturbances, become public property, a subject of perpetual ribbing, a cause sometimes for murderous hatred. There is no door that can be closed, no escape, mental or physical, no respite from the violent manhood of many men, overtrained, bored to desperation, looking for trouble, crowding the dance halls and night spots, oppressed with a hunger that has no relation to food, with an inner yearning that seems to squeeze the intestines to the size of a walnut. If not overcome by the immensity of battle, temporary relief can only be found in anything from going AWOL to murder, by way of rape, liquor or war-weddings.

It is not fear of death or wounds, nor boredom, nor absence of mail, nor fed-upness with the rank and file. It is a composite. And it is the uniform . . . "You're in, ain't you? And you can't goddam-well get out of it for duration . . . the uniform which means you've signed away your self for keeps. Yes, Sergeant! . . . Yes, Captain! . . . Yes, Major! . . . Goddammit, where are you yourself in all that? You haven't got a self any more. They've taken it away from you. You belong to them, body and soul. You might just as well be in Sing Sing. You're cut off from everything you ever did or felt or thought. You're just another goddam number! It was your life, wasn't it, before they drafted you? You could work, or go fishing, or ride a subway, or buy a sandwich, or feel good, or feel lousy, or go some place with the girl friend, or do what you goddam-well felt like when you felt like it, couldn't you? . . . Nuts to you, Sergeant! . . . Go jump in the lake, Captain! . . . Yoohoo, Major!"

There are other sides to that stifled self too — odd sides which never could get put into words — the sense of protection you felt when you watched your mother-cat suckling her kittens; the fierce gentleness that made you go hot and cold when the girl friend put her hand inside yours; the stupid lump in your throat when you gave a kid a stick of gum . . . if only sometimes you could goddam-well cry! . . .

To many millions of such normal men living abnormally in England in the spring of 1944, the immensity of battle was still denied. Everybody knew that it was the spring of invasion; that one day, any day, might be D-Day. Every inch of the island was crowded with these millions, of different races and colors, all waiting, waiting, nerves twitching to breaking-point. Now and then a murder reached the headlines, a sex crime, a fierce explosion of rioting in a city dance hall. Throughout the countryside every green hedge hid beneath its tender leaves thousands of piled shells, every clump of trees sheltered a unit of tanks, or guns, or planes . . . also waiting.

In Friar's Dene, the paratroopers were in no way different from the rest, except that there was nothing to do and no place to go when the day's training ended. Nothing to do except to investigate the charms of the young women of the place. Those who were in the outlying farms came in, all dressed up, in the evening, ostensibly to go to the movies. It was a moot point whether the shopgirls, who lived in the town, had an advantage over the others. But whether field workers or town workers, all of them reacted to the virile soldiery as did the Greek maidens a thousand years before Christ, or their Hittite sisters before that. In official language they fraternized. In the more truthful phraseology of the G.I. they were pushovers. In due course, the Vicar of the pseudo-Gothic church, horrified at this gay, if helpless, getting together of youth, took it upon himself to utter grave admonitions from the pulpit; the Baptist minister, sharing his anxieties but not his somniloquent diction, let loose upon his congregation the thunderous threatening of the ancient prophets. . . . Neither man thought of praying to his God to stop the war.

As the urgent spring days slipped by, and the routine of training began to fit like an old glove, there was hardly a household in Friar's Dene whose door was not open to the paratroopers, whose hospitality, over and above such scrappy things to eat and drink as they could scrape together, did not include a gathering of girls and young women eager to "entertain the American boys," to offer their incalculable crumb of femininity upon the altar of sweet charity . . . and with, perhaps, at the very back of their minds the wisp of thought that possibly they might be one of the eventual thirty thousand war wives to be transported to the wonderland of America. It was not time yet to consider the statistics of Unmarried Mothers. . . .

Major Wainwright had said that eighteen months was long enough to mark a man. Having come by his knowledge the hard way, he could have said one month, or one minute, with equal truth.

A particular minute occurred exactly thirty-one days after the coming of the paratroopers to Friar's Dene. And in that minute they began to receive their first "briefing" for a landing in enemy territory on D-Day, whenever that might be, many hours ahead of the main landing.

It was announced under the most solemn zip-your-lip conditions. Not a word, not a murmur, not a breath, must emanate from any man. On their silence depended what might be the turning-point of the entire war . . . a grave responsibility to carry round in the loneliness of their hearts, the imperative necessity of making their faces look as they had looked yesterday, of writing home only in terms of inanity, of wisecracking as usual in public, of making good the pretense that in the fullness of their youth death had not taken a step nearer.

From that minute, odd values asserted themselves, perceptions became razor-edged, appreciations swelled to passions, living became an urge. The abnormal normal was shocked to a new abnormality.

Had you, like Jack Wainwright, suffered the First World War, you would not have been in any degree amazed at the spectacle of a hard-faced paratrooper stopping in his tracks to stare up at a bird singing in a tree, to see him motionless so as not to scare the bird away; and, when it did fly, you would have understood when you saw him swallow and heard him mutter "Jesus!" It was the same prayer you had muttered once, and you knew he would take it with him — the vision of that bird, and the memory of the emotion it gave him — into some far-off slit trench.

And in the bar parlor of the Monk and Paunch, foul with the reek of beer slops and sawdust and cigar butts and the frowst of unaired rooms, you also knew with deep knowing that where yesterday darts and billiards had been stale and unprofitable, comparable to the dreary exercise yard of a prison, tonight, in the white light of their "briefing," they would take deep breaths of the ripe friendly-smelling haven from which they were about to be wrenched, but to which, one day, by God, they would make a pilgrimage and drink the barkeep under his counter for old times' sake. . . .

And Bill Thatcher?

In the case of Bill Thatcher, at the advanced age of twenty-six, Salerno had been the second turning-point. The first was induction. Softly brought up, accepting all the advantages of a comfortable home and a good education as a matter of course, of right, the herding with his fellow humans in the army had shown him a quite other world than the one he knew, a world with all the cotton wool removed. Instead of shrinking from it, as the weak man will, Bill Thatcher had used his brains, won himself a place in the harsher world, and in the doing acquired the stature of a man.

As he left the camp on the evening of the "briefing," only his feet had any contact with the soil of England. He had gone home. The inside Bill was back in the Berkshires, a passionate ghost staring through the windows, seeing and hearing his mother, father, the kid sister . . . reaching for them, and unable to communicate . . . clutching achingly at the swelling hills and burnished maples, the noisy brooks that leaped so foamingly over the round white stones, the slim young cedars that advanced like infantry upon a hillside, the rich and satisfying splash of sun that lit it all and shaded it too . . . sunsets . . . moonrises . . . magnificent thunderstorms that scoured it all clean with tropical violence.

He knew now that it was not just a part of him, but the major part, the roots of him, from out of which had sprouted the dream of that pastorale to end all pastorales, in payment of his debt to life, which had let him sense the beauty of which it was capable . . . and now the inconceivable ugliness of which it was equally capable. . . . This horror that they called D-Day . . . and he was twenty-six, like the rest of them . . . a bunch of good guys who hadn't begun to live yet, any of them, with everything ahead— ambition, success, a home, wife . . . and kids who must never be called on to take a "briefing." . . . And the pastorale? Hell, it was dead before it was born! There wouldn't be time for it afterwards . . . even if there were an afterwards . . . and there was something wrong about that too. . . .

He was scowling as he stumped along the English country road, trucks swooshing by on the wrong side of it. It was a lonely road, inside him, and he was vague-eyed, his thoughts still turbulent, as he came into the market place of Friar's Dene. . . .

So what? . . . Beer? . . . He glanced uncertainly at the inn. Should he or shouldn't he? . . . Why not? There wouldn't be many more times.

He shouldered his way through the swing-doors, nodded to the barkeep, glanced into the parlor.

A dart game was in noisy progress. Four men were banging balls about on the mended baize of the billiard table. Along the wall, on a leather-seated bench, sat a group of his buddies, each with a tankard of beer in his hand, their eyes following, but perhaps not seeing, the rolling balls.

Bill looked at them, the angle of his vision shifted from its usual acceptance. . . . As if we'd all been shaken up in a sack, he thought. Look at them . . . Tom Kamenakis, who can rattle the patois of Crete, although he'd never been nearer to it than South Boston till the draft caught him; Lester Thornhill, Mayflower, Andover, Yale, Elihu Club, Phi Beta Kappa, stuffed shirt with guts; Reub Vargoulian, who, at the drop of a hat, starts reciting the ancient history of Armenia as though he were telling you the plot of an exciting film he'd just come from; Nick Salvaggio, a second Caruso, California type; Harry Oldfield from the Texas ranges, and he'd give you the rest of the world for a plugged nickel . . . a swell bunch!

Bill went back and bought himself a tankard. He blew the foam off, took a sip and then carried it over to join the group.

Reub glanced up at him, grinned. "H'm-h'm!" he said. "Another sad-sack! Guess we're all sweating it out, Wise Guy! Me, I stay here till the beer runs out of my ears!"

"Me too!" said Harry Oldfield. "An' Ah hope it'll drown all the butterflies in ma insides!" He laughed, moved over a little on the bench, spoke lower. "They sure did hand us one son of a bitch of an assignment! Sit down and rest up, boy. You cain't afford to waste your strength, standin' there, when we-all have to go out and personally win this yere war!" He laughed again.

Bill shook his head. "Thanks, Harry, but my kind of jitters is something else again. If I sit on my fanny I'll go crazy — "

"Ah, nuts!" broke in Tom. "I know what he wants! . . . C'mon, bud! Let's you and me leave these guys and go get us a coupla dames!"

Nick leaned over and slapped his knee. "You're on, Tom!" he said. "Leave-a me finish this beer and we get-a the hell out of here. . . . O.K.-a, Bill?"

This time Bill Thatcher shrugged his shoulders. "If you two can get something that way, you're lucky. I don't know what I'm looking for. Wish I did! I'm as jumpy as all hell! . . . Think I'll go and tear off about ten miles of this country on my two feet. Maybe that'll do some good. Feel like joining me for a workout, Thorny? You seem to be the only one of the gang not otherwise employed."

But Thornhill took another sip of beer. "Not on your life!" he said. "We'll have all the walking we need . . . soon enough! And besides, I've thought out a new grip at darts, and when those boys get through I'm going out there and make a clean-up!"

Not without a feeling of relief, Bill Thatcher nodded. He wanted to be alone . . . and yet he didn't. "Well," he said, "O.K." For a moment he stared into his tankard, unseeing. Then he emptied it in one long drink, took a deep breath, murmured, "I'll be seeing you!" He took the mug back to the bar, nodded absently to the barman and stumped out into the street again.

He stood for a moment in the doorway, his eyes getting tuned to the darkness. A violent tang of perfume hit his nostrils. A hand fastened on his elbow.

"Hullo, dearie!"

She must have been laying for the first man who came out. "Hold it!" said Bill. "But if you want to stand by, there's a couple of boys inside who'll be looking for you in a minute." He side-stepped past her. . . . If they'd all been Krauts instead of Yanks, she'd have been waiting just the same, poor little devil! And at that, a little later on the German girls will be queuing up in the darkness for Nick and Tom in some bombed-out village on the other side of D-Day. . . .

He gave an odd laugh, and kept on walking past the shops, not a single window of which caught his eye. Presently he muttered, "The hell with this walking! Where am I headed for anyway? . . . This D-Day stuff has got me down! . . . I wonder if I could trust myself to face Minchen tonight without showing anything. . . . My God! . . . Minchen!"

He stopped dead on the sidewalk. Things were happening inside him. It was as though the furniture of his mind had suddenly become changed all round, had shifted completely, and in the dark he had banged into Minchen standing where she had never stood before.

He remained staring at an invisible cobblestone . . . seeing her strong hands commanding the notes, and the bobbed curls at the nape of her neck, and her changing eyes as she looked up at him, and the way she walked — her skirt lilting from side to side like the kilt of one of those lean Highlanders with no hips — and the way she put her head back and closed her eyes when she laughed, so that the V made by the chords of her throat became an enchantment. . . . And it wasn't just that. All that was merely a series of pleasing externals that a lot of other girls could have, the physical "what-it-takes." But with Minchen there was a million times more to it than that. . . . There had been a month now, and instead of seeing her once or twice, he had found himself going down to the Recreation Center every single night for those thirty nights, and not for the sake of playing the old tin can of a piano . . . he knew that now. . . . Somehow Minchen stayed with you. You did a lot of thinking about her up at twelve thousand feet . . . and saw her too . . . and remembered things about her that had hit you. When she played, for instance, she played from her belly. In other words she said things — like that line from the Saroyan play about the Arab's flute: "That's crying a thousand years old!" Minchen had that. It did things to you. It reached out to you, and had you all tied up inside. It was like a bridge she lowered, so that you could cross over and get to her . . . and not the surface stuff either, but layers and layers down! And when she stopped playing the bridge was gone, because what you said to each other was never anything but words. They gummed up always what you really wanted to say, and you couldn't be sure you'd even won a beachhead with her . . . or could you? If you hadn't, would she have taken you home, cared what you thought of her family, her village, her music? Would she have treated you like a buddy in the sense of sympathy, understanding, recognition? Why should she have bothered after that first evening, if not? And why would you have been carrying her around? Why . . .

"Hi-ya, Wise Guy! Changed your mind about that marathon? Or are you back already?"

"Aw, c'mon-a, Bill! We're not having any cheap-a stuff tonight. We go to Duke-a Street . . . you know . . . wine and everything, top-notch-a!"

Bill Thatcher didn't have to turn round. Darkness or light, eating or sleeping, in a foxhole or in a latrine, those two voices were a part of life, his G.I. life. . . . Over his shoulder he let fly in their common vernacular. "Nuts to you!" and stepped off the sidewalk to get away from them.

Ahead were the dim beckoning lights of the Recreation Center.

AN icy wind made the barbed wire red-hot to the touch. For the while it also blew away the stench of offal, stale urine, disinfectant.

The prisoners huddled in groups behind the flimsy cover of buildings, stamping their feet on the frozen mud. Chow time in five minutes—lukewarm dishwater and stale black sawdust . . . Jees! What would it feel like not to be hungry for once? Why, for Crisake, don't the Red Cross or somebody send over some parcels of food from home? Home? . . . Crise! Ma would be home from work now, banging around in the kitchen, frying up a swell mess of hamburg with onions for herself and Gert . . . Gert! . . . Jees, I never thought I could love a woman like I love her! Three weeks was all we had together and now two goddam years of this! Gert! Gert! . . . Holycrise, if I let myself think of her I'll go nuts!

A pretty slattern stepped up to the mike in the crowded People's Court, glared at the judges. "It's like this, see! We was married three weeks and then he went across and I lived with his mother till the baby was born paying board reg'lar and now I want my husband's insurance. I'm entitled to it ain't I? I support his child only it's made out to his mother and she won't give it me . . ."

"Was your husband killed in action?"

"Killed nuthin'! He's in a prison camp but I . . ."

"If he's not dead, you're not entitled to any insurance."

"Yes I am too entitled to it supposin' he dies only as I was saying his mother won't make over the money to me. It's ten thousand dollars and she ain't got no right to it. I'm his wife and it's his child and I've got certificates to prove it so you can't tell me I ain't entitled to it . . ."

Over there, an icy wind blew away the stench of offal . . .

CHAPTER NINE

BILL WENT UP THE STEPS OF THE RECREATION CENTER TWO AT a time. There was no sound of music inside. He jerked the door open and went in. . . . Ah, so it was like that — three of the boys joshing her at the piano . . . three of the roughnecks. They'd better beat it down Duke Street with Tom and Nick where they belonged! Maybe they didn't think he could handle it! . . .

He went over at top speed and fetched up beside the piano bench, facing the three men. "You'll pardon me for butting in," he said icily, "but I have an urgent message for Miss Wainwright from her father!"

Minchen swung round to him quickly.

The three eyed him blankly. One said, "Is zat so?"

And another, in a hard voice: "All right, spill it quick, bud, and scram! We're on the floor, see!"

Then Minchen took hold. The tone of Bill's voice was odd, and there was something in his face . . . She rose, smiled at the three of them. "Listen, boys! If you'll wait a moment, I'll probably come straight back. But this is something I've been expecting and it may be important." She turned to Bill. "Would you mind coming over to the window?" She began to lead the way there, talking. "I suppose Dad came tearing down the hill on his bike. Is it the answer from . . ." She kept the trickle going till they reached the window and were out of earshot. Then she said, differently, "Is anything the matter, Bill?"

"Yes," he said, and his voice was still icy. "Plenty! But those guys are all set to make trouble if we stand here and talk. Let's get out of here, and quick!"

"Out of here?" Minchen's eyes searched into his. "All right. I'll go through the kitchen, as if I were just fetching something from my coat, and I'll go out through the back. You can pretend to read a magazine for a minute and then go out the front way. I'll meet you outside the chemist's across the street. I don't believe they'll follow."

"They'd better not!" said Bill. "I might start something!" He left her, strolled ostentatiously past the piano to the magazine table, picked up an ancient *Saturday Evening Post* and sat down. He lit a cigarette first, and was astonished to find that the match shook in his hand. He began riffling through the pages with an impatient finger. . . . She hadn't fussed or hesitated! She'd looked at him straight and snapped into it! Wouldn't you know it? . . . At the piano one of the three began picking out a tune with one finger. . . . After a minute or so, Bill flung down the magazine and, with his hands in his pockets, strolled across to the door. As soon as it had swung to behind him, he went down the steps in two leaps and made for the drugstore. Dimly he saw her, standing by her bicycle at the curb.

He joined her. "Come on!" he said. "Let's beat it!"

Once more she didn't fumble the ball. She was in step with him right away, pushing her wheel.

They were headed back towards the market place, went like shadows threading their way among other shadows, catching now and then a word or two from mouths they barely saw.

Presently Bill said, "Know where we're going?"

"I've been wondering!" said Minchen.

"The Berkshires, I hope!" said Bill.

Minchen stared at him, trying to see his face in the dimness. It couldn't be done . . . and there was still that difference in his voice. She tried a laugh and said, "Sorry! I'm awfully bad at riddles."

"Think I'm kidding, do you?" snapped Bill. "Listen, for Pete's sake let's go somewhere where we can sit down. We can't talk this way, and I've got to talk fast. Isn't there some place, one of these tearooms, where there won't be anybody? There are too damn many soldiers in this man's town!"

"The nearest place I know," said Minchen, "is just behind the fountain. I imagine that at this time of the evening it ought not to be full."

"It's got to be empty," said Bill, "or else . . ."

Dollar-gleaners had sprung up in every side street — people who had turned their front parlors into tearooms, stuck a sign in the window, and fed all their homemade jam, and water cress, to an eternally hungry soldiery. In some of these places other things were obtainable than jam, so that their reputation spread like wildfire and the gleaning was good — until the day when the Provost Marshal put them out of bounds to the troops.

The one behind the fountain boasted no more than six tables. The arty note in the checked tablecloths, plus a large colored lithograph of "September Morn," supposedly raised it at least one degree above drabness, and at night there was always half a scuttle of coal ready to have a match touched to it.

They found the place empty.

Minchen promptly annexed the table nearest to the fireplace and sat down. She could see Bill's face now — drawn, frowning. . . . Could it be anything she had done, or not done? And what on earth did he mean by going to the Berkshires? . . . "We'll have to order something," she said, "even if we don't want it. Why not make it two pots of tea?"

Bill nodded.

The waitress who appeared in the doorway smirked at him, pulled herself together at sight of Minchen. Thin, already a trifle gone at the knees, attempting to do the impossible with a perfume called *Nuits Exotiques,* she made you think of Dali, and then try not to; but, once you had, you could almost see thwarted desires, like snakes, twining and writhing from her navel, finding nothing on which to fasten save the distorted shadows projected from her mind.

Minchen smiled at her absently. "May we have two pots of tea, please?"

"Any jam or cress?"

"No thanks. Just the tea and a little milk."

Dali nodded and removed herself.

Minchen put her elbows on the table and her chin on her clasped hands as she watched Bill fidgeting at the mantelpiece, opening a new pack of cigarettes, crumpling the cellophane nervously into a tight ball and then flicking it onto the coals, his fingers fumbling as he tore a hole in the top of the pack so that the cigarettes would shake out one by one. . . . Usually he was so neat. . . . What could possibly be the matter?

He turned to her abruptly, held out the packet, one cigarette sticking out ready for her to take.

She tried to catch his eye as she took it, but he kept staring at the match flame as he struck it under his thumbnail, put it first to her cigarette and then to his own.

So she said, watching him, "The chairs are not nearly as hard as they look, Bill. . . . Incidentally, do I get a good mark for coming away without a single question . . . leaving those men flat . . . ? I thought it was pretty good staffwork . . ." She stopped. It seemed to her that it was about all she could manage of pseudo-bright drool. And she wasn't sure that he had even heard.

But apparently he had. He turned from the mantelpiece and looked at her, for the first time. "It was tops!" he said. "I knew you'd come through like that. It wouldn't have been you if you hadn't. It wouldn't have been us either. . . ."

In spite of herself Minchen's eyes dropped. "Us?" she repeated, but even to herself her voice seemed small, from a suddenly dry throat . . . now that she knew.

Bill jerked his cigarette into the fire, tweaked a chair out and sat down facing her across the small table, leaning towards her, tense as a wound-up spring. "Yes, us!" he said. "At least that's how I've been thinking of it. . . . I hope you're going to tell me you have too, because I've got to tell you something that . . . that's going to change everything. . . ."

Now that she knew, hadn't everything changed already? Minchen could feel her heart banging against her ribs, loudly, insistently; and the hand holding the cigarette trembled so that the smoke was making odd jerky patterns. . . . Changed? Why, it wasn't Friar's Dene, or even England; there was neither time nor space. All feeling and thinking and living could never be the same again. . . .

"In the old days," said Bill, "I mightn't have had the nerve to take a chance quite so soon, but you're in this war too and you know the kind of things it does. . . . I mean, the fact that we happened to walk right into each other the way we did . . . as though we were both . . . ready. And the fact that you made me want to come down every evening so as to check up on what I'd been thinking about you all day. Did you know I've been doing that? I didn't realize it myself until this evening, and then all of a sudden it hit me with a bang and there wasn't a thing to do about it except to tell you . . . and here I am, trying. Tell me, did I . . . find you all by myself, or did you find me too?"

. . . A few streets away, champagne corks were popping in a brothel. A few miles away, twelve hundred bombers and fighters were blasting the coast of France. A few days away, and it might be D-Day. . . . But on their tiny pin point of isolation this boy and girl were held by a force greater than them all.

In her changed world, Minchen had already progressed. She

had a queer sense that she was not sitting there for the first time, not hearing these words for the first time. It had all happened before. It was as though all the years of her life had been merely a pause, a waiting, perhaps a preparation, for her to hear them again now. . . . Curious that he should have used the word "ready"! What else could she be? As ready as the earth when the sun rises on a new day, or the rain falls upon the waiting fields. . . .

Nevertheless her voice was shaking when she answered. "I feel as if I'd been expecting you," she said. "As though we had known each other all our lives . . . but didn't recognize each other immediately."

Their hands were on the table, a bare inch apart. Up to now he had never touched her, never even shaken hands. They had always met each other with "Hi!" and a grin. Up to this moment the inch had been a mile. It was nothing now. Bill's hand moved to hers and took it . . . and it was not simply that the touch of it was as cool and soft as the petal of a flower . . . it was Minchen's! And immediately things in him were melting and breaking down and quickening and changing their character and leaping. . . . Unusual words like "trust," "communion," "faith," flicked through his mind, and a surge of fierce pride and unutterable tenderness. . . . All he could muster to say came in a gasp. "Minchen! . . . Little Minch . . . oh my God!"

Minchen's eyes were like stars. "Isn't it wonderful that it's happened?"

"It's the greatest moment in the history of the world!" said Bill. "There's never been anything like it! . . . I just want to go on staring at you so that I can believe it. . . . Do you know you've changed? You don't look a bit the same as you did a minute ago! And it's incredible how much more beautiful the Berkshires are now that you've come!"

Minchen nodded, smiling. "Ah, I see now! . . . But of course I've changed. You have too. Nothing's ever going to be the same again—us, Mother and Dad, tonight, tomorrow, anything!"

"You're dead right!" said Bill. "It's the nearest thing to being born all over again that I've ever experienced—only born grown-up, with everything hitting on all eight . . . and with your foot right down on the gas! Why, until we . . . found out, we were just idling! We've got to step on it to catch up. Hang on to my hand, tight, while I make the next jump. . . . That's right! Now listen. You said something one night . . . it seems a million years ago now!" He laughed. "But anyway, it was the second time I came to the cottage and your father proposed that toast. Remember?"

"Of course!" said Minchen. "And I remember that you touched your glass to mine."

"And you remember what I said to you—that your dad was handing us a tough assignment? And you said 'I'm not afraid!' Remember that?" He laughed again. "Judas! It's extraordinary what a past we have already!"

Minchen moved her hand a little in his. "I'm less afraid than ever, now!" she said.

"That's what I wanted to hear!" said Bill. "I knew you'd come through with that! And I'm going to take you up on it. . . . Now, hold tight!"

Minchen smiled. "I'm ready!"

Bill leaned forward. "What do you say we get married tomorrow?"

Her eyes widened, but didn't leave his. "Tomorrow?"

At the gasp she gave, Bill tightened his grip on her hand. "We know, don't we? We're not just a couple of kids any more. Not now! This is the moment when we begin to live! And it's for the rest of our lives! Haven't we the right to make up our own minds? God knows they haven't left us many rights these days, but that's one of them! They can't stop us if we really want it . . . that is, if you really want it! I'm not trying to jerk you into this, Minch!

It's for you to decide, and I want you to use all the brains in your head! If you say no, I'll take it, and I won't say another word! . . . You see, things move fast in this war, and I'm . . . on the production line!" He smiled, made a gesture towards his uniform. "You know as well as I do that they're liable to call on me to produce at any time, and when they do . . . well . . . the going's going to be tough! And so there's the question of my coming back . . . or not coming back, as the case may be. . . . You know! . . . Your father would say that I don't stand a dog's chance. But if I hadn't a terrific hunch that I am coming through, I wouldn't have breathed a word of all this to you. I happen to believe it. I feel it. There are too many things to be done, afterwards . . . and it seems to me that our names may be written down somewhere to do them . . . yours and mine, Mr. and Mrs. Bill Thatcher! Think of it, Minch! Think hard! And remember, if you say no . . . why . . . that's fine, and you'll see me come leaping back to get you as soon as the show's over. . . . I think even your father would give me time out for the wedding!"

He broke off with a grin that was intended to be cheerful, casual.

But Minchen knew. She knew herself too. Everything had changed. She wasn't a girl any more, belonging to herself, untouched. She was a woman, and a man wanted her, wanted her for his wife, wanted to marry her tomorrow, before the call would come . . . at any time . . . to go out and "produce" . . . and the man was her man, and she was his "for better or for worse, till death do us part." . . . They said that to each other even in peacetime! But they didn't think about death then. It was merely a word, a poetic thought. Now it wasn't. . . . She would wake every morning and look out of the window and ask "Is Bill all right today . . . please?" And when she went to bed she would be asking, "Is Bill still all right tonight . . . please?" And somehow, in that way, they would be together . . . and even if she were only engaged to him it would be a sort of . . . protection for him. But if she were his wife, wouldn't that make it doubly strong . . . chain mail . . . surrounding him, enfolding him, keeping him . . . perhaps? And what if they only had a week together? Or it might stretch to a whole month. . . . For Bill it might be forever . . . if her thought, her prayer, were not strong enough. And she belonged to him now, not to herself. She mustn't think of herself any more, only of him, for him. . . .

She tried to smile. Somehow it only succeeded in matching Bill's grin. "I lied to you!" she said. "I am afraid now . . . but not of getting married!"

Bill made an odd sound in his throat. "Then it's . . . tomorrow?"

There wasn't any need for her to say anything. Her answer was in her eyes.

Bill could read. He found himself on his feet, her side of the table . . . and Minchen stood up . . . and then they were in each other's arms. . . .

REPORT from the Chinese Council of Economic Research:

"Since the outbreak of the war against China, Japan's war imports are as follows:

From the U.S.A.: 54.4%
From Great Britain: 17.5%
From the Dutch Indies: 7.4%
From Germany: 3.8%

"If our allies should cut off their sales of war materials to Japan, the annual loss of trade would be:

To the United States: two hundred million dollars.
To Great Britain: sixty-seven million dollars."

Matthew 27, 5–6:

"And he cast down the pieces of silver in the temple . . . and went and hanged himself.

"And the chief priests took the silver pieces, and said, It is not lawful for to put them into the treasury, because it is the price of blood."

CHAPTER TEN

JACK WAINWRIGHT SNAPPED OFF THE RADIO BUTTON. THE NEWS was Italian, and Russian. "My God," he said, "I don't understand it!"

Muriel glanced at him over her embroidery. "Understand what, dear?"

"This business of D-Day!" said Jack. "Have we got a General Staff or haven't we? I can't imagine what they're waiting for. In a couple of days it'll be June. I'm convinced that the ground's dry enough in France by now to operate guns and tanks, and surely to God we must be ready! . . . Do you suppose it's all part of the war of nerves? Or do you think we're not really going to attack this year at all, and rely on bombing? I can't believe it, but June makes it so desperately late. They'll have to plan on getting bogged down by November. . . . I confess to you, my dear, that I find myself praying for D-Day and loathing it at the same time. Like all wars — and that's the bitter paradox — this one has to be fought and has to be won . . . by us. But I know the frightful slaughter D-Day means. The only admissible thought is that a break-through will bring the end of the war that much nearer."

Muriel's work went down on to her lap. "The end of the war!" she echoed. "Oh Jack, if only we dared think of it!"

Jack shook his head. "We can't yet. The whole bloody world's got to be bled white first!" He gave a laugh that was like a bark. "And to think also that you and I won't be dead before they start another one! We may be in a couple of wheel-chairs, but, by God, we'll see it! And Minchen's potential children will be the exact age to go first. Incredible spectacle of helplessness!"

"Ah, no! Please!" said Muriel. "I won't think about that. I refuse. This one is so awful, I can't believe they'll ever want another. Let's not talk about it."

"I'm sorry, dearest!" said Jack quickly. "Forgive me. I didn't mean to unload on you like that . . . but, somehow, I can find no escape from it all. . . . Shall I turn on a little music?"

Muriel shook her head. "No. Let's go outside. It's such a perfect evening, and a breath of air will do us both good. You go ahead. I'm going upstairs for a moment."

As she rose, Jack also got up from his chair. He reached out and caught hold of her by the shoulder, a smile at the corners of his eyes. "Would it surprise you to know that I admire you very much, Mrs. Wainwright?"

Muriel smiled up into his face, a foot and a half above her own. "Not a bit," she said. "And if you'd take that pipe out of your mouth I'd show my proper appreciation. . . ."

Jack laughed, tilted up her chin with two fingers. Then he removed the pipe, bent down and kissed her.

"And now," said Muriel, "why, especially, at this moment?"

Jack shook his head. "I should have to begin twenty-five years ago," he said. "It's a long time to have lived with a gloomy devil like me. I often wonder how you stand it."

Muriel laughed. "It's a military secret. . . . Wait for me at the gate, darling, will you?"

Jack nodded, patted her shoulder. As she went towards the stairs, he strolled to the cottage door. It was open as usual. He stepped down on to the brick path. Halfway along it, the yellow cat was sitting, performing his evening ablutions.

"Hullo!" said Jack. "Waiting for Minchen? You're a trifle early, old lad. She's not due back for a couple of hours yet." He bent down, scratched the cat between the ears for a moment, then went on to the gate and leaned his elbows on it. . . . Minchen . . . and her potential children . . . He made an empty gesture with his good hand, shook his head, frowning. The sky was full of stars, and silent. Too early yet for the bombers. . . . It gave one a moment, thank God, in which to hear the village breathe, the untouched village, the lucky village! And the beech leaves were quietly rustling, and somewhere a dog barking, and faint music from somebody's gramophone . . . rather pleasant in the distance . . . one of those old Viennese waltzes too, lushly sentimental, reminding one of a table for two with the champagne being twirled in the ice-bucket. . . . God, how far away! Back even before the other war had completely knocked the props from under everything, the sham, the hypocrisy, the greedy jockeying . . . and then they had done nothing . . . nothing . . . and there would be the inevitable wheel-chair in which to chew a bitter cud . . . But not any more tonight. Grant me at least a moment out!

Behind him came the click of Muriel's shoes on the bricks, short, brisk, birdlike . . . he would recognize it on any bricks in the world, recognize it with a profundity of emotion that was inexpressible.

He turned to her, watching her come. "Hullo, dearest! I thought you were never coming. And it is so perfect out here tonight. Would you like just to lean on the gate, or shall I get a couple of chairs? Or what about strolling to the edge of the beeches?"

Muriel tucked her hand through his arm. "Let's just lean," she said. "I've often thought that the man who built this gate used to come out every evening and smoke his pipe here, just as you do. It invites, doesn't it? And he made it just wide enough for two, bless him."

"He probably sported a wig and knee breeches," said Jack.

"And a lovely ruffle to catch all the snuff he spilled," said Muriel.

"And the chances are," said Jack, "that he was just as outraged at the coming of the Spanish Armada as we have been by the Germans. The more it changes, the more it's the same thing, eh?"

Muriel ignored that one. She said quietly, "And perhaps he had a daughter too, and worried about her . . . not all by himself, but to his wife."

Jack turned to her quickly. "You mean . . . Bill?"

Muriel nodded.

Jack said, "What do you think we ought to do?"

"I was going to ask you that," said Muriel.

"And I was hoping you'd tell me," said Jack. "Has she by any chance confided in you?"

"Good heavens, no!" said Muriel.

"Then what's your feeling?" said Jack. "You know a great deal more about these things than I do. Is she only very much interested, or is she in love with him?"

Muriel hesitated. "My dear," she said, "it's such a fine line between the two. My feeling is that she has already crossed it, but of course I don't know for certain. All one can say is that her manner, her interest, her approach, are all something we've never seen in her before. And you have to admit that Bill has everything to attract a girl, good looks, tremendous personality—plus, in this particular case, their mutual passion for music. And more than all that, I happen to know that in addition to his having come up here every Sunday, he hasn't missed a single night at the Recreation Center!"

"And Minchen has always said that the piano down there is no good. The inference is pretty obvious, isn't it?" said Jack. "All I can say is that for Minchen's sake I pray to God that she isn't in love with him."

"Oh Jack, that seems such an awful thing to say."

"It is an awful thing." Jack banged his fist on the top of the gate. "It's a crime against life to have to say it. Why shouldn't those two fall in love? Isn't Minchen the sort of girl that any man would be damned lucky to marry? And Bill is one of the nicest lads I've ever met, as clean and straight as they come. I'd have chosen him as an officer in my battery out of a million others. By all the laws of nature they're absolutely made for each other. But they have to meet and fall in love with a thing called D-Day hanging over their heads. D-Day . . . Death-Day! Can't you see the beaches littered with the corpses of all the Bill Thatchers? Can't you imagine all the Minchens with their hearts broken? Another two generations have to be wiped out . . . for nothing again . . . for a slogan that's a lie, just as our slogans were lies. Freedom! Great Christ, whose freedom? If we are lucky enough to win our own freedom from the Germans and the Japs, are we going to give a damn about anybody else's freedom? Will the Indians be free of us? Or the Javanese from the Dutch? Or Indo-China free of the French? Ask Churchill! It's going to be a Limited Liability Company, that's all . . . Freedom Incorporated . . . with fat bonuses to a jealous board of directors!"

Muriel tugged at his arm. "Oh, my dear, I hate to hear you say these things. You only torture yourself . . ."

Jack gave a dry laugh. "One is supposed to enjoy masochism," he said. "Perhaps I do subconsciously. Perhaps it's a form of punishment that ought to be only mine, but which I'm always inflicting on you. It's in the air . . . everywhere . . . every gesture . . . one is without escape. It's a sort of mental concentration camp. . . . If it hadn't been for you . . ."

Muriel's hand crept into her husband's. She said quietly, "And what about Minchen?"

"It would have been better if she had fallen in love with a cripple!" he said violently. "A nice bright boy minus an arm or a leg is the only safe kind for a husband these days."

"Isn't there anything we can do?" said Muriel.

"Do?" Jack laughed again abruptly. "My dear, you don't ask

that question seriously, do you? There's nothing to be done. We're as helpless as corks in a stream. All we can do is hope and pray . . . or curse . . . and stand by her. And if your own heart gets broken in the process, I suppose that's just part of the game."

"That's ridiculous!" said Muriel. "I refuse to be so utterly helpless. I'm going to talk to her tonight. I think we both ought to talk to her."

Jack shook his head. "My dear," he said, "perhaps you have faith as a grain of mustard seed. Perhaps you can stop the tide, or switch the moon from her course, or turn the mind and heart of man from making war. But for Minchen and Bill there has to be D-Day!"

"Hush!" said Muriel. "Listen! . . . I thought I heard Minchen's voice."

Both remained silent, their heads turned towards the end of the village, where the trail began down the hill. The distant dog had stopped barking, but another Strauss waltz had been put on the invisible gramophone. It came like an echo. And then they heard the crunch of quick steps, an eager laugh and not only their daughter's voice, but Bill's.

"It's too early," said Jack. "I wonder . . ."

Muriel caught her breath sharply, for the two young ones emerged from the trees on to the village street, and even in the soft starlight it was obvious that they were hand in hand.

It seemed to Jack Wainwright that a cold grip had closed on his stomach . . . the sour-sweet smell of that oozy shellhole was in his nostrils. He pressed his wife's hand urgently. "It's come!" he whispered. "We . . . we mustn't let them see!" He turned his head towards them and raised his voice. "Hullo, you two! What on earth are you doing here? Did you bust the piano or something?"

It was Minchen who laughed and answered. "Hullo, Dad!"

They were not more than twenty paces away now, and coming

fast, tingling, radiant, wonderful, their clasped hands swinging, openly, triumphantly.

At the gate they halted, shoulder to shoulder.

Minchen said, "Oh Mother, I'm glad you're there too. Bill and I have news for you. It may seem like rather a bombshell. You see . . . we've made up our minds to get married . . . tomorrow . . . and here we are to tell you all about it. Don't you think it's wonderful, Mother? Don't you, Dad?"

Even corks can get dragged under for a moment . . . when they hit a rock . . .

"Tomorrow! . . . Minchen!" That was Muriel, coming up to the surface.

Jack Wainwright passed a hand over his face. It rasped deafeningly.

Minchen put her hand on the gate. "Let's all go in. We can't very well tell you about it here."

It seemed an eternity before Jack Wainwright came up. He heard himself say, "Would it be in order for me to have a word alone with Bill first? There may be one or two things . . ."

Bill leaped at the opening. "Thanks for suggesting that, sir. I was going to ask if I might talk to you."

Minchen laughed. "Oh well . . . if you must! But don't be too long, even though Mother and I have heaps to say to each other."

Her father moved from the gate and the two young ones came in, and then Minchen slipped an arm through her mother's, and the two women went up the path together and into the cottage.

Bill shot a quick glance at the older man's face, took a deep breath. There was something in Major Wainwright's face . . . He couldn't tell, but this wasn't going to be easy. Had he better wait? Or should he jump in first? . . . First! "You see, sir," he began, "I . . ."

But Jack Wainwright held up a restraining hand. "Would you

mind, Bill?" he said. "I'm . . . still trying to pull myself together. That was something of a haymaker you two landed."

Bill laughed apologetically. "I suppose it was," he said. "But we both felt you would understand."

Jack Wainwright raised his eyebrows at the slight emphasis on the word "you." How much and how little he understood! And the boy was so sure . . . and so right to be sure. It was such a magnificent disregard, a sort of defi . . .

The Strauss waltz was still grinding itself out, and the dog had started barking again . . . but the sound of the leaves seemed to have changed from a rustle to a shiver . . .

He turned quickly to the boy. "Look here, Bill," he said, "I'd like to say at once that I've never met a man whom I'd rather see Minchen marry. In these four very pleasant Sundays that we've all spent together, both my wife and myself have felt that you have become one of the family."

A great wave of relief loosened Bill's muscles. He wanted to laugh, to shout, to celebrate. Instead, he stammered out, "I . . . I can't tell you how much that means to me, sir! Why that . . . that makes it . . ."

Jack Wainwright interrupted. "Not altogether," he said. "I want to ask you something first."

"Yes, of course," said Bill quickly.

"You see," said Jack Wainwright, "although my wife and I were weakly human enough to bring a child into this incredible world, we happen to . . . be fond of her, and we would like to save her from being crucified . . ."

Bill gasped. "Crucified?"

Jack Wainwright spread his hands. "It's all in the point of view, isn't it? Of course I realize that it's damned egocentric of us and without the slightest importance in view of what's taking place in most other countries at the moment. Nevertheless, as her father, I think I can be forgiven for not wanting to see her in a concentration camp, or in the hands of the Gestapo, or, for that matter, married to a soldier."

Through dry lips, all Bill could find to say was, "I don't see . . . I don't know what you mean . . ."

"That's what I was afraid of," said Jack Wainwright. "To me they're all the same. It's just a question of degree. What about D-Day, Bill? Where will you be? If you marry Minchen, don't you think you'll be dumping the whole war into her lap as a wedding present, that you'll be offering her a refinement of torture that is the special privilege of all married women in wartime, especially brides? Of course"—he shrugged his shoulders—"I don't pretend to know anything about women, much less about the modern angle on war marriages. Perhaps war affects their psychology and they like the excitement, the glamour of it. Perhaps most of them can return to their bridge and cocktails, merely pretending to be suffering heroines. I don't know. But I do know that Minchen doesn't know how to pretend. . . . Do you like the idea of your bride's listening to the radio descriptions of the fighting on D-Day, Bill? She will be doing that, you know. And I'm old-fashioned enough to think of it as a form of crucifixion. . . . You must have other ideas."

He saw that the boy's face was getting tighter and tighter. It was what he wanted. The answer wouldn't come from the surface.

"You already have Sicily and Salerno behind you, Bill, and D-Day just ahead. You'll agree that there are several things a soldier has to face, whether married or unmarried. Only, being married underlines them rather. The first is death, which is simple. The second is mutilation, and that's . . . not so simple. There's a third thing, one of the intangibles. Let us call it mutilation of the soul. It can damage a man just as badly as lopping off his arms or legs. Nothing shows, of course, but it's a nice private little hell. . . . One or two of the fellows I fought with finally preferred suicide. Not so good, eh? . . . Anyhow, those are the three main gambles, aren't they? And of course, lots of men, the lucky ones, perhaps, are really non-sentient, purely animal. They can face those three gambles as if they didn't exist. The others — and I include you among them, Bill — are the unlucky ones. They're really fighting double. They not only have to face the enemy, but their own understanding of the odds against them. It takes . . . added guts. But when one of them, knowing these things, contemplates marrying a girl during a lull in the fighting, it implies, to me, only one of two things. Either he is really the other kind, purely animal, and wants her body at the only price he can get it; or else, momentarily, he has lost command of himself, been pushed too far, is trying to bolster up his courage with hers, and offering her practically nothing but the early prospect of widow's weeds. It strikes me as tragedy for both of them."

He glanced again at the boy's face, began tapping his pipe out against the open palm of his hand.

"Nice of you to have listened, Bill!" he said. "Feel like giving me your ideas?" He pulled out his tobacco pouch and the noise of the zipper was sharp in the silence between them.

Perhaps it was the sight of another man about to smoke. Perhaps it was merely nervous tension. Almost without being aware of it, Bill produced cigarettes and lit one, flipped the extinct match out into the street, took a couple of deep drags. . . . The ancient waltz was still playing, but he hadn't heard it. All he had heard, behind the devastatingly quiet stream of opposition, out of which projected such rocks as "crucifixion," "dumping the war into her lap," "bolstering up his courage with hers," was the flood of unuttered words that had surged through his mind — words that it was so hard to make mean what you wanted them to, especially when almost every one of Major Wainwright's had a barb in it. How could he argue with a point of view that had been twenty years in the making? What chance had he of making him see that, even if the things he said were true, they couldn't possibly apply to Minchen and himself? Not a chance in the world!

The palms of his hands were sweating, cold and sticky . . . Maybe there was one way out of this spot — the simple truth. He'd have to see that. He'd make him see it.

He turned and looked straight into Major Wainwright's waiting eyes. "Look," he said. "I'll try and tell you how it is between Minchen and me. . . . I know about D-Day. I went into that. And I want you to know that I questioned my right to say anything to Minchen before I told her. And when I did tell her . . . I said that I was willing to wait till after the war. I also told her not to say yes or no till she had decided whether she was willing to take the gamble on my coming back. . . . I — I didn't mention . . . mutilation. Perhaps that was a dirty trick. Also I didn't know about what you called the inner kind. So I didn't go into that either. . . . If you think I wasn't fair with her, didn't really come clean with her, I wish you'd do it . . . now . . . right away. I don't want to marry her under false pretenses. She has to know what it's all about. But when she said yes, I . . . I felt that she really did know. And so of course it was I who suggested our getting married tomorrow. It didn't occur to me that I was . . . trying to bolster up my courage. It doesn't now. And as for what you call the animal side of it . . . I suppose it would be pretty hard to deny that, up to a point. But it wasn't in my mind when I asked her to marry me. I asked Minchen to marry me for the same reason you had when you asked Mrs. Wainwright to marry you . . . because I love her, because she's the only girl I shall ever want to marry, because when we get back to the Berkshires we can start all over together, try and accomplish something worth while together, at least face life and bring up our children together. It all seemed so . . . so simple, so natural. And I felt so certain that I was coming through. And Minchen did too. So we both wanted to hurry. We felt that we . . . that we had the right to spend the rest of the time together before D-Day, before our personal gamble begins. . . . That's how we stand at this moment, sir. But I wish you'd . . . talk to Minchen."

Bill Thatcher stopped, as abruptly as he had begun, and stood waiting.

Jack Wainwright's fingers were turning and twisting on his pipe, as his mind turned and twisted to dodge the vision of shell-holes, rain, machine guns, the million-to-one chance. . . . What was it he had said to Muriel? Faith as a grain of mustard seed. Here it was again, flowering, pathetic, magnificent. Might it be strong enough to triumph? After all, many would come back, whole, undamaged within or without. . . . He himself had only been . . . well . . . a little dog-eared! And the boy was clean, and straight, and not thinking only of himself, and had already acquired the germ of understanding. He was the type they would need afterwards, honest and strong, bringing with him that quickened sense of life and its values that only contact with death and an escape from it can give. . . . If there were any sense in the scheme of things, Bill would be one of those destined to come back. . . .

He put his hand on the boy's shoulder, gave it a little shake. "Thank you, Bill!" he said gravely.

Bill swallowed. "But you're . . . going to talk to Minchen?"

For a moment Jack Wainwright didn't answer. What was the good of "talking" to Minchen now? And yet . . . How much did she really understand? Had she weighed terror, and the steady daily pressure, wondering, waiting, hoping against hope? She was no bridge player, little Minchen! There would be nothing between her and the crown of thorns . . . and nothing that either Muriel or himself could do to help. She didn't even belong to them any more. She was Bill's. From now on, all they could do was stand by on the side lines, praying . . . or cursing. . . .

"I suppose it's a father's job," he said, "but I hate it."

"I wish you would," said Bill.

Jack nodded. Without another word, he marched himself up the brick path and into the cottage.

His wife and daughter were standing by the table, face to face — the girl's alight, vibrant as a plucked harpstring, so that the whole room seemed filled with the overtones of her emotion.

Muriel's eyes leaped to her husband's face as though to read his verdict.

Minchen said quickly, "Where's Bill, Dad?"

The beauty in her eyes made him catch his breath as though a sharp pain had pricked him. She was indeed Bill's! "He's all right," he said. "It's just that I . . . am ass enough to think that I ought to ask you a question. . . . May I?"

Minchen nodded. "Anything, Dad darling."

"Then," said Jack Wainwright, "must it be tomorrow? Couldn't it be . . . after the war?"

For a moment she didn't answer. And in that moment it seemed to Jack that another and older woman were standing there. He didn't need any answer.

But Minchen said quietly, "I know what you really mean. And that's why it's got to be tomorrow, Dad. You see . . . in a way, I don't count, now. It's Bill . . . just as he is. Nothing's going to happen to him, but . . . if it does . . . well . . . he won't have been cheated. Life owes him that . . . and so do I!"

It was all so simple, so natural. Bill had said it, and now Minchen, whose simplicity was fundamental, asking nothing, giving everything . . . Jack Wainwright took her in his arms and kissed her. "God keep you both, my dear!"

MAN does not live by bread alone . . .

In their prison cage, living skeletons muttered together, a flame growing at last in their eyes.

For the pounding of friendly guns was coming nearer . . . and nearer.

Like shadows the starved ones gathered at the barbed-wire gate, innumerable, feeble, but cloying as flakes of snow.

The two last guards came running, shoving — the rest had made their getaway.

To these two a thousand withered arms and legs felt like the beating of moths' wings and they laughed as they sought to punch a way through. . . .

But those eyes were flame throwers. . . . It was under them that the guards screamed and went down beneath a pile of skeletons whose bony hands went to their pleasant work. . . .

Gouging, blinding, strangling, satisfying . . .

Man does not live by bread alone.

CHAPTER ELEVEN

BECAUSE WAR HAD NOT SCARRED OXFORD, AND BECAUSE IT WAS near, they picked it for their honeymoon. Honeymoon? Even that tender word, implying thirty days of bliss, had suffered streamlining at the hands of brigadiers. All they granted Bill Thatcher was from Friday afternoon to Monday at dawn — fifty hours in which to change back from hard to soft, in which to find the self that had been reshaped. For soldiering not only robs you of privacy and self, it demands that you bang the lid down on all your tendrils of softness. You have to learn — don't you? — that to yield for a moment will give you a week's suffering, that, for example, to let yourself go in a letter home by expressing love or longing is to tear open a wound that heals slowly and whose edges grind in the process; and yet you want to hold the damn thing open and let it bleed; and at the same time you curse yourself for being such a weak fool as to open it; and you swear you won't do it again. But you do. And it hurts. Every time. . . . You've got to get tough — haven't you? — inside particularly, to harden everything over, to seal it off behind barbed wire, to dry it up, to kid yourself that it doesn't exist, to shove it as far back in abeyance as is inhumanly possible. And in the end you become a soldier. . . . Thanks a lot!

And the process of unhardening? That doesn't come so easily either — does it? Don't you know you're going to tear yourself on that rusty wire? Don't you know you're going to be played for a sucker by everyone who's never been out there? And that isn't so hot — is it? But if you don't, or can't, tear down what you've had to put up, God help you, soldier!

Bill Thatcher had Gela behind him, and Salerno, and Anzio — three stiff courses in the process of graduation. Call him a sophomore, still on the way in, still puzzling at the dimmest glimpses of what a man like Jack Wainwright knew by heart, but, as he himself had said, learning fast. It was natural that, being only a sophomore, his reaction to the secret briefing for D-Day had been violent, a subconscious revolt against outrage, a rush from the extreme of hardness to the opposite extreme of softness. It was, though he didn't know it, the ultimate gesture of nonacceptance. The honeymoon was the urgent summons of life, and he answered it exultantly, guard down, wide open, reckless — a young Icarus at last on his way to the sun.

Some fifty hours . . . like grains of sand running out.

Bride and groom in the ecstasy of their discovery of each other, filled with wonder and awe, and reverence and tenderness, and strength and softness, and hunger for each other, giving and receiving, "wounded by beauty in the summer night" . . . man and wife, alone together in the crowd, eyes alight, hand in hand, aware only of each other; Oxford a mere carpet unrolled for them to walk on by their servant, life; time in suspension in spite of Big Tom and all his satellites; ancient quadrangles and stately gardens their own private pleasance, from echoing cloisters to the windings of the river where the sun tossed largesse of gold upon the ripples for them alone. . . .

Fifty hours . . . imperishable, all-pervading.

It was on Sunday afternoon that a college porter said to Bill, "Are you enjoying Oxford, sir?"

For a moment Bill blinked at him. Then, with a grin, he said, "I think it's the most marvelous place in the world. We're coming back after the war to see it. I mean . . . to see it again!" And when they were out in the street once more, he laughed to

Minchen and said, "That was almost a break, wasn't it? I should have hated to hurt the guy's feelings, but let me tell you something. I haven't seen a thing but you! It's all been just a blur, a setting for you, Minch, a running accompaniment to the music of you! I haven't the slightest idea where I am and I don't care, so long as we're together! Oxford will keep. One day you and I will make a pilgrimage here and really look at it. We haven't time now, have we?"

And Minchen, staring straight ahead, squeezed his hand tightly. "Not a second to spare, Bill darling!"

There was a moment of absolute silence between them — the projecting shadow of the train that in an hour would be taking them back to Friar's Dene.

Bill frowned at his wrist watch. "Fifty minutes now! If only to God it was fifty years!" He took a deep breath. "Listen, honey! Something darned important. I've been thinking about it. I want you to do something for me . . . for us. Promise?"

"Darling!" said Minchen.

"I've . . . I've thought up a way we can be together, every day, at the same time, when I'm . . . across the Channel."

Minchen's spare hand came up to her throat.

"This is what you do," said Bill. "Every afternoon as the clock strikes five, you sit down at the piano. Play to me for an hour . . . all the things we both know . . . everything we've made a stab at together. And whatever I'm doing out there, I'll be singing them to myself inside, and in a sort of way I'll be sitting close beside you on the piano bench in the living room, close. . . . What do you say, honey?"

Minchen couldn't say anything, could hardly see anything. . . . Only her grip answered him.

"I knew you would!" said Bill. "And it isn't that I shan't be thinking about you the rest of the day. You're not going out of my thoughts any hour of my life, but over there from five to six will be . . . special . . . ours. I'll be whispering all the things I shan't be able to write. I'll be telling you all over again that I never knew I was alive till you came along."

He ended with what was meant for a laugh.

But there were tears spilling down Minchen's cheeks. "Oh, Bill!" she said. "I promise! I promise! And every note I play will be telling you how much I love you and want you. And nothing in the world will ever make me miss a single day. . . . Bill! Turn your head! Look at me!"

With a wrench he did so, smiled into her eyes.

"Oh my dear," she said, "you . . . you looked as if you'd . . . already gone. I couldn't bear that! We mustn't think of it. We're not going to think of it . . . either of us! We're here and I . . . I love you every minute, even when you . . . when you make me cry like a perfect fool in the middle of the street . . . Oh Bill!"

THE colored boy was on his knees in a cell.

"Jesus, help me! You know I ain't done it! Help me! Save me, Lawd!"

Outside the jail, the mob was like an angry sea in the night.

They broke in and laid hands upon him, gagged him, bound him with ropes and dragged him forth.

"Jesus, help . . ."

Whooping and cheering, the procession of cars streaked through the town.

The field was not far. There was a scorched tree in it. To it they tied the colored boy.

"Take the gag out! Let's hear the raping rat squeal!"

They took the gag out.

Five gallons of regular was enough for the job. . . .

Then they stood back and flipped lighted matches at the screaming boy. . . .

"Jesus . . ."

CHAPTER TWELVE

WHAT DOES A SOLDIER TAKE INTO HIS FOXHOLE? JUST A rifle and a bunch of grenades?

You might think so when you see him lying there, queerly flatter after the shell with his name on it has found him. Bits of the rifle may still be around, broken and useless. But the impedimenta of really important things he had with him — equally valueless now — have disappeared. They might never have been.

And yet it was a crowded foxhole, jam-packed with items of infinite value — his life, for instance; greatly augmented by his expensive army training, his potentiality as a killer, his possible aftervalue as a worker and father. . . .

"So what?" you say — you a fat civilian, or a thin one, or luckily too old, or holding a key job, and anyhow plugging yourself on black-market beefsteaks and kicking to the ration board for more gasoline.

Well . . . Take another look into the foxhole. You won't have to gag, because it hasn't begun to smell yet, and try to imagine that it might have been yourself if you hadn't had a break, or were smart, or something. . . . What else was there before the shell came? You can't imagine. Or maybe you don't give a damn.

That soldier, in addition to his life, had fear with him . . . cold, sweaty blinding terror; and he had to take it alone, and come out of it alone, and somehow transmute it into courage — or at least into the savage calm that lets a man kill. . . .

"Ah blah!" you say. "A G.I. scared?"

Ask a live one. He won't be scared to tell you.

But this one's dead now, and terror is over. Other things are over too, just as big as life and fear, and he had taken them all with him into his crowded lonely foxhole—everything he had stored up of love and ambition and pity and God and loyalty to his family and friends and his cleanness and dirtiness and his capacity for pleasure and misery and longing and remembering . . .

"Blah!" you say again. "Every man has a good healthy ninety-to-one chance of survival! The official limit on war casualties—killed, wounded, missing—is ten per cent!"

Wonderful! But doesn't it mean that, in an army of ten million, there will be a million occupants of foxholes whose photos will never appear in the glossy magazines being kissed by excited females when the army marches into a "liberated" town? Has it occurred to you where they'll be? Under a wooden cross, or on an operating table, or being slowly starved as prisoners. . . . But, after all, what's a mere million?

Bill Thatcher—like practically every man in every war—was convinced that he was not going to be one of the ten per cent. He had told Jack Wainwright so. He had told Minchen so when he asked her to marry him. He was "coming through." He knew it. And, now that Minchen was his wife, it just wasn't possible that . . . well, that anything could happen. The Major had certainly painted a grim picture, and he knew what he was talking about, all right! All too many poor devils were going to get theirs! D-Day, and afterwards, was going to be the toughest thing yet . . . but when you had a girl like Minchen waiting for you . . . why, this marriage was absolutely meant . . . as if they'd been led to one another . . . so of course everything was going to be all right . . . but meanwhile this damned D-Day. . . . It was already something to drop like a falling leaf where you knew the enemy wasn't . . . but this time it was going to be right in the thick of the dug-in Krauts who would give themselves a time plastering them with ack-ack and machine-gun fire as they floated down. . . .

In the manner of a man facing the inevitable — whatever it did to the pit of his stomach — he allotted the fact of it a given place in his mind, like a can of bitter pickles on the back pantry shelf, well out of the way.

But from the moment of his return from the honeymoon it was off the shelf. During all the daylight hours he was faced with it, working for it in the dirt of built-up fortifications exactly similar to those which they would have to storm on the day itself, timing it, memorizing it, absorbing it, getting more and more tightly ready for it.

After three nights and two and a half days away from it all with one woman, it was a shock to him to get back, a violent awakening from a dream, a growing awareness of the profundity of the emotional disturbance that had taken place within him. He found that he had been using different senses, different perceptions, had laid himself wide open.

The inevitable kidding, Chaucerian in its allusions, was hard to take. It seemed almost as if something had happened between him and the rest of the outfit. It was as if they didn't recognize him, treated him as a different man, as a stranger who would have to make good with them all over again. And he knew that they were right. He had left them all behind, escaped from the day-to-day conglomerate life of the unit, emerged on to another plateau of living. He found that his need for their companionship was outgrown, that he couldn't be bothered with the Monk and Paunch any more, its darts, its billiards, its craps, its beer. Every need and thought and desire was canalized to Minchen, heightened and satisfied by Minchen, by the sight of her, the touch of her, the realization even of the existence of her. It began to seem as if he were two Bill Thatchers — the unreal one training for D-Day; the real one in the cottage with Minchen.

Up there, there were so many things to be stored up . . . he had tasted the bitterness of foxholes . . . and it had to be done quickly, almost frantically, yet with the appearance of casualness, as though he were not reckoning every minute there with her, and with them, above the price of rubies.

It was not easy to grin cheerfully each morning as he kissed her good-by before tearing down to camp, for he carried with him the difficult knowledge that it might be the last morning. And all he could say to her was, "So long, Minch, honey! I'll be back up at the usual time this evening."

And Minchen, cheerful as a grig, not less calm than a commuter's bride, would reply in kind. "Of course, darling! Take care of yourself!"

And then they kissed . . . and off he would go, quickly, steel-hard.

It wouldn't have helped Bill if he could sometimes have seen his wife, standing where he had left her, motionless, only her eyes giving her away. In a moment she too would have to button on a smile and go downstairs to another day's pretending.

He never did see her, for when she had him back with her again, to see, to hear, to be with, Minchen didn't have to pretend any more. She had to be herself and more than herself. There was so little time, and Bill must not go away empty. He must be full and pressed down and running over with everything that she had to give. He must be completely enwrapped with her, her love, her youth, her courage, her mind, her faith, so that, in a sense, he would never go away at all. She would always be with him, in him, the other half of him, the non-soldier half that he would be yearning to come back to, so that at last they could go on together, whole again, one . . .

There was so little she could do . . . to be waiting for him at the gate when he came up, so as not to lose an instant of him; to lay the supper with him; to sit beside him at the table; to wipe the dishes as he washed; to feed the cat while he stood there talking; to hold him tight for an infinite second before going back to the family in the living room; to darn an army sock for him while he told her secret things on the piano; merely to listen as he talked to Dad and watch the expressions on his face and be ready for his eyes that reached for hers all the time; to go out walking with him in the woods in the moonlight when all the cottages were asleep; to stay awhile together after Mother and Dad had purposely gone up to bed; and then to turn out the lights and creep up with him soundlessly to her room which was now forever theirs, could never be hers again . . . so little, and yet heaven could hold no more.

"I *ALWAYS say you have to be a* part *of a war to understand it, and it's very very close to us! Of course, Albert and I do our bit —I'm in our Ambulance Corps, you know, and we cover the district between East Amelia and Grove Manor,* always *in uniform from noon on; and Albert is on the Draft Board and has to bear the brunt of so many people unwilling to do their simple duty! Oh my dear, the farmers are simply terrible, pretending to be needed! But Albert simply ignores them! . . . But as I started to say, we're closer than most, because Albert's sister's oldest son, Malcolm, holds an extremely important post in the WLB, and her younger son, Felix, is a lieutenant-commander in the Navy and has an office all to himself in the Pentagon! Then his cousin's daughter, Amy, is a WAC and right in the thick of it, a most responsible position driving a General, my dear, in one of the largest hospitals in England! . . . So you see how terribly,* terribly *interested we are in* all *the war news!*"

CHAPTER THIRTEEN

JUNE IS THE MONTH OF BRIDES AND ROSES.

On the breakfast table in the cottage there were as usual dark red roses in a silver bowl. Muriel had just cut them. There were beads of dew still on their petals.

The bride this morning was late.

Her father smiled as he sat down and unfolded his napkin. "No Bill last night again," he said, "therefore no Minchen this morning. I don't blame her. She's leading a strenuous life." He glanced at his wrist watch. "Eight minutes to go, for the news. . . . What are we eating?" He raised the lid of a dish. "Kedgeree! Wonderful!" He spooned up a couple of helpings, passed one to his wife. "There's no one in the world who can make this as you do, my dear. Toast?" He handed it to her, took a piece himself.

Muriel passed him his coffee—if one could still dignify it by that name. "Why do you suppose Bill couldn't come up last night?"

"Even a bridegroom in uniform has to be on duty sometimes!" said Jack. "He oughtn't to have a kick in the world. They've treated him pretty handsomely, I think, letting him off practically every night like this. It's only the second one he's missed since they were married."

"And this morning is the eighth day," said Muriel. "When he comes up tonight we ought to celebrate their first week. You know, Jack, we're awfully lucky!"

Her husband's eyes twinkled at her across the table. "I've known that for twenty-five years!" he said.

Muriel smiled. "I didn't mean that. I meant about Bill. If any marriage was ever made in heaven, this one was! They simply adore each other. . . . If only, when the time comes, Bill's father and mother become as fond of Minchen as we have of Bill! Have you faced the fact that one fine day she'll be going to America?"

Jack Wainwright didn't answer for a moment. When he did, it came somewhat slowly. "No, I . . . hadn't quite reached that point in my thinking. All the same . . ." His eyes softened again. . . . "I promise you, my dear, that when that day comes we'll trail along with them — if they'll let us."

He was rewarded for the suppression of his real thoughts by the glow that came over his wife's face.

He went on. "Looking to the fact that when Hitler and Company will have been successfully wiped out, the U.S.A. will have more to say in the shaping of the immediate future than any other country, I should like to go over and take a personal course in democracy. We haven't the faintest idea of it here in England."

From upstairs came the sound of a closing door. It was followed by quick feet down the stairs. Minchen came swinging into the room.

"Hullo, darling!" said Muriel.

Jack Wainwright watched her coming. You'd have to be blind, he thought, or an idiot, not to be able to read what was in her eyes, her walk, her manner. Even before Bill's coming you had to take a second look at her quiet loveliness; but now she was changed from quietness. She was alight, transfigured. It was as though radiance emanated from her, flooded the room. . . .

"Hullo Mother!" Minchen put an arm round her mother and kissed her, touched her father's shoulder and kissed the top of his head. "Hi Dad! . . . How were the early worms this morning without me?"

"Good morning, Mrs. Thatcher!" said Jack. "I don't have to ask if you enjoyed your extra nap. You look as if all the roses in the garden would have to fold up when you step out, in envy, hatred, jealousy and all malice."

Minchen laughed as she pulled out her chair and sat down. "Do you think I ought to blush and make him a deep curtsy for that, Mother? . . . What is there this morning? I'm starving!" She helped herself to fish and toast while her mother poured coffee for her.

Jack glanced at his watch again. Still three minutes to go for the news.

Muriel said, "We shall all starve tonight if I don't go down to Friar's Dene this morning. There literally isn't a thing in the house to eat."

The yellow cat came marching in, tail high, tip slightly bent. He went straight to Minchen and landed in her lap, his nose near the plate of fish.

"No, Frankie!" said Minchen. "I'll give you some when I've finished . . . Curl down, and sit still . . . That's right . . . By the way, Mother, I'm thinking of going down when Dad and I finish work. I'll do the shopping for you, if you like. I thought I'd meet Bill at the camp. Why on earth do you suppose they kept him down there last night again, Dad?"

"I suppose," said Jack, "his name was on the roster for guard duty. Every man has to take his turn you know, corporals or not."

"Yes, but . . . two nights running?"

Jack dodged her eyes. "It might be remarked that he has done an excellent job of wangling to have been able to come every night as he has." He reached out and snapped on the radio. While the tubes were warming up they went on talking.

"Wangling!" said Minchen. "I think it would have been utterly beastly if they hadn't let him come! . . . If we're a minute or two late this evening, Mother, you won't mind, will you? I thought we'd walk up over the fields. And don't lay the table. We'll do it as soon as we get here . . . Shall I tell you what Bill said about you the other day?"

"I can't imagine," said Muriel, "that he'd waste time talking about me."

"Well, he said that you had the most exquisite taste of anybody he'd ever met! How's that for a son-in-law?" Minchen laughed.

The radio tubes began to hum.

Muriel smiled. "A remarkably observant young man. . . . More coffee, darling?"

"Please!" said Minchen.

"I'll have some too," said Jack, "if the pot will stand it."

"I'll divide it between you," said Muriel.

"*This is D-Day! The invasion has begun! An hour before dawn Allied troops were pouring onto the beaches . . .*"

The one word "God!" tumbled from Jack Wainwright's lips.

The coffeepot remained on the table, but the knuckles of Muriel's hand were white with the intensity of her grip on the handle.

Minchen's fork stopped halfway to her mouth, then described a slow arc back to her plate while she stared wide-eyed at the instrument which was changing the world.

"*. . . of France. Thousands of planes are covering the landing. The guns of our battleships have knocked out many of the German coastal forts, but savage resistance from mortars and machine guns is reported to be causing casualties in some sections of the beaches. . . .*"

Jack Wainwright took one look at his daughter's face. He kicked his chair away and began marching up and down while the relentless excited voice went on pounding.

"*In other sections our troops have already fought their way in-*

land for several miles and have joined up with the paratroops who had succeeded in spiking the German defenses . . ."

The front paws and head of the yellow cat appeared above the table. Delicately he began eating the rest of Minchen's forgotten fish.

Suddenly he received the shock of his life, found himself scrabbling with his claws trying to hang onto the tablecloth. . . .

Minchen's chair had gone over backwards. . . . She couldn't listen any more. She mustn't. . . . She made for the door, blind and sick. It seemed a mile away. . . .

Muriel cried out: "Minchen! . . . Wait!"

But Minchen didn't hear or stop. At last she reached the door, fumbled for the thumb-latch, was out. . . .

"We can't let her go like that!" gasped Muriel. "I'm going to follow her! She might . . ."

The radio went on and on, tearing down, searing, destroying . . . building up, recreating, giving birth to wild hope . . .

Jack Wainwright's eyes were on the open door. "Oh my God!" he muttered. He turned to his wife and caught her by the hand. "No!" he said. "No, my dear! Not even you can help her now! Wait till she comes back!"

"But, Jack, she . . ."

"Steady now!" said Jack. "You've got to hang on to yourself! . . . Look! She's headed for the beech woods. That's as good a hole as any. She won't want anybody to see. . . . I wonder," he gave a harsh laugh, "I wonder if there were any beeches in the Garden of Gethsemane?"

[illegible] and going [illegible]

[illegible]

[illegible] "As she comes down!"

[illegible]

[illegible] gently down," said Jack. "You see [illegible]

[illegible] Stick handed [illegible]

[illegible]

[illegible] of education?"

Part Two

ON the open beaches of the world
The dead,
Sharing the democracy of youth.
Through the open windows of the world's ration boards
The quick,
Sharing the democracy of the home front—
Like strip-teasers, tearing off the final G-string of decency,
Exhibiting a naked ego,
Mean, lying, timorous, bullying,
Greedy, angry, self-righteous, pathetic . . .
With full bellies lusting for more meat,
With crowded pantries demanding more sugar,
With squandered mileage howling for more gas,
With well-shod feet itching for more shoes,
More this, more that, just more, of anything . . .

CHAPTER ONE

IN LITTLE MINCHEN THE LONG SUMMER MONTHS, TO ALL OUTWARD seeming, might as well have been about to occur in the reign of Henry V. In those days, the local farmers had probably just received the news of the battle of Agincourt, mumbled appropriate oaths, spat, and gone on with their farming.

In the reign of the present George, the names had changed, if not the locale — Caen, St.-Lô, Isigny, Carentan, Avranches. There were more of them, that was all, and the news came faster.

But Little Minchen was off the German bomb-run, and not even susceptible to the wild caprices of these new things called "doodle-bugs." So, as in the old days, the "good old days," the crops ripened and were somehow duly harvested. And people died, mostly of old age, or ailments that go with it; never of "frightfulness," Gestapo or tommy-guns. And babies were delivered into a quiet sunny world. And the children rushed clamorously out of school at the appointed hours. And at the end of the monotonous sweaty days, the land army came straggling back to billets from the fields; and then from cottage windows came the sounds of radio and gramophone.

To all intents and purposes peace was theirs, and, because of it, the inevitable egocentric gripings. . . . There was barely enough to eat, wasn't there, with the damned rationing and all, and little to smoke and nothing to drink; and if they broke even so much as a harness-strap they couldn't get another, could they? They had to make do with a bit of bale-wire, a bit of anything, a bit of nothing! They could tell you all right what was meant by blood, sweat and tears! It was nothing but a bloody sweat to get anything done with all these 'ere regulations to try and read, and coupons that didn't mean anything, and papers to fill in, and questions to try and answer and become muddled up proper and all for nothing, and them out there in the fields anywhere from fourteen hours a day trying to harvest the crops with nothing but a lot of girls screaming and laughing and jabbering their heads off and always in trouble with the soldiers. . . . The sooner they licked them damned Germans the better! Give it another year and the whole of England would be overrun with unmarried mothers and their brats . . . speaking of which, that Wainwright girl had at least had brains enough to marry the man, even if she was fool enough to marry a soldier, and not just a soldier either, but one of them Americans that all the girls were so wild about. Wasn't England good enough for her? She could 'a' had the pick of any one of the English officers down there before them Yanks came. Must be all that foreign education she'd had! Never did believe in it anyway. If her father hadn't 'a' been so cockeyed, he'd 'a' told her off proper! Chances were that if the feller came through, which wasn't likely, he'd forget all about her when the war was over and go back to wherever he came from. How could you tell about them Yankees? Friendly-like, yes, and outspoken — even if you could only catch the half of what they said with their funny slang and all — but could you trust 'em? Not if you were a girl you couldn't, judging by what you saw a-goin' on. . . .

Agincourt . . . St.-Lô; Henry V . . . George VI. What difference? Their task had always been the same — to scratch the earth between two blades of grass in order that they and their fellow man might live.

But in the end cottage, St.-Lô was the more important.

The morning after D-Day Jack Wainwright and his daughter were both out at six o'clock as usual. As usual? Stretching away from them were the same long rows of peas, string beans, carrots, beets, lettuce, tomatoes, but same only in point of time, appearance, surroundings.

It was another world today.

No one had seen Minchen yesterday, except the beech trees, and to them the sight of her was nothing new. They had seen the hawk strike the rabbit, the owl drop onto the mouse, and the fox crunching the bones of the pheasant. They had seen wounded animals that had crawled away from the sportsmen's guns, painting the small leaves with blood as they dragged themselves along, mutely frantic to drop deep into their hole before the inevitable dogs would start to whimper and dig. . . .

She was kneeling this morning in a pair of ancient brown corduroy trousers and a green sweater, her hair done up in a red bandanna. As usual she made a brilliant splash of color, as though, at the given spot where she knelt, the tame vegetables had burst into a wild blossoming.

Her father, on his blue-jeaned hunkers at the same pile of tomatoes that had to be sorted, had his pipe in his teeth as usual. But this morning it became cold once he glimpsed his daughter's face as she came out to him. . . . Anything he said to her would be a damned lie, a ghastly impertinence. She would never see Bill again . . . but . . . Christ, you couldn't leave her strung up on the barbed wire! . . . He said, with fierce anger, "He's all right, Minch! He's all right, I tell you! . . . They're off the beaches. They've really broken through. They're well inland. It's . . . it's going splendidly . . ." His voice trailed off. As if it mattered to her how the hell it was going! . . . He couldn't be sure that he'd even got through to her. But at last she did nod. That was something!

And then Minchen knelt, dipped her obedient hands into the red fruit. But she didn't see them. She wasn't there. She was in Normandy, trying to see Bill in the fields that she knew so well, the fields that she had biked through; Bill among the apple trees and poplars, the hedges, the cows, the iridescent magpies. . . . Where was Bill, now, this moment, how was he, what was he doing? It was like a heavy dew, a mist . . . you couldn't see him, find him. You only knew he was there. Something inside you insisted, urged, cried out, that he was still there . . . although it was impossible that anyone could stay alive if you listened to that ghastly radio. . . . But Bill was! You knew it! You knew it . . . had to believe it . . . you must believe it. . . .

A tomato missed the basket. Then another one.

Minchen sat back on her heels. Her shaking hands, disobedient now, went to her face, covered it tightly. . . . "Oh God, please take care of Bill! You must! You must! He hasn't done a thing. . . . Please! Oh please . . ."

Her hands dropped into her lap. "Dad!" she said.

Jack Wainwright was apparently as far away from the tomatoes as his daughter, but he hadn't allowed his hands to stop. He had more years of this kind of training than she. He came back to her from across the Channel.

"Um'hm?" Then his eyes touched hers. It was more than enough. He bit hard on his cold pipe stem, scowled down the long rows — backbreaking, neat, weedless, fruitful . . . fruitful in more senses than one. From the beginning they had been his own private hole, an opiate, a daily dressing for his inner wounds, a poultice to draw out not only sweat but the abject misery of a man whom war had stripped to the bone. . . . Good God, was there no end to it? Must Minchen now be stripped too? The damned wheel had given a full turn. . . .

Minchen's fingers were digging and twisting into the earth. "Can't you . . . help me somehow, Dad? I . . . I've tried to pull myself together and I . . . I can't. I don't know what to do. I just feel deathly sick. I keep on telling myself every minute that Bill's all right but it . . . it doesn't work. I'd told myself that I was going to be with him out there, but I've . . . I've lost him!

I can't find him. I can't get there. He's . . . he's gone! Can't you help me find him, Dad? You've got to! You've been through all this. You know! You can tell me . . ."

As the words hit him, Jack Wainwright's face looked as if it were carved out of rock. It seemed to him that everything had stopped—the birds, the sun, his capacity to bleed. . . . It had taken days sometimes before they died in No Man's Land . . . and this was a girl . . . this was Minchen! And whenever a sparrow droppeth, the Father knoweth . . . Oh Christ! With the market price of sparrows about three for a penny—the cost of their training, say—and Minchen on her knees in the dirt, a million Minchens all over the world, as they would be on their knees in the next war and the next, sparrows without end, amen . . .

Minchen was still speaking—as much, it seemed, to herself as to him, as though instinctively holding the wound open to let the pus flow out.

"I'm a coward! Bill's out there in the middle of . . . of something I can't even imagine, and I sit here and shake! I hate myself. I loathe myself. I made him a promise and I've broken it already! He might forgive me for yesterday, but not if I don't keep it today . . . every day. It's frightfully important and I . . . I can't get hold of myself. It's all so different. I'd told myself what I'd do when Bill . . . went, but they wouldn't even let him say good-by and it . . . it hit me. It's queer, as though something's gone inside. I can't seem to make myself obey. And I must because of Bill. He needs me. He wants me, and I can't get there! Tell me where he is, what he does. I've got to be able to see him. Is there any night out there? I mean does he ever sleep? Is there any shelter, any place that's . . . that's safe, even if only for a minute? He was so sure he was coming through, but all I can see is millions of guns firing at him all day and night. How can anybody live through that? And yet you did, didn't you? So somehow there's a chance for Bill . . . isn't there? Some possibility? Some miracle? Isn't there? . . . Tell me, Dad! Tell me!"

"A chance? Of course he has a chance!" He answered quickly, firmly—but he didn't dare look up from the tomatoes. "He'll come through all right. It's written in his face. He's the kind who always comes through. He's already come through Sicily and Italy, hasn't he? Well then! And besides, Bill believes that he's coming through, and that makes a hell of a difference! It was generally the man who felt that he wasn't going to last who didn't last. So pin your faith to Bill's, Minch! Believe it and hang on to it through thick and thin! Don't let it get away from you, whatever you may hear on the damned radio! Keep on saying to yourself: 'He's coming through! He's coming through!' . . . No one knows the power of the human mind, the impossible things that it can accomplish, cures that defy all the doctors. So put your whole mind and will on Bill, with every ounce of faith that you can muster up. You've got to make it work . . . got to . . . not only for Bill's sake but your own!"

Minchen nodded. "Thank you, Dad! I'll try. I promise I will. . . . And now tell me about him."

Jack Wainwright swallowed.

Every minute of his four and a half years of the other war gave him a sort of television of the fighting in Normandy. He had already lived Bill Thatcher's life, seen a thousand Bills die . . . and now, because the war had been dumped into his daughter's lap as a wedding present, must it be his pleasant job as a father to break her heart by telling her what Bill was really up against? . . . Good God, no! It was too much. Better tell her about rest periods and life in billets rather than hit her again by telling her what it took to advance under crossfire from machine-gun nests and snipers, through artillery barrages and bombing, over the not-yet-cold bodies of men smashed by shell, by bullet, by grenade, by flame-thrower, by anything that would destroy life. . . .

He said abruptly, "All right, I will. . . . But look here, don't sit on your heels! Drive yourself to keep your hands moving while we talk! You'll find it damned helpful after a time. . . . It's a method used in all the best insane asylums, you know, so God knows we need it!"

He struck a match and put it to his pipe.

Minchen's lips were moving. . . . "He's coming through! He's" — her hand reached out for a tomato — "coming through!"

WHAT fun to play soldier in Finland!
A brief winter sun paints the frozen earth,
Touches the eager button-eyed children as they come rushing out to the end of the village. . . .
Toys everywhere, toys for the picking and poking, toys to climb in and out of,
Tanks and wagons and horses and guns, a little broken certainly, but spilled in such exciting confusion, with piles of soldiers to choose from. . . .
Such wonderful toys, all the way from Russia, all life-size, big ones with bushy beards, young ones without even mustaches, lots and lots of wooden legs sticking up, stiff arms pointing everywhere.
Just look at them all!
Some clutching their bellies as though they had eaten green apples,
Some with big holes in them and funny things hanging out,
Some making faces as if they didn't like something,
Some who had just closed their eyes and gone to sleep in the snow.
All such a pretty mahogany-color, and you could jump on them and poke them with sticks and roll them over now that they were frozen solid, now that they didn't stink any more. . . .
What fun to play at soldiers!

CHAPTER TWO

BY D PLUS 24 THE WORLD HAD CHANGED.

Roosevelt, Churchill and Stalin knew that the war was won. Hitler, Goering and Goebbels knew equally that the war was lost.

Refugee kings and governments in exile began to dust off their traveling bags. State Departments in all the peace-loving countries began to burn the midnight oil in their efforts to establish the right man in power in all the little countries — the man who would play ball afterwards.

Field marshals, admirals and visiting firemen were being safely jeeped around the Cherbourg peninsula.

The tanks were ready to roll.

The rest was a mere matter of routine — that a few million more soldiers would have to die; that a few million more prisoners, civilians and otherwise, would perish of cremation, starvation, torture; that robot bombs were raining on London; that a thing called an atom bomb was nearly ready to show how the job should really be done; that all the harlots who had helped to make life tolerable for German officers and men were now helping the morale of Allied officers and men; that the stock exchanges of the winning nations would drop many points because of the danger of a quick peace.

The man in the street was unaware of these things. All he knew was what he was allowed to know — that de Gaulle had really paraded in triumph through the streets of Bayeux; that the Canadians had reduced Caen to a bloody bulge ready to burst;

that the Yanks had successfully gutted and captured Cherbourg; that St.-Lô might be cleared of the last Kraut next time the radio was snapped on . . . and then for the big push . . . the break-through . . . breathless hope . . . a rush for Extras on the streets . . . the radio left tuned in. . . .

For the fighting soldiers, however, D plus 24 was just another day, of potential survival, or otherwise. And it was sufficiently long after the landing for their brides to be receiving a few postcards, spelled out in foxholes and barns and hedges and broken villages — "Everything fine. Hope you are fine too." And that meant a moment of heaven. But the date was many days old. You couldn't tell . . .

When the first one arrived from Bill Thatcher, Minchen was out working.

It was just after nine o'clock in the morning when Muriel appeared, framed in the roses that surrounded the back door. She called and waved the postcard.

As if her hoe were red-hot, Minchen dropped it and ran, her eyes shining. She gasped an excited "Oh Mother!" as she took the card. . . . "Your letters are like water in the flames of hell. Thank God for you honey. Bill." And then, as though a dam had been blown up, something gave inside her. She found herself sobbing her heart out in her mother's arms.

Was it possible that she was only twenty-four days older? How could it be, when nothing was as it had been before — the cottage, the days and nights, herself?

Prior to Bill, her daily life had been concerned, naturally, solely with her own identity. Every thought, every opinion, every action, was the result of what made its way into the inner fortress, that remote place in which, unconsciously, one screens and sifts, rejects and stores up — a feeding process, haphazard, without arrangement, but in blind obedience to the need we have, to the essential ego with which we are born and with which we shall inevitably die. Then marriage had burst upon her suddenly, like a hurricane, causing the most violent displacement of her inner furnishings, creating needs of which she had never dreamed, exciting desires that she had never openly recognized, grafting another identity upon her own.

Between wars there would have been assimilation, fulfillment, completion, a gradual recognition of the normal on a different plane. But, as abruptly as he had come, Bill had gone. Minchen was left sitting alone, and not alone, in the devastation of her former self, bewildered, shaken, spent; new things, enormous things tossed there among the rubble — sex, frustration, her man in "the flames of hell."

A tough assignment for a girl to take all at once, and all alone. Only to her pillow in the dead of night could she yield the secret of a suffering body to which a tormented mind could offer no comfort. And if the empty night hours were bad, daytime was little better. Slow word by slow word, her father had taken her back with him to the Somme, to Ypres, to the Gargantuan break-through of March 1918, and though he had underlined the fact that men could live, and had lived, through those "flames of hell," it still called for all the courage she had to contemplate Bill among the bloodstained hedgerows of Normandy. Nevertheless she felt that it had dispersed the fog, that, however faintly, she could see him out there. So now at last she was able to keep her promise to him, to play to him every afternoon from five to six. She even added a touch of her own by getting into her prettiest frocks and dabbing herself with the perfume that Bill had given her. Hadn't he said he would be sitting beside her on the piano bench . . . very close . . . ? There had been many things to push aside, many ghastly obstacles and possibilities to eliminate, too many slow hours in the course of any one of which something could have happened out there. . . . But other post-cards came trickling in, and eventually two letters from somewhere in billets—real contact again, as though, almost, she had heard his voice on the phone. After them, she found that she could draw a longer breath, could find an hour's peace at the keyboard in the conviction that Bill was hearing her, was drawing strength and comfort . . . and protection . . . from the knowledge of her sitting there canceling out space between them, giving herself to him spiritually.

He had said to her once—a thousand years ago—"If ever I have kids away from home I'm going to write them every single night . . . and air mail!" Every single night she wrote to him now, alone in her bedroom, their bedroom even though he was away from home. For there was no moment in which she could be alone in it now. That was impossible. It was on that corner of the bureau that Bill had kept his hairbrush and comb; on that chair every morning he had put each foot in turn to tie up his shoelaces; and on the back of it had hung up his trousers, carefully folded, each night; this the drawer in which his "undies" had been allowed to take the place of hers . . . how trivial, but how unforgettable . . . and there was everything they had said to each other, mostly in whispers, before they had got into bed and turned out the light. . . .

Minchen could never again be alone in that room, more especially because now physically she was alone. If Bill's presence there had forever annihilated her old self, his absence was equally annihilating to her new self. Her physical aloneness was appalling, almost frightening. She wanted Bill, needed Bill, was passionately hungry for Bill. Every sense that he had waked in her refused to go to sleep again. Nor, by giving orders, could she obtain obedience—perhaps because the orders were not too sternly given. The changes of condition had been so abrupt that it was asking too much of herself, the more so in that every moment of the day she was in Normandy as close to Bill as she could get in thought, in heartache, in prayer, in fear, in longing.

She put what she could of it in her nightly letters — all except her fears, and those he must never know, not even guess. It was the nearest she could get to talking to him, and they had had so little time together in which to try to say all the things that mattered, all the things that normally would have been spread over many months of daily companionship, confided glimpse by glimpse, shared tenderly, delighted in, laughed over, stored away for the long domestic pull. She had known nothing of gentle give and take, of gradual discovery and adjustment. She had known only a leaping flame, burning up everything . . . and now the flame was removed.

The task forced upon her through the endless summer days was to pretend that there were no charred ends.

BROKER'S *ad:*

"Controlling more than half of the proved oil reserves of the world, the United States petroleum industry is a major business enterprise. Our new survey presents an over-all picture of this huge industry, discusses problems of supply, demand and production, provides investors with a comprehensive view of the many varying factors which affect oil securities. They will find this survey gives a straightforward, unbiased assessment of the industry's prospects — both present and future."

Some of the "varying factors": The recent $250,000,000 American deal in Saudi Arabia, with an expectation of twenty billion barrels. At the moment, however, Arabs are tearing up pipe-lines; Jews accuse the British of supporting the Arabs in the hope of getting the oil; and, last but not least, there is a new oil concession in Persia, a bare three hundred miles from the American and British fields, which, unfortunately, belongs to Russia.

Some other well-known "major business enterprises": Caesar, Napoleon, Hitler. . . .

CHAPTER THREE

THE ENDLESS SUMMER DAYS . . . OF THEMSELVES INFINITELY beautiful, the hot persuaded earth yielding its crops, the trees in all the vanity of their full leaf, the gardens a flaming pageant of succeeding blooms, the starry nights like a cool perfumed bath . . . an invitation to kindly living, to horse fairs and festivals, to peasant dancing and water carnivals, to holidays and harvest thanksgiving.

But thanksgiving was now for the bloody break-through at Avranches; and for water carnival, dead-sprinkled beaches of the Riviera; and the only dance was the *pavane* of the tanks on their sweep to the Seine, and, if you could call it a festival, the corpses in the streets of a freed and frenzied Paris.

And like a weird accompaniment to break-through, to sweep-up, to landing and to liberation, was the daily trickle of piano playing in the cottage of that remote village. . . . The humble tumbler did his tricks to the Virgin Mary. It was all he knew. Minchen's hope was not less great than his, and her music was all she had to give during that summer which for her was no summer at all.

Her mother, sitting inconspicuously in her chair listening, knew something of what was behind that music, could sympathize with the statements it flung out wildly, at least guess at the increasing questions it posed to which no answer came.

She knew that the girl was keeping her tryst with her husband. . . . That much was like a voice from the past; for the last war had conditioned her as this one was conditioning Minchen. The only difference was one of marriage, for, while Jack Wainwright had gone off without a word or a sign, Muriel had been in love with him. For her, in all those four years, there had been only one thing in the newspapers — the casualty lists. . . . Every day, after the others had done with the paper, she had taken it off to her room and locked the door. In case Jack's name should be there she had to be alone. And twice she had found it in the wounded column. . . . So now each afternoon as she listened, it seemed to her that Minchen was saying aloud all the secret thoughts that she had sent out to Jack so short a while ago, but had never been able to write because they were not even engaged. How could she tell if he would ever come to her . . . if he even wanted her? It had been like four years in the dark, four years of "solitary," of secret hoping . . . and when at last he did come, it wasn't the old Jack at all, alert, eager, responsive. The one who came back had to be learned all over again from the beginning. It was almost as though she had married the imprisoned ghost of someone she had known in a previous incarnation, who could only be brought back to earth by years of digging under the piled ruins. . . . Minchen would never have to go through anything like that! It couldn't possibly be, since Bill and she were already man and wife, had thus already established a past together on which they could build . . . whatever happened. . . . And when he did come, Bill would find her . . . what was the word? . . . purified, stronger, leaner, spiritually speaking, because of what she was going through now. It was in her music already, a cleanness, a refinement, a more controlled emotion, an increased authority. . . . Please God, it would not be all spilled, wasted. . . . Perhaps, now that they had reached Paris, one might dare to begin to hope. . . . Even Jack was more excited than she had ever seen him!

"Excited" was only one of many words necessary to describe Jack Wainwright's feelings. For him that summer had been a most curious one, a summer of self-discovery and self-contempt.

He found himself unable to approach any action or solution in terms of black and white. He convicted himself for being a contemptible streaky-gray.

For him the rushing sweep that led to the freeing of Paris was just plain miracle, and like all miracles was hardly to be believed. He likened himself to a skeptical guest at the marriage feast at Cana, half expecting that the water which had been turned into wine would suddenly revert once more to water. There must come, he thought, some moment when the Germans would uncork a stroke of master-strategy that would rock the advance back on its heels, back to the Channel again, and so to defeat. And even if not, there still lay ahead not only a stretch of country that in his war it had taken four years to conquer, but in addition the now well-prepared Maginot and Siegfried lines . . .

Thus he found himself alternately chess player and pawn, commanding general and "poor bloody infantryman"; fiercely exultant when thinking in terms of armies and victories, the next moment hating himself for being exultant; and hating again that in him which made him hate himself; bleeding internally when he broke it down and remembered the suffering of the individual soldier, and then justifying himself by praying for a faster and faster break-through so that killing would come to an end the more quickly.

Behind the radio he had pinned a large-scale map of France. Whenever he came in from work, he marched straight to it — like a drug addict reaching for the syringe — stood glowering at it, hands jammed in pockets, pipe going full blast, cursing himself for drinking in the quiet well-modulated voice of the BBC speaking like some damned Peeping Tom from stinking foxholes, from plastered gun positions, from inside tanks, from the comparative safety of warships off the beachhead, from dripping cellars in hideously smashed French villages . . . in a word, from the core of terror, destruction and death, into the comfortable untouched cottage where he, Jack Wainwright — and for God's sake why, he asked himself, by what right, by what fate? — would sit quietly down to lunch, or dinner, with his family, eat from a table with a cloth on it and flowers and knives and forks . . . sleep at night with his wife, unafraid . . . wake next morning to another peaceful English summer day, birds singing, bees booming, cat purring . . . thanks to Russian privates and American G.I.'s and English Tommies, and Canadians and Australians, and the Maquis and all the rest . . . world youth dying by the hundred thousand to keep him comfortable; and all the rest of them who were not in it, idiots like himself who had been content to eat the lotus after the last war . . . and so, he went on tight-lipped, there he stood, hidebound, running the gamut of his fatuous emotions, egocentric and gloating and superior, and thanking God on his knees that he was out of it and mentally urging on the lads whose turn it was to do the filthy job . . . and of course he shouldn't let himself think even in deep secrecy that those poor lads were being slaughtered simply because man is a lousy animal, because greed is his strongest motive, because his plodding second-rate leaders could offer him nothing more than "blood, sweat and tears" — that ultimate confession of abject failure that had won its maker not bitter ironic curses but a crown of glory throughout the cockeyed world! . . . Ah, no indeed! He mustn't on any account think that. That was treason. And it was equally treason, to say nothing of loathsome hypocrisy, to mumble "Father, forgive them! They know not what they do . . ." They knew damn well what they were doing! And he himself was one of them, for didn't the animal side of him, the human side, make him flush with fierce pleasure every time the enemy was blasted out of one more place, had one more tentacle lopped off? Wasn't he filled with hard cold satisfaction every time thousands of tons of blockbusters were unloaded on Berlin regardless of women and children? . . . A streaky gray, the battle as much within as without — that while half of him wanted to weep, the other half was rejoicing; that while the first bitter half made him yearn to escape from the whole shameful business, the human half rounded him up and drove him back unresisting into the herd where he belonged!

There was no escape anywhere. Every day he went out without a shirt into the generous sun, thanking God for it, loving the glow of it on his skin, basking in it . . . and yet, he told himself, it wasn't right. It was cheating. There was, somehow, blood in it . . . as there was in every gesture of daily living — in the food he had no right to enjoy, but did; in shaving in a clean bathroom, in the soft pillow that he didn't change for a hard one; in the luxury of a shower and a fresh towel when he had finished work among the vegetables; in the nightly putting on of slippers and settling down into a deep armchair; in the companionship of a wife and daughter sheltered and untouched; in the aching loveliness of sunrise, and sunset, and the harvest moon . . . although one had no right to beauty any more, or pleasure . . . and laughter was sacrilege. It could belong now only to children. . . .

And when five o'clock came and Minchen began to send out her call to Bill, Jack Wainwright had already taken himself and his uncomfortable thinking into the farthest corner of the garden. Her playing tore him. It was not just music. In a decent civilized world, it should have been a Te Deum, but this lapse into barbarism had made it a De Profundis. Every chord she played was the voice of all women trying to reach husbands, lovers, sons, in fear, anguish, pleading. . . . What was a war marriage but a private crown of thorns? It made no difference that they put it on their own heads. How could they help doing so? It was the common offering made to their generation. It was their present-day finishing school, the home-front torture camp, needing no barbed wire or guards since there could be no escape till the shambles stopped . . . and then the ones whose men did come back, whether whole or not, would get a sort of pass degree, because in the nature of things they would be able to forget. The others in this sweet system of higher education would graduate *summa cum laude*. They would not be allowed to forget. For them the days and the years would be empty. For the majority of them there would be no other man. The number of wooden crosses would nail that, as it had after the last war; and once again all that civilization left them would be the choice between polite prostitution and quiet Lesbianism. . . .

Would Churchill and Eden have these things in mind when they sat at the peace table gypping the rest of them for trade routes, oil concessions, so-called "life lines"? Why should they? The dead in a war were always an infinitesimal minority, utterly without importance. A mere sprinkling of half-dead women was not worth a thought. Theirs was the weighty task of seeing that the right king should go back to the right throne, that the right party in power — their own — should at all cost remain in power, that civilization should thus pursue its well-ordered course towards World War Three. Wasn't that the function of government? It would smack of *lèse-majesté* to disturb them at their sacred task with the rude mention of corpses, male or female. . . .

And Minchen in all this, how was she coming out? Pass degree, or *cum laude?* Merely because she was Muriel's and his one child, because she was of his blood and bone, because he loved her, had he the right to desire passionately that she should be numbered among those whose man would come back, whose future life should be granted a modicum of happiness? . . . Happiness! How egregious after one glance at the world map! What inconceivable impertinence to stand out there among his ridiculous vegetables and raise his face to the sun, muttering "Let Bill come back to her!" . . . As if it mattered!

OVER *the air:*
A cry from the women of Poland,
Of Russia, of France, of Belgium
Of Holland, of Czechoslovakia . . .
"Where are our children?"

Over the air:
Tangos and Dietrich's legs and rationing,
Jazz and Haw-Haw and Nylons,
Symphonies and strikes and FOREVER AMBER,
Rhumbas and black markets and hepcats jiving,
The crooning Voice and college football and the liquor shortage,
Hymns and Ex-Lax and Hollywood divorces,
Boogie-woogie and three-hundred-and-sixty-thousand-dollar bonuses,
"America the Beautiful" and Quick Relief,
O.P.A. and W.A.C. and C.I.O. and S.N.A.F.U. . . .

"Where are our children?"

CHAPTER FOUR

ON A CERTAIN UNFORGETTABLE AFTERNOON AT THE END OF August Minchen rose from the piano, closed it as usual, stood for a moment, her brown hands still touching the wood as though aware of lingering vibrations. Presently her eyes came back into the room and found her mother, whose chair had just been reached by a beam of sun.

Minchen crossed the room and stood behind the chair. Then she bent down and kissed the top of her mother's head. "I'm going to bike down to . . . to Friar's Dene, Mother," she said.

Muriel's head came up quickly. For a moment she looked into her daughter's eyes. Then she said, "Would you like me to come too?"

Minchen shook her head. "I'd . . . rather go alone."

Muriel said, "You're quite sure? . . . All right, darling. . . . Bless you!"

Minchen thanked her with a smile, paused for a second at the door as though she were going to add something, then changed her mind and went on. In the hall she reached out and touched the flowers in the big vase . . . Bill had always paused there to take a sniff. . . .

The sun was like an envelopment as she stepped out of the cottage door. . . . What was Bill going to say if . . . the handles of the bicycle almost burned her as she pulled it away from the hedge and wheeled it out into the street . . . if this were really true?

The yellow cat came running up to her, talking loudly.

Minchen bent down and rubbed his head. "I'll be back soon," she said. Then she mounted the machine.

There were half a dozen children playing in the street. They called out to her, grinning and waving as she threaded between them. Minchen smiled back at them, left them behind, the crunch of gravel under her wheels more loud as her speed increased. . . . Would it all look the same when she came back? It had seemed out of focus ever since Bill went. Would it be more so than ever if . . . if she . . .

There was a gathering question in her eyes as she made the turn at the end of the village—the turn where she had waited for Bill the first time he came up on her father's bike and he had laughed and said, "Your left hand looks awful bare to me!" And she had laughed too and said some stupid thing or other . . . but only with her outer voice. Her inner voice had been shouting to her, shouting the most incredible and marvelous discovery. . . .

She was dropping like a bullet down the steep hill, her hair streaming out behind her, her frock plastered tight against her body. . . . When Bill and she had swooshed down together, he always left her behind, had to brake and wait for her at the bottom by the big elm tree. Once he had already lit two cigarettes before she had caught him up, one for her and one for himself. . . . There was hardly an inch of the road that he had not made his and given back to her for a memory. It was now almost like following a film of them both, subtitled for her by things he had said, things she hadn't known she was going to remember but which she knew now she was never going to forget. They were so vivid, so aural, that as she came pedaling into Friar's Dene, it was not into the town of reality, of that particular August evening, but of those other exciting days when Bill used to come storming into the Recreation Center, when Bill had met her in the dark outside the "drugstore," when Bill had proposed to her in the queer dingy tearoom. . . . "Tell me, did I find you all by myself, or did you find me too?"

The town's pace had relaxed to an amble, since the departure of the main body of paratroopers. But, as the girl rode along, a couple of "Yoo-hoo's" came at her — almost like echoes — from the doorway of the Monk and Paunch. Her eyes, completely detached from the present, registered a slight going and coming at the Recreation Center, a group of only three or four outside the movie, and the market place seemed almost hushed now that there were only one or two army trucks instead of the unending stream. . . . "Too damn many soldiers in this man's town!" . . . Minchen smiled. How she had wondered what was the matter that evening! Bill would like the town this evening, especially if . . .

She turned out of the market place into the road that would take you — if you followed it far enough — to Oxford . . . fifty hours . . a thousand years ago. . . . But he's coming through! He's coming through!

The old house in front of which she dismounted was of red brick, ivy-covered, an iron railing in front of it, two steps up, a recessed white door, a small brass plate above the bellpull. Looking at it, Minchen saw none of those familiar details. The bricks might have been transparent, for all she saw was the thin wrinkled kindly face, under a puff of white hair, of Dr. Merivale, who had brought her into the world, joked her through measles and mumps and vaccination and scarlet fever and . . . and now, in a minute . . .

She stood a moment, staring, then took a deep breath, her heart banging against her ribs. Then, quickly, she dropped her bicycle against the railings and ran up the steps and gave the bell a terrific pull. The inner jangling was a cataclysm. . . .

Were the men and women of Paris at that moment shooting wildly at the last remaining Germans? Or were the last pockets of resistance already pounded to pieces by the tanks and the people shouting and sobbing and embracing?

How should Minchen know? And why should she care? When she came down the steps again, the question in her eyes had been answered. The jangling had become a carillon, all-pervading, claiming the universe.

Nobody knew, passing by, that she was in any way different from the next girl—"A nice brown kid in a pretty frock," they would have said, not knowing that her apprenticeship was over, that, for better or worse, she was an entrant in the blind gamble of motherhood: boy, girl, genius, moron, average, delinquent, sickly, strong, wanted, not wanted—in any case another unit in an incomprehensible herring-run, remorseless, awful, beautiful, pathetic, bloodthirsty, gentle, wise, ignorant . . . and, at this particular moment of its peculiar rhythms, wholeheartedly engaged in the arts of slaughter.

HAVE you seen their bodies —
Of these "displaced" children of the world —
Bloated with starvation,
Running with sores,
Smelling like hell?

Have you seen their hands —
Of these "displaced" children of the world —
Bloody with murder,
Foul with thieving,
Savage as hell?

Have you seen their eyes —
Of these "displaced" children of the world —
Blinded with hurt,
Glaring with hate,
Older than hell?

CHAPTER FIVE

THE NICE BROWN KID," AWARE ONLY OF THE CLAMOR OF BELLS, was presently on her bicycle again, her legs obeying subconscious orders to take her somewhere. She might as well have been a sleepwalker strolling unconcernedly along the parapet of a sky-scraper as the machine rolled between buses and carts in the market place, turned in the opposite direction from home and carried her safely once more out into the country, past the army camp, until she found herself at the point where the field trail began . . . the trail up which Bill and she had walked, holding hands, finding each other. . . . Oh, of course! . . . Bill! Oh Bill, I've news for you . . . such news! Wonderful news! . . . Can you hear me? . . . Wait till I get up to our stone and I'll tell you. . . .

She was off now, pushing her wheel along the footpath that climbed the hill. There was a point up there, nearly at the top, where, when you turned round, the view stretched away to in-finity; and always they had stopped there, and sat down, as Bill said with a grin, "to admire the view of each other." Their stone was a flat one—flat enough, and big enough, for two, if you sat close enough.

Her strong brown legs were like a couple of pistons driving her up in a fury of hurry. By the time she reached the stone, she was hot, flushed, gasping for breath. She lowered her bicycle onto the ground and, facing the view, stood gulping infinity into her lungs. . . . Perhaps he would be still humming what she had played him that afternoon . . . still near enough to be able to hear her now if she concentrated hard enough, willed it with everything she had. . . . It was so important . . . and it wasn't asking much. It couldn't possibly interfere with any of the important military messages that were crisscrossing each other out there . . . so please let it go through! You must let it go through! . . .

She sat down on their stone . . . a sort of contact . . . and, with her hands clasped round her knees—that was how they had always sat—began her message. "Bill! . . . Bill, darling, listen! You must hear this before anybody else in the world! We're going to have a child . . . a child!"

She repeated it aloud, her eyes tight shut this time, as if, in the hush of that August evening, the air waves might somehow cheat war for a minute and carry it. . . . Why not, since I'm carrying a child? It would only be a sort of mutual courtesy, and not really cheating . . . haven't we earned it? Neither of us has ever done a thing but obey orders. . . . We haven't kicked or squawked . . . ever . . . not even when we were only given fifty hours for a honeymoon, not even when Bill was kept on duty two nights in the tiny handful of days which was all we had till D-Day, not even when he was whisked off without a sign or a word. . . . We both accepted all that, took it for granted just like everybody else . . . but they expected more than that. They expected you to behave as though you enjoyed having your husband go and not knowing from minute to minute whether he was killed . . . you were expected to smile and chat brightly at meals and eat your food as though it weren't choking you . . . and when you went up to bed you mustn't on any account curse or scream, oh no! You had to read half the night, force yourself to make stupid words have meaning, because if you were fool enough to yield to the thought of Bill . . . and you couldn't even write to Bill and tell him how many times you dressed again and spent the night walking and walking through the fields and the beech woods. . . . Oh no, there hadn't been any squawking. It hadn't even entered their heads. . . . They were supposed to accept all that! And it wouldn't have been the slightest use to squawk. Who would have listened to a couple of kids? That's what they would have called us, war-age kids! . . . But they can't call us that now! Not any more. Not with this child coming. Kids! Why, we're parents! We . . . Why, Bill! . . . Oh, Bill, my dear! . . .

The jumble of half-expressed emotions came to a sudden dead end at the impact of an entirely new concept, as simple and clear as inspiration. As definite as though the air waves had brought her back an order. It snapped her up from the stone, bicycle in hand, and sent her on her way—not in a tearing hurry this time, but in a steady purposeful frowning-thoughtful trudge which took her not only up the rest of the hill but far along the way to a new attitude, a different approach to her entire problem.

The yellow cat was waiting for her at the picket fence, but for the first time in his life he didn't get picked up in answer to his salutation. It seemed as though she had neither seen nor heard him. He had to follow on the run into the cottage, and even there had to proceed as far as the kitchen before he could rub his head against her leg.

Minchen went straight to her mother.

The question in Muriel's eyes was obvious.

Minchen nodded. "I was right, Mother," she said. "The doctor thinks March. Did you say anything to Dad?"

Something remote about her daughter made Muriel catch her breath. "Yes. . . . Is everything . . ."

"There's not a thing to worry about, Mother! I'm glad you told Dad. I've something desperately important to ask him. It may . . . change everything. Let's go and see what he has to say!" She stepped round the cat and made for the living room.

Muriel moved the soup on the stove so that it wouldn't boil and followed her.

Jack Wainwright was standing in the streets of Paris outside the gray Hôtel de Ville . . . the crowd surging . . . a machine gun chattering . . . Minchen walked into it. . . . No, she mustn't. Not tonight! . . . He reached out and snapped off the radio, looking for the answer in her face.

She went up to him. "It's true, Dad. I've just told Mother. . . . Sometime in March, the doctor thinks."

He had his answer — but he was still looking for it in her eyes, to see, if he could, what lay under the bald statement . . . whether those machine guns made any difference. . . . They were perfectly steady, without fear, thank God. . . . "You are . . . very wonderful, my dear!" he said. "You . . ." A smile creased the corners of his lips. "You remind me strongly of your mother!" He bent forward and kissed her forehead. "We must send a wire to Bill tomorrow . . . or have you already attended to that?"

Minchen shook her head. "Not a wire exactly. . . . It's all pretty terrific. . . . But I've been sitting out there on the hill for a long time, doing a lot of thinking, or trying to . . . and probably only succeeding in smashing my head against a brick wall, I suppose!" She laughed, went over to the table and helped herself to a cigarette from the always lean supply.

Muriel perched herself on the arm of one of the big chairs, her hands, for once, unoccupied in her lap. "I thought," she said, "that it was one of the recognized methods of breaking them down — the walls, I mean, not the heads — if one went at it long enough."

In a cloud of smoke Minchen turned and leaned her hips against the table. "I hope you're right, Mother," she said. "Dad, you ought to know all about this particular one. . . . How does one get one's husband out of the firing line?"

Jack Wainwright's eyebrows went up. He gave a surprised laugh. "That's an easy one — or it was in my day . . . if only he had a title! Earl Thatcher, or even Sir Willard Thatcher. Either of those would wangle him a pretty safe Staff job. Or of course, one could tell him to get himself shot through the foot. . . . Better not do it himself! That used to be a court-martial offense, but if it's done from a distance it looks authentic. Incidentally, how's his French? A battalion interpreter's job used to be soft, arranging billets behind the lines and doing little shopping errands for the officers and so on. . . . Any of those things what you mean?"

"No," said Minchen, "they're not. I was thinking about the camp in Friar's Dene. There are still officers and men there — lots of them unmarried too. As far as I know they're training reinforcements. Bill's been out there long enough to make a marvelous trainer. Is there anything wrong with that?"

"It's a perfectly honorable job," said Jack Wainwright. "They need fellows who can train men, and Bill, God knows, has had plenty of experience by now. But they don't dish out a job like that to a good man in the line. The longer he's been out, the longer they'll keep him there. Either he has to be wounded and passed unfit for action, or else he has to have . . . influence, friends at court, the old wangling game . . . You can't hurry it either. There is a precise formula laid down, almost, you might say, a routine — that is, of course, if things haven't changed since my time. The fact, for instance, that Bill is only a corporal, is distinctly against him. A noncommissioned officer is next to nothing. For that matter, lieutenants are pretty small beer — unless they've the luck to have an uncle who is at least a Chief of Staff, or a titled aunt who entertains generals at her country place . . . but of course, those are British niceties. I don't know the first word about the American Army. They may do things differently. Even our own Army may be different in this war, though I wouldn't bet on it. We like to preserve our ancient institutions." He shrugged a shoulder.

Minchen swallowed another lungful of smoke, blew it out, thinly, violently. Her fingers were drumming on the table behind her. "It may have to come to wangling . . . I don't know yet. It never occurred to me that I was begging for favors. It seemed to me just plain sense. Doesn't it make any difference that Bill isn't expendable any more? That's the incredible word, isn't it?" She laughed, but it didn't sound much like Minchen. "For that matter, I'm not either! It seems to me that there's a shade of difference between being a Land Girl and having a child. Incidentally it's utterly different from being merely married. Bill had to go, on D-Day. And I had to let him go. We were expendables then . . . we both knew it. And there hasn't been a single squawk in any of Bill's letters, and it never occurred to me to do anything else than shut up about it . . . not until this evening. But there's every reason now why I shouldn't shut up any more. And I'm not going to! I don't know how they run this beastly war, and I don't care. I suppose they think children are expendable too! I don't. I'm not just a cat that's going to have kittens. I'm a woman, and if I've a right to have a child then that child has a right to have a father! Bill can't be allowed to stay out there. They'll have to send him back. He's the father of a child. Doesn't that count in their scheme of things? Isn't it of the slightest importance? Don't they care if they let all the fathers be killed off? Suppose we didn't care whether these children of ours lived or died? Don't you see? If they can't see it, if Bill has to be wangled back, then all I can say is that it's a ghastly crime and they're all a lot of fools! I'll wangle, I'll do anything, but I won't go on digging their damned vegetables and see them throw Bill away!"

She ended as abruptly as she had begun, with not more than a slight tremble in her voice at the end.

While you could draw three startled breaths, the silence was profound.

Then Muriel went to her daughter. "I know it's going to be the most wonderful child in the world!" She put both her hands on Minchen's face and kissed her.

Jack Wainwright cleared his throat, with a lot of noise, dived frantically into the wrong pockets for pipe, tobacco, matches. "If only I could tell you that I thought you had a chance! Of course you're right . . . but you're up against the system, and you're on the outside. We both are. . . . One might have to reach Eisenhower, and how the hell can you do that? . . . My God, why aren't you mothers all organized, married or otherwise? There's no difference as far as the children are concerned! Why the hell are you all sheep? Why don't you boycott this bloody business of war? Why do you get a kick out of nursing the battered wrecks and rolling bandages and making shells too? How many million asinine women are preening themselves in snappy uniforms, vastly proud of having released that number of men for the shambles? . . . Why, for God's sake, don't they go and chain themselves to the railings of Downing Street or the Kremlin or the White House and make such an international stink about it that the politicians won't be able to do it again? And why am I such a damn fool as even to think of it? It's fantastic, ridiculous, impossible! In the next war they'll all be—"

Minchen's body jerked up from the table. She threw her cigarette into the fireplace. "Oh . . . damn the next war! And this one too! Bill and I are nothing but rats in a trap! But I tell you, if I'm going to bring a child into this world, they're going to give me back its father! And if that means reaching Eisenhower . . . somehow I'm going to reach him!"

[illegible] in the world [illegible]
Adams [illegible]
But [illegible]
[illegible]
[illegible] and I thought [illegible]
[illegible]
[illegible] We [illegible]
[illegible] and how the [illegible]
[illegible]
[illegible]
[illegible] Why [illegible] forget the [illegible]
[illegible] Why do you [illegible]
[illegible]
[illegible] remember [illegible]
[illegible]
[illegible] Why [illegible]
[illegible]
[illegible]
[illegible]
[illegible]
[illegible]
[illegible]
[illegible]
[illegible]
[illegible]
[illegible]

1941–1945 *THOSE marvelous Russians! . . . Our great allies! . . . Let us send every available supply to the Soviets! Moscow, Stalingrad, Leningrad—the bloodiest fronts in history! 'Uncle Joe' creates 'scorched earth' tactics, has Hitler bewildered! . . . Glorious Russian soldiers break the German might! . . . Millions of Soviet civilians moved to Siberia make stupendous war production without water, food, shelter, or fuel. Heroes all! . . . Full of proud confidence, their magnificent offensive clears Russia of the invader, sweeps into Berlin!"*

1946– . . . *"Get tough with Russia! Stalin betraying the Atlantic Charter behind his Iron Curtain! . . . What are they doing in the Balkans? And the nerve of asking for bases in Spitsbergen! . . . What is this veto anyway? . . . Watch out for Communism! . . . How about a European bloc against Russia, with Germany made strong again? . . . Do we fight them now, or what?"*

CHAPTER SIX

BY EIGHT O'CLOCK ON A SUNNY LATE-SEPTEMBER MORNING THE light mist has disappeared; but every blade of grass is still pointed with a pearl of dew, iridescent as a soap-bubble; and if you are only twelve years old, a small girl doing a boy's job in wartime, there are a million fascinating things like that to see and wonder about as you pedal slowly along on your bike from, say, Frier's Dene to Little Minchen — as slowly as you can, even though your errand is to deliver a telegram at the Wainwright cottage.

It isn't too late in the morning to catch sight of a rabbit in a clearing . . . and he might easily be talking to a pheasant, even if the pheasant was awfully busy and pretending not to take any notice. And then, when you came to the hill and couldn't possibly ride any more, there was a place, just inside the five-barred gate, where there was a fairy ring! Of course, in the daytime, you couldn't possibly expect to see any fairies, but you couldn't ever tell if one of them hadn't dropped something there in the moonlight and forgotten to pick it up again; and it didn't take a minute to prop your bike against the gate and climb over and make sure. . . . Bother the old telegram! It could wait!

Did young Mercury ever unfasten the wings from his heels and take time out for a swim, or a moment's amorous dalliance, while Jove was busily hurling his thunderbolts?

On this particular morning an intent Alice nipped over the high gate and disappeared into her private wonderland, heedless of the wartime gods of whom she was the messenger; her concern the investigation of the elfin world of childhood — an enchanting sight if you could have seen her, shoes kicked off, herself the fairy dancing barefoot in the bejeweled ring of grass.

It was nearer nine than eight by the time she came trudging and blowing to the top of the hill, happily empty-handed, and, now that there would be other children to see her, oozing awareness of the importance of her status — Telegraph Girl. Before mounting her bicycle at the outskirts of the village, she produced the yellow envelope and held it in her hand for all the world to see. Then she rode along, her bell ringing loudly to clear the way. . . .

In Little Minchen there would be such intense traffic!

Two children stared at her from a doorway as she passed them on iron wings.

A dog wagged his tail at her and refused to budge from the middle of the road. She called out: "Naughty dog!" . . .

A plodding horse in a farm cart merely shifted the angle of one ear as he clip-clopped along. She told herself that the horse was very rude not to pull over. . . .

And then she was alighting from her own fiery steed at the end cottage, the Wainwrights'. As she was propping her bicycle against the picket fence, the yellow cat stepped delicately into her crowded world. "Oh you lovely pussy!" she exclaimed, and bent to do homage and establish friendship, her chubby hand deep in his golden coat. Even when confidence was established to their mutual satisfaction, it wasn't possible, apparently, to walk gravely to the cottage door. Flagstones were made for hopping. Still Alice, she hopped.

It was Muriel who answered the knuckle-rapping.

At sight of the yellow envelope, she failed completely to see what would have brought a delighted smile to her lips — the child dipping one quick knee to her in salutation, a twitch of survival from more ancient days. What she did see, through the immediate drumming of her heart against her ribs, were the almost inevitable official phrases: "The War Office regrets . . . Killed in action."

All unconscious of her real importance, Alice piped up: "Please, there's sixpence to pay." Muriel swallowed. There was something macabre about that sixpence. . . . The warm, sticky, somewhat rumpled envelope shook in her hand. It was addressed . . . of course it was . . . to *Mrs. Willard Thatcher, care of Major John Wainwright.* . . . "Care?" What care could they take of her now?

She heard her own voice from an infinite distance. "Wait. There may be an answer." . . . How ridiculous! . . . As if there could be an answer . . . Wasn't this it? . . . But Minchen mustn't open it! I can't let her. . . . I won't!

Her finger pried at the envelope, as she turned away.

The yellow cat stepped up behind the child and with arched back began to rub himself against her warm bare leg. With a squeal of pleasure Alice promptly sat down on the step and scooped the cat up in a great armful into her lap, her world a constant harmony, while behind her the grown-up, whose face she was not interested to see, was dreadfully alone with her daughter's telegram.

But even as the potential blow had been withheld for at least an hour by the dillydallying of its unconscious bearer, so now the envelope entered into the seeming conspiracy of delay. It was too well stuck down. There was no interstice for an anguished finger. Muriel took three would-be steadying breaths while she dislodged a hairpin. . . .

Minchen was in shorts this morning, face, arms, legs the color of horse-chestnut. She glanced at her father across the row of string beans. "You know, Dad," she said. "I thought of another angle last night — Bill's father."

Jack Wainwright was tanned to a crisp from the waistline up. His lean body was hard and muscular. The mechanical hand was the only false note. "What about him?" he answered.

"Well," said Minchen, "I've wasted a whole month bombarding Eisenhower with letters. Don't you suppose that Bill's father could get some action? After all, he is a lawyer. That ought to entitle him at least to get an answer from somebody at Headquarters."

"Good scheme!" said Jack. "His two letters to you couldn't have been nicer. He might be very useful. It's conceivable that he might know some senators or congressmen, and be able to work it through them. One gathers that they are pretty powerful people, infinitely more so than our niggling M.P.'s."

"Then I'll write him today!" said Minchen. "I'm absolutely fed up with this waiting! . . . And that frightful brute down at the camp yesterday was too awful! I could have killed him!"

Jack Wainwright frowned. "My dear, don't forget that his job is to shovel men into the line, not get them out of it."

"Yes, I know," said Minchen. "But he needn't have laughed at me!"

"That was pretty unnecessary," said Jack. "But he might be a good officer at that. And the better the officer, the less sympathy you're going to get! . . . I'm not saying this to discourage you, old thing, but you must realize that you're up against something! It's going to take time. You've got to be ready to take some frightful smacks in the face, even when you get to the higher-ups. So by all means write to your father-in-law. . . . Hullo! There's your mother coming. Looks as if you'd clicked for a letter . . . or perhaps . . ."

He didn't finish his thought.

Muriel's practice, when a letter came for Minchen, was to call from the back door and wave; and then, every time, Minchen ran, like an antelope. . . .

This morning there was no wave, no call. She was coming to them.

But nevertheless Minchen was out of the row of beans already, running, her face alight.

For the first time Jack's hands stopped working. It was not a letter that Muriel had. . . . "Oh my God!" he muttered, and stood rigid, his teeth clamped on his pipestem, his eyes on the telegram.

Muriel saw Minchen's face change as she ran. She called out quickly: "It's from Bill! He's in England!" She had to swallow before she went on. "He's . . . slightly wounded but quite cheerful. In a way it's almost . . . good news, darling! . . . Here. You'll see . . ." She thrust the telegram into Minchen's hand. "I just had to open it . . . you know . . ."

But Minchen had the yellow sheet unfolded and wasn't hearing her mother's voice any more, only Bill's. . . . SUCCESSFUL LANDING WEATHERSFORD HOSPITAL ONE ARM SLIGHTLY BANGED UP NOTHING TO WORRY ABOUT HOW ABOUT YOUR HOPPING NEXT TRAIN CRAZY TO SEE YOU WIRE YES BILL.

Slightly banged up . . . one arm . . . nothing to worry about . . . slightly banged up . . . Weathersford! Where they took the serious cases! *Nothing to worry about* . . . Had he lost an arm? Was he hiding it from her? . . .

Down through the rows of beans limped Jack Wainwright, his wife's words—"slightly wounded, quite cheerful"—fading into sounds that were twenty-five years old, twenty-five years unforgotten: strangled sounds from a long double line of beds . . . the click and rattle and smell of all the dressing gadgets on a wheeled table that the orderly pushed along following the doctor from wreck to wreck. . . . And then you lay staring up at the ceiling hour after hour, plastered with bandages, while it went on hurting, dully . . . and even through the deep atavistic absorption in yourself it entered your consciousness that they'd put screens round the fellow on the next bed . . . and the doctors fussed for a while, and then the orderlies came again with a wheeled stretcher and loaded the body on it and lugged it away . . . no further use to King and Country. . . . and you thanked Almighty God when they dished you out another couple of pills that would put you out for a merciful hour or so. . . . Oh yes, just a "blighty." . . . And quite cheerful . . . with the added cheer of knowing that when the thing was healed they'd send you back into the line to stop another one. . . .

He came to them and, with a sneer at himself, deliberately held out his cork hand. "May I read it?"

Minchen looked up from the telegram, turned an odd face to him. She said, and her voice wobbled, "Oh, Dad! . . . What do you think?"

Jack Wainwright took the telegram. At the name of the hospital his jaw muscles stuck out; but he read on, and then reread it; and finally handed it back to her. "Do what Bill says. Wire yes and get to him as fast as you can."

"Of course, but . . . his arm? And they flew him to Weathersford! Does that mean . . . ?"

Jack interrupted with a hard voice. "It means that you don't need to reach Eisenhower! It means that when he leaves hospital he'll get sick leave and come down here! Don't waste time wondering! Go and look up a train and pack the smallest bag you've got. You may have to go from door to door in Weathersford before you find a place to sleep. Stay as long as you can. It'll make all the difference to Bill. Hurry now! I'll come in and write you a check. And you'd better take all the ready money there is. If I were you I'd take your bike too. You never can tell. It might come in damn handy. There are all sorts of errands Bill'll want you to do for him. . . . Go ahead! Action! Jump!"

Minchen gasped, and turned and ran for the cottage.

Muriel caught hold of her husband's arm. "That was . . . wonderful! But, Jack, what do you really think?"

Jack Wainwright put his hands on his wife's shoulders. "None of us can afford to think until Minchen gets there."

"Even though Bill said there was nothing to worry about?"

"Would I send you a wire saying 'Arm amputated'?"

"Oh, Jack . . . then you . . ."

Jack shook his head. "All we can do is wait!"

EPICURES' DINNER, *October 1946, Waldorf-Astoria, New York, U.S.A.:*

Turtle Soup with Madeira. Lucullus Crusts. (Dry Sack)
Channel Sole, Sauce Auguste, Special Fennel. (Chablis 1929)
French Partridges in casserole with slivered greens and fritters. (Château Margaux 1940)
Foie Gras from Strasbourg and Riviera Salad. (Château Margaux)
Real Peach Melba "Escoffier" with Hazelnut Biscuits. (Champagne)
Caribbean Coffee. (Brandy)

[*The partridges were specially flown over for the occasion from starving Europe.*]

CHAPTER SEVEN

THE AMERICAN HOSPITAL BUILDING AT WEATHERSFORD WAS ONE of a number of historic landmarks taken over by the government. It had previously been "taken over" by William the Conqueror in 1067. Legend had it that he himself had lived there for a time. Subsequently, however, the call of Les Andelys became too strong. He gave Weathersford to one of his yes-men and departed. In the ensuing eight hundred-odd years, rival barons had also taken it over, plugged it full of cannon balls, put the defenders to the sword and the building to the torch. Always it had risen again out of its own ashes. Cavalry had stabled their horses in its vast halls which had run the gamut of murder, rape, weddings, births, music and festivals.

Today, ivy-covered but again at war, its acres of meadowland had been given to the plow, its forests scientifically stripped, its innumerable rooms denuded of tapestries and armor, paintings and rugs: the only decoration now a frieze of cots each burdened with a broken body.

Ambulances collected these casualties from an airfield in the grounds and also from the railway station a couple of miles outside in the small town. Originally a mere baronial dependence, a service station almost for the nobles and their retainers, Weathersford had become once more a supply depot, this time for the hospital.

By map, Friar's Dene was only seventy miles away: but it was cross-country, and it had taken Minchen three mortal hours to get there. In point of moral wear and tear it was a journey that she would not soon forget. Her fellow passengers, released from their national inhibited silence by the impact of war, did what Britishers always do when they emerge, or are thrust, from behind their stone wall. They opened the floodgates; and, when they found that she was on her way to a wounded husband of whose condition she was still in ignorance, Minchen became the target of horror stories of such opulence that the compartment reeked of mangled corpses and sawn-off gangrened limbs.

Metaphorically speaking, she drew her telegram tightly around her as a protective cloak against the sadistic discharge. She clung, as to a couple of spars, to the doubtfully encouraging words "slightly" and "nothing to worry about"; but her own uncertainty was like a dead weight that threatened to pull her down into the verbal deluge.

It was like a release from a life sentence, rather than three times sixty minutes, when at last the train stopped at Weathersford and she was able to stumble out into a recognizable world, into the comforting rattle and bang of goods being unloaded by American soldiers, the grinding of immense baggage trucks missing her by inches as she struggled to get at her bicycle between boxes, bales, people . . . exasperating people who, in her state of nerves, seemed deliberately intent on getting in her way.

Her plan was a simple one — to strap her bag to the back of the bicycle and ride straight out to that awful place, painted to her with the pigments of Doré, where Bill would be lying. . . . She didn't care where she was going to sleep that night. She might not sleep at all. They might let her stay on a chair beside Bill's bed. . . . They couldn't possibly be such brutes as to refuse to let her. . . .

And then, through the intensity of her concentration which nullified the platform din, she had a vague sense of her name being called, from far off, like a whisper. Before it could reach her consciousness, her arm was gripped and she heard her name again, heard it this time not only through her ears but through every pore of her body. Only one person in the world could say it like that. . . . She let go her suitcase and swung round . . . and every other thing in the world vanished, was silent, did not exist.

All she said was "Bill!" and it was the huskiest monosyllable that ever got lost on a railway platform.

It wouldn't have mattered if she hadn't said it, for Bill's lips silenced hers and Bill's arm crushed her to himself fiercely, like a cable tying them together, and Bill's buttons dug through her blouse and hurt, and she loved it and wanted to go on feeling it because they were Bill's buttons . . . unbelievably, ecstatically Bill's . . . and time was wiped out . . . and he'd never really been away . . . and if he had it didn't matter now . . . nothing mattered. . . . Nothing? . . . Suddenly she tried to strain away from him, remembering. . . . "Bill! Your arm . . ."

But Bill merely tightened his grip. "Minch!" he said. "Minch, don't move! God, have I been waiting for this!" And he kissed her again, her lips, her wet eyes, her cheeks, her hair . . . starved for tenderness, the winter ice crashing and grinding at the surge of spring. . . .

And then a voice broke in. "Sorry bud, you picked a bad spot! How's about beginning again somewheres else? Guess it'll keep, won't it?"

The sweaty grinning G.I. had already disentangled three large crates from their very elbows. He had also put the girl's bicycle more or less in safety against the station building. But there were more crates, and his reluctant utterance was forced upon him. He stood waiting, and looking. "Jeez!" he muttered, his chin dripping with admiration and envy.

What he said to them was like a delayed-action bomb. It took seconds to explode . . . and incidentally to shatter the only touch of eternal beauty in all the dingdong humdrum cacophony of that station.

Bill's arm slowly relaxed from the small of Minchen's back, slipped down and away. His hand found hers and held on. "You make it all worth while!" he said.

Minchen clung to his hand. Heaven was a blur . . . Bill too.

Then Bill's head moved. He became aware of the waiting G.I., glared at him, realized the situation. He turned to Minchen again. "Let's get going."

Minchen groped for the suitcase somewhere at her feet. "My . . . my bicycle's somewhere."

The G.I. said, "I leaned it against the building." He pointed.

Bill nodded at him. "You're O.K., brother. . . . Thanks!" Then he led Minchen away, urgent to have the world to themselves. . . . She hadn't changed! She was still Minch . . . even more Minch if that was possible. . . . It wasn't that she was just tanned to a turn, infinitely more beautiful than the snap of her that was the most precious thing he had had on him all the time. There was something . . . else; something . . . deeper . . . some new quality . . . He gave her hand a squeeze. "I've thought of this a million times, out there . . . meeting you, I mean. And it was always in the village . . . just at the top of the hill and just you and me. But I wouldn't change it for this platform! It's still you and me, isn't it? . . . Specially you. And I knew it was going to knock me, but . . . not like this. I . . . I can't tell you what you're doing to me, Minch. It's . . . it's the damnedest thing! You . . . you've put my swallowing gear completely on the fritz! I . . ." He made a noise that was meant for a laugh. "Guess we'd better beat it out of here, honey, and quick! . . . Look, let me take your suitcase while you push the wheel. We haven't far to go. As soon as they brought me your wire I came whooping downtown in a jeep and I've found a place for us to stay. Us! . . . Did you get that?"

Minchen's face showed that she had. She was having difficulty with her own swallowing but she managed an answer that was entirely satisfactory. "Oh, Bill! . . . Darling! . . ."

Whatever else she intended to say died suddenly in her throat.

Bill was reaching around to take the suitcase from her and for the first time his left arm came into full view. The sleeve of his battle jacket had been cut off at the shoulder. The arm itself, right down to the finger tips, was swathed in bandaging.

Minchen's stomach shriveled. "Bill!" The word was the nearest thing to a cry. And then, almost fiercely, she demanded, "How much have they hurt you?"

Bill's eyes flicked once. Then he laughed quickly and said, "I wouldn't swap that for anything in the world! It has given me you again. . . . They can have the rest!"

There was a note in his voice . . . She couldn't be sure. . . . Nothing to worry about? . . . They can . . . have the rest? . . .

Bill snapped out an order. "Grab your wheel! We're on our way!"

OCCUPATION:

Did the German soldier pay for a woman in France, Holland, Belgium, Norway?

In Germany the current price for a woman is quoted at one pack of American cigarettes in all zones.

Recruiting sergeants take note.

CHAPTER EIGHT

A CLOUD NO BIGGER THAN A MAN'S HAND . . .

It remained over Minchen's head as they walked through the town, talking jerkily on account of people and jeeps and trucks.

The rooms Bill had found were in a small red-brick house on the edge of the community, set back from the main road. Behind it was a field bordered by pines, open country beyond.

As they walked up to it, the front door opened. In the frame a woman stood smiling.

Under his breath Bill said, "Mrs. Green's the name. Nice old gal. Opened right up when I went to town on her."

She was gray-haired and pink-cheeked and blue-eyed and "comfortable" and, for no apparent reason, was wearing a shawl over her shoulders.

Minchen lowered her bicycle on to the plot of grass and went up to her. "It's awfully kind of you to take us in, Mrs. Green!" she said. "We're terribly grateful and we'll try not to be any bother."

Blue eyes looked into brown and melted. "You can be all the bother you want, dearie, and I'll be glad of it. I know how you feel with your husband just back and all!" She put spontaneous hands on the girl's shoulders and kissed her on both cheeks. "There! I feel the better of that! . . . Now, you come along in and make yourselves at home!"

Minchen took Mrs. Green's hand in both her own. "That was . . . sweet of you! Thank you!"

Mrs. Green beamed and led the way into the sitting room. Like herself, the place smelled of lavender. The sun seemed to be coming in at all the windows, touching antimacassars on ancient armchairs and a horsehair sofa, glinting on an array of framed photographs that littered, neatly, the top of an upright piano in the corner. There was a table in the center which had the appearance of mahogany. On it was a maidenhair fern in a terracotta pot. The walls had a gay figured paper, and the cream-colored hangings at the windows were looped into broad sash-like bows.

"How very nice it all looks!" said Minchen.

Bill nodded. "I told you my wife would fall for it as soon as she took one look."

Mrs. Green's hands were folded across her stomach, in deepest satisfaction. "I've never taken lodgers before," she said. "My son has always sent me enough to keep the home going after Mr. Green passed away. But with this war and all and you an American, I just couldn't bring myself to refuse. And I'm glad I didn't!" She smiled from Bill to Minchen. "If there's anything you want now, you just tell me. I tried to think of everything but as I said I'm not used to it so you'll have to make allowances. When my son comes he likes to light up his pipe, so you're welcome to smoke anywhere in this house. Mr. Green never felt right neither until he'd put on his slippers in the evening and was settled down in that chair with his tobacco jar right to his elbow. And then there's another thing I'd like to ask as a favor. If you either of you care to play the piano would you leave the door ajar so that I can hear? Mr. Green always liked me to play to him of an evening but of course I can only manage a few simple tunes and you wouldn't want to hear them! But it is wonderful what a comfort music can be when . . ."

Minchen looked at Bill with a smile, just in time to see him bite his lip and turn his back deliberately on the piano. Her face went white. She knew what "all the rest" was now. . . . She wanted to run to him, to fling protecting arms around him, to weep with him, to curse with him. . . . She stood perfectly still, frozen, rocking on her feet, not hearing a word as the old woman babbled on and on. . . . Then, somehow, she reached her, broke into the stream by clutching her arm. "Mrs. Green, I . . . Forgive me . . . my husband and I . . . It's been so long and it's . . . it's dreadfully important. . . ."

Mrs. Green took another look into those anguished brown eyes. "I'm an old fool!" she said. "And him wounded and all! Don't take on so, dearie! Everything's going to be all right, you'll see!" She turned to Bill. "You take good care of her, Mr. Thatcher! Don't you let her make herself sick a-worrying!"

And then at last she left them . . . looking at one another . . . searching. . . .

Minchen's hand was on her throat. She could hardly see him. She stumbled to him, and her arms went carefully round him, and she put her face against his. And then it seemed that the small cloud burst upon her as she clung to him and sobbed.

Bill held her to himself tightly. He was wide open . . . now that she had guessed. "Minch! . . . Darling . . . Don't cry like that!"

"I . . . I won't believe it!" cried Minchen. "It isn't . . . human! Oh Bill, they haven't done *that!* Tell me I'm wrong! Tell me it's going to heal. . . . Tell me!"

Bill had known it — that she would be torn to pieces when he had to tell her. But now that it had come, now that her whole body was a shaking misery against his, his own moment of revolt — when they had told him — came back again, this time worse, because it was for Minchen. . . . Minchen who had never pulled a trigger, never seen a man drop, never done any of the lousy things he'd had to do. . . . God damn it . . . now they reached out and got her into this thing! He was the one to take it . . . not she! They hadn't any right to touch her. . . . "Listen, honey, you mustn't let it get you. I'm one of the lucky ones . . . and I mean lucky! If you saw that hospital down the road you'd know it all right! All I've clicked for is a few holes and a couple of fingers. There are a million G.I.'s who'd give their souls to swap with me. . . . I'm not saying it wasn't tough. Believe me, I sounded off! But when you stepped off the train, you fixed it. I don't suppose I'll ever be able to tell you what you did. It was like a miracle. It washed it all away. If I've learned nothing else that's good out there, I've learned that you're the only thing there is!"

But Minchen's sobbing still shook her. "Lucky" . . . how horrible! And to have to mean it . . . when they had taken away his music! Never to be able to play again . . . all the years of work that he had done, all of himself that had gone into it . . . thrown away, wasted . . . no more "someday" and the concert platform. . . . "Lucky!" How infinitely sarcastic!

"My dear . . . my dear . . . I love you! I love you! . . . Oh Bill, it isn't fair! It's damnably cruel! You mustn't ever go again! Promise me you won't go again! I won't let you go again! You've given them enough! They can't have you any more. . . ."

"Enough?" Bill broke in with a savage laugh. "Thank God you don't know anything about it! A mere couple of fingers? Why there isn't a man who wouldn't pray for a stroke of luck like that!" He laughed again. "Believe me, I know when I'm well off!"

Minchen shivered as though something slimy had walked over her. What was the horror that made Bill say things like that?

Bill went right on. "Why, I'm such a joke as a casualty that they'll be kicking me out of this hospital in a few days. They need my bed for the real ones. Anything that looks halfway like a doctor can handle me now. So you see, honey, I'm all right! . . . And listen, there's another thing. I'm going to see to it that I get shifted to Friar's Dene. There's a medical officer there and they won't be able to return me to duty for quite a while, either! So if your father and mother can stand to have me around, that'll mean . . . our room in the cottage! Think that one over . . . Mrs. Thatcher!" He was patting her, his cheek hard against hers. "Ah, my dear, pull yourself together! It's all right! We're going to make it all right, you and I!"

Soon Minchen was able to swallow down the hard lump of rage and hatred and injustice — enough at least to be able to get hold of herself for the time being, to straighen up and take a long breath again and wipe her eyes and blow her nose and manage to say to him, with a choky laugh, "Mrs. Thatcher's compliments and she's . . . she's taking it very hard!"

"But she's taking it standing up!" said Bill. "And I knew she would! . . . And now that you've got a mere walking case on your hands. would you like to hear some of the chores you've got to do for me? . . . You're going to be awful busy, Minch! You've got to cut up my victuals every time we eat, and help me button my clothes, and tie up my shoes . . . and I don't mind saying that shaving isn't such a cinch with one hand! How are you with a razor?" He grinned at her. "You must have had some training on your legs, or do you belong to the wax school?"

Of course! Those things too! But somehow the grin made it worse. "You don't want me to start bellowing all over again! . . . Oh, Bill, I . . . I didn't mean to go to pieces like that, but I simply couldn't bottle it up altogether. . . . You didn't really expect me to, did you?"

Bill shook his head. "Shall I make a confession to you?" he said. "Believe it or not, I did a little bawling to myself yesterday . . . right in my damn pillow, just like any kid!" He laughed and began fumbling for cigaretttes in his jacket pocket.

Minchen moved quickly. "I need one badly too!" she said, and took the packet out of his hand. She put a cigarette between his lips and took one herself.

Bill smiled. "Neat!" he said. "Here's a light." His hand went into his pocket again and he flipped a lighter in front of her. "Snappy teamwork, I call that! I knew we were going to be able to handle it together! . . . And now we've got that all straightened out, let's try and not slip off one of those horsehair contraptions. They look just like New England to me." He pulled a small table in front of the sofa and put an ash tray on it. "There are only about twenty million things to catch up on, and we haven't even made a beginning! D'you know you've . . . changed somehow? You look lovelier than I've ever seen you—tearstains and all!"

Minchen smiled up at him as she sat down. "I feel as if I look a wreck!" she said. "But you've changed too. You're awfully brown and fit but you look . . . older."

Bill shrugged a shoulder. "Yeah!" he said. "It does that all right! You either grow up fast or . . . you don't! Let's forget it! Tell me all about yourself. I want to know everything you didn't put in your letters. And did you do a swell job of writing! I don't suppose you could guess how many times I read each one. I could almost recite them to you one after the other!" He laughed. "I guess they're pretty dirty now, but I've got the whole bundle in my kit."

As he sat down beside her his left hand hit the sofa arm. It made him hiss with pain. . . . This damned swinger! He pulled it cautiously into his lap.

Minchen saw. Her own hand clenched. Then she took a furious pull at her cigarette. She mustn't say anything. He wouldn't want her to. . . . So she said, "And some of yours are all blurry where I cried onto them! . . . How . . . how long is it since you had my last one?"

"Heck!" said Bill. "It must be well over a month. We've been hopping like a bunch of fleas. They couldn't keep up with us. I'll probably get them here sooner or later. Then we can read them together. . . . But there's another thing, just as important. Your music, Minch! It really did come through. I heard it . . . and I knew what you were saying. . . . There were times when it nearly drove me crazy . . . I wanted you so much . . . and I could see you sitting there . . . all clean, and we were so much a part of each other that I . . . I knew that even if they rubbed me out I'd get back to you . . . somehow!"

For a moment they remained looking at one another. Then

Minchen slid an arm round his neck and put her lips to his. Presently she said, "It's like a heavenly echo to hear those things. . . . Oh, Bill, darling, doesn't it almost begin to feel as if you'd never gone away? . . . and you mustn't ever go away again. Not now. You haven't had my last letters. They told you why, the special reason, I mean, that changes everything. . . . I only knew myself a month ago and then I wrote you pages and pages about it . . . and I played it to you every afternoon . . . and I thought it to you every single night, almost letter by letter, as if we'd had a private wireless. I almost succeeded in convincing myself that it must have got through. And now I'm glad it didn't! Out there in all that horror it might not have seemed so much. It might have been . . . tarnished . . . out of key . . . I don't know. This way is better . . . with you . . . so that I can tell it to you . . . or do you know, now?"

Her face was very close and her brown eyes were more direct than any wireless. But, at the impact of her unmistakable meaning, it seemed to Bill Thatcher that he was seeing, and understanding, from an infinite distance—from the other side of terror and brutality and agony and violent death, from the other side of what he himself had done and witnessed and felt and thought—strange new sproutings as yet uncatalogued, forced in that fantastic hothouse. In that other stranger world, from which physically he had only just emerged, a thousand guns, wheel to wheel, a thousand planes unloading bombs, had made the earth tremble at man's hatred of himself, at man's joy in killing, at man's animal courage in facing death, at man's continuous belief in his own godhead. In this world in the brief hour that they had been together, he had not let her out of his sight. It was she who was pulling him back, holding him back from "out there," giving life again to all that he had stored up. He knew that if she went out of the room for five minutes, left him alone, the film of what he had lived through would begin to unroll again in his mind in color that refused to fade, with the appropriate sound effects and even the smells. They were an integral part of him, kneaded into his being. It was only Minchen who could help him push them into the background, Minchen who would bring him to a proper perspective, Minchen who would be the music that he had lost . . . Minchen . . . Minchen! And now she was telling him that there was going to be a child. . . . He wasn't ready. He couldn't spare her. He didn't want the interference of an unknown element coming in between them . . . and a child in this ungodly mess . . . there were the bodies of dead children plastered along the cobbles . . . and Minchen had been carrying one while he was pumping out tracers from a red-hot machine gun. . . . It didn't tie up . . . it was "out of key" . . . it was somehow infinitesimal . . . impertinent. . . . He wanted to push it away, refuse it. . . . And damn it, why? Why did he have to feel like that? What had happened to him? It should have been so wonderful, so terrific, completely out of the world! And it would have been, if only he hadn't known the things he now knew . . . as Minch didn't know them, would never know them if he could help it. . . . It wasn't her fault. It wasn't his either. It was simply the way it was. . . . And to Minch this child must mean everything that he couldn't make it mean . . . yet. You could see it in her eyes, feel it in her voice. . . . He mustn't let her even guess . . .

"Minch!" God, he had to lie to her! . . . It couldn't be done, not with her looking at him like that. . . . He pulled her head down on his shoulder. Even then it couldn't be done. "Minch," he said, "it's too big. I can't take it yet. Give me time. I know it's the most marvelous thing in the world . . . for you, but I'm all mixed up. And I'm . . . jealous. You won't let it . . . interfere, will you? Right now, I've only got room for you!" He gave a sort of laugh. "I seem to keep on saying that, don't I?"

Minchen left her head where it was. She sighed contentedly. "Yes, but I happen to like the way you say it!"

November 1940 — "*Perhaps the most murderous of all the attacks on industrial centers was the great night-long bombing of Coventry.*"

July 1943 — "*Pure, naked, bloody terror! . . . Set your teeth and do not forget who it was who brought you such misery! Let hatred glow in your hearts! Walk through the streets of Hamburg, among its 30,000 dead, and from the smoldering ruins of houses see for yourselves at whom bombs and phosphorus were aimed. Forgiveness and conciliation are no longer possible here. . . .*"

December 1946 — "*This week two cities, recently mortal enemies, and both of them terribly bombed in the late war, will exchange Christmas greetings by radio of 'foregiveness and rebirth.' The cities: Britain's Coventry, Germany's Hamburg.*" (Time.)

CHAPTER NINE

WHEN BILL BECAME CONSCIOUS IT WAS FOUR O'CLOCK IN the morning, faintly luminous although that was of the least importance.

He was only barely awake, and his whole awareness was of one thing — pain, waves of it, rhythmic, pounding. Had he been lying on the arm? . . . Didn't matter. It hurt. . . . Why in hell didn't they come and give him a shot of dope? . . . Have to do something. He shifted, felt Minchen's body beside him, started up, fully awake. Her head was a black splodge on the pillow . . . little Minch, dead to the world! . . . Mustn't make a noise. Might wake her. Be stinking mean, that. Barely light yet . . . but this arm was pretty fierce.

With extreme care, he untucked the blanket and sheet on his side of the bed, found the floor with his legs and edged himself up on to them. He turned then and pulled the blanket up so as not to leave Minchen's shoulders uncovered. . . . Minch . . . Judas, only three days ago and those tanks had come rolling at them! He'd been a whole man then — for the first part of it anyhow. Then that damned mortar had opened up. And now he could creep around on his bare feet so as not to wake Minch. Even if the lousy arm was throbbing like all hell, what of it? It really was Minch lying there! They could have the whole damned arm for that!

His fingers explored the bandage, squeezed lightly here and there. It didn't help a bit. He made his way to the dressing table where he had left his lighter and cigarettes, felt around . . .

touched something soft and silky . . . hers! . . . then her handbag . . . what a million priceless things she carried in it! . . . Ah, there were the cigarettes. . . . Thank God, there were a lot of things you could do with one hand, specially when it was your right . . . and as soon as this stinking pain had gone out of the other one, you could develop some sort of technique.

He snapped on the lighter, dragged at a cigarette, inhaled a vast lungful. Technique? . . . He blew out the smoke violently. Minch's father would be able to offer suggestions and criticisms, wouldn't he? . . . He gave a sarcastic snort, then suddenly saw himself in Little Minchen that first day . . . He came out and I saw his hand and said, "They can't do that to me!" Guess we all said that . . . suckers! . . . God, if only Minch would wake. This thing's beginning to get me down. . . . He glanced at his wrist watch. Suppose if I went and stamped up and down that living room, the old girl would think I was a burglar and die of fright! Light enough here anyway. Shan't bang into anything.

He began wiggling the arm warily, experimentally, then held it close to his body, began to walk, smoking furiously. . . . She's there I know, but it's . . . tough out here by yourself. Shut up, you fool! You've got to take it, and a lot of it. What was it they said? Bloodstream to readjust itself, nerve tissue . . . a long business. Thanks! . . . No more lousy tanks to stop anyway! Guess that thought ought to hold me for a while! Even if it does feel as if a couple of tanks had gone over it. . . . Judas, why can't I wake her, talk to her, sneak down with her and make a cup of coffee . . . be damned if I will. But, gee, kid, you don't know . . .

Another cigarette.

Guess I'll have to learn to cover up. Minch is too smart. I'd meant to ease her into that piano business, but she tumbled so fast it might have been her own hand! . . . Wonder how Kreisler'd have felt if they'd got his bow arm? H'm! Well, why not? I know I hadn't begun yet, but someday . . . The hell with it! It's up to me to forget that from now on. Suppose I won't really believe it till these bandages come off. . . . Hope to God they put 'em on right, that's all. Not so damn sure they did. . . . Suppose the stump has started bleeding again? Or they didn't clean it properly or something? Why the heck don't they tell you a few of the things you can expect? Lying on it probably didn't help, either. . . . How does gangrene start, anyway? Suppose they have to chop another lump . . . You fool, you don't know the first thing about it. Turn it off. You'll scare the pants off yourself! Concentrate! . . . Minch! . . . And there's this kid that's coming! Queer how hard that one was. March she said . . . March, and between now and then they'll bump off about another million, while this child is quietly coming along into our "brave new world"! Yeah! How do they write that stuff? They ought to go out and take a look . . . or a walk through the wards right down the street! Our "way of life," eh! . . . Jees, I think this has begun to bleed! Pumps like . . .

"Bill! What is it? What's the matter?"

Minchen's eyes were wide open. She sat up with a jerk, alert, anxious.

As Bill looked at her, the beginning of panic, the four-in-the-morning aloneness, went out of him. Her voice gave him back himself, put everything under control again. "It's all right, sweetness!" he said. "Nothing's the matter. I woke up and the arm didn't feel so good, so I thought I'd have a cigarette."

He went to the bed and sat down on the side of it.

"How long have you been up? Why didn't you wake me?"

"H'mh'm!" Bill shook his head, smiling. "But I'm . . . glad you woke up, even if it's only for a minute."

Minchen frowned. "Is it hurting badly now?"

"Oh, so-so!" said Bill.

She reached out and touched his face. "Does that mean . . . it's awful?"

Bill kissed her hand. "You go back to sleep, honey!" he said. "I'll just have another cigarette."

Minchen leaned away and snapped on the electric light. Her eyes reached for his face. "I will not!" she said. She looked at her wrist watch. "We're going to get dressed and go straight to the hospital. Somebody'll be on duty who can do something."

She slid out of bed on the other side and began hauling on her garments.

Bill watched her, and through the agony of his arm, he laughed. "You know," he said. "You make me feel like your cat. I want to purr. You don't make the same noise as a top sergeant when you give orders."

Minchen said, "I'm so furious at myself that I'm fit to be tied! I'm no earthly good! I've never rolled a bandage. I've never been inside a hospital. I'm as much use to you as a sick headache! And worse than that, I even went on sleeping while you were out there alone! I hate myself for that. I ought to have felt it. I ought to have known immediately!"

"You don't have to kick yourself," said Bill. "You did, didn't you? You woke as if I'd called you. And I guess I was calling you . . . in my mind. Seems to have worked almost too well, doesn't it? At least one part of me wanted you to go on sleeping, and here you are giving orders!"

"Yes, but I might have been helping all this time!"

"You work quickly," said Bill. "You've already done your bit for the morning. My mind was tearing around like a diseased rabbit. It's human again already."

Minchen came round to him, kissed him. "That's to keep it human!" she said and went down on her knees and pulled on his socks, held out his trousers so that he could stick his legs into them, laced up his boots, eased him into his one-sleeved shirt and finally the battle jacket.

The last two made him grit his teeth audibly. Minchen caught her breath. "Did I hurt you?"

"You couldn't," said Bill, "if you tried."

Minchen smiled. "Are you all ready? We ought to go down like a couple of mice."

They did so. It was Minchen who burgled the front door open, with its chains and latches, letting in the emaciated grayness of that small hour.

For a couple of breaths Bill stood rooted. The all too familiar beginning of light took him back . . . but the buildings were unsmashed and there was no sweetish smell of stiff bodies, no tommy guns stuttering at distant windows. . . . You could walk through this place singing and shouting if you felt like it . . . only you didn't. Why didn't you? What was wrong with the idea anyhow?

Minchen said, "Are you all right, darling?"

Bill let his breath go, took another look at her . . . just to make sure. . . . "All set, honey!" he said quietly. "Let's go!"

PALESTINE, Anno Domini 33:

"Foxes have holes, and birds of the air have nests; but the Son of man hath not where to lay his head."

And the Romans sent soldiers to apprehend him. . . .

Palestine, Anno Domini 1946:

"Give us a piece of earth that is not stained with the
blood of our people.
Give us a piece of earth under a sky unclouded by hate
and fear.
Give us a piece of earth that will yield to our labor
and longing for freedom.
Give us a piece of earth that will heal our wounds and
make us whole again."

And the British sent soldiers to apprehend them. . . .

CHAPTER TEN

MURIEL WAS IN THE FRONT HALL. ONE BY ONE SHE inserted into the tall vase branches of just-cut marigolds. Their tawny orange flowers made a blaze of light. She said aloud, "He always used to put his cap beside them and take a sniff!"

From the living room Jack answered. "I don't seem to be able to lay my hand on the corkscrew. Any idea where it might be?"

"Good Heavens!" said Muriel. "We haven't used it for so long. Have you looked in the sideboard?"

"Top and bottom," said Jack, "and every drawer. I've also tried my desk and the tobacco closet. It seems to have vanished into thin air."

"I'll take a look in the kitchen," said Muriel, "just as soon as I finish the flowers."

"The corkscrew has the priority," said Jack. "But you go ahead. I'll look out there myself."

"I suggest the knife drawer," said Muriel, "and you'd better probe under everything. It's the only place in the house I can never manage to keep arranged."

"Well," said Jack, "as they ought to be here in half an hour or so, let's hope that my probing efforts won't take too long."

Muriel went on with her marigolds, hurrying a little. Presently from the kitchen came sounds of upheaval, the crash and jangle of kitchen knives, forks, spoons, strainers, funnels, all being emptied on to the kitchen table. She smiled, carefully poked in the last three long stems and then went out in the direction of the continuing cataclysm.

In an isolated position on the table was the missing corkscrew.

Jack was holding the knife drawer with his good hand under the edge of the table and sweeping the loose pile back into it with the other.

For a moment Muriel watched him. His gesture was so distinctly unfeminine. When he had got the drawer back and there was quiet once more, she said, "One so often has to envy a man's way of getting things done."

Jack picked up the corkscrew. "It was, of course, at the very bottom of that remarkable collection. I have a feeling that from now on it had better occupy a niche among my pipes. . . . Are the glasses and water out there?"

Muriel laughed. "You fetched them yourself fifteen minutes ago. I believe you're really as excited as I am!"

Jack's eyebrows went up. "Excited? . . . I suppose the word is admissible, but it doesn't go far enough. You see, my dear I hate to confess it, but I never expected Bill to come back. . . . I might add that there have been moments when that thought was a severe handicap in my talks with Minch! Thank God she won't have to ask me any more questions now!"

Details of that interminable summer stood out black and white in her mind, details that nobody knew but she knew. How many times had she waked in the night and heard Minchen creep downstairs and go out? How many times had she read Minchen's face when the radio was in full description? How many times had she watched Minchen go through an elaborate pretense of eating, in reality feeding everything to the cat on her lap? And how many times had she not dared to look at Jack's face as he answered Minchen, holding forth on the speed of the advance, on the demoralization of the Germans, on the possibility of the war's ending almost from day to day, on the fact that in a war of movement casualties were reduced to an absolute minimum. . . . All the time he hadn't really believed a word of it. But he had kept it out of his voice . . . at what effort!

She went up to him and took him by the lapels of his coat. "My dear," she said, "you've done a wonderful job! Minchen will never know how much she owes you."

Jack shook his head. "You put it the wrong way round!" he said. "She will never know how much I owe her! It's she who has done a wonderful job. While there are a few Minchens on this earth perhaps the race has a chance after all. I know that if I'd been in that girl's shoes I should have cracked! And then, as a last straw, with Bill's chances about at zero, to find that she was going to have to bring a child into all this! . . . Will you ever forget the look on her face that night? I don't know when I've ever been so moved. . . . For her, at that moment, there was no war. It was insignificant. She was Eve . . . the creation, the mother of us all. . . . Quite extraordinary! And quite humbling!"

Muriel nodded. "Yes!" she said. "And it must have been equally wonderful news to Bill. Poor boy. I hope it will help him now!"

Jack's glance dropped to his cork hand. "You know," he said, "I've been asking myself whether it really is Bill who has come back. Minchen didn't put that in her letter . . . naturally. But how can I help being a pessimist about anything to do with war?"

"Ah, my dear!" said Muriel. "But you were older than Bill when you came back!"

Jack shrugged a shoulder. "In my experience it isn't altogether a matter of age. And you don't have to be wounded either. After all, this boy didn't come out of the Sicilian show scot-free. And this has been a dozen Sicilies rolled into one. Added to which, they've lopped off the career he'd mapped out for himself, his one passion, the thing that brought Minchen and him together in the first place! Don't you see? . . . Any fool can dig vegetables!"

Behind her back Muriel's tiny hands were fists. "Oh, Jack . . . please!" She turned quickly. "I . . . must go and get ready. They'll be here any minute now . . ." She hurried out of the kitchen, negotiated the stairs, and then with the door of her room safely closed, pressed her hands to her face. . . .

But, alone again—and it was striking how much every individual was ultimately alone—Jack Wainwright paced the floor, uncomfortably, savagely treading the mill of his thoughts. . . .

The boy would be here, in the house, at any minute now, facing what you had had to face so long ago. . . . The wheel had turned full circle. Here was another generation, destroyed and wasted in the game of fools . . . and the fools would be in power still when half the world lay dead! In their various insane institutions of government was there the slightest perceptible change in their thinking? It was not to be detected. And between them all was the same thin veneer of highly advertised friendship disguising the same basic distrust which would set them all clawing at each other's throats again once the fighting stopped. They would say it again—"Gentlemen, there are bargains to be had in Germany!" And the national-international game would be on, the scramble across the corpses for the booming markets which, for a while, perhaps, would stave off the inevitable crash! Couldn't you almost hear the avalanche of high-flown political verbiage by all the old-timers and their hangers-on? Couldn't you see the unfortunate plebs, bilked again, surging to their "free" elections, to vote once more for the very system and the very groups that had always destroyed them, and must inevitably do so again? . . .

He dragged a match under the mantelpiece and lit his pipe, snorting sarcastically. . . . Harrow would retain its prehistoric straw hats, and Eton its "toppers"! And when the little bastards were marched off to their various moribund churches they would be treated to a hot anxious piddle of anticommunism, each minister claiming that it was his own pet god who had won the day and who must now be thanked for the inestimable boon of being spared from the holocaust to enjoy the privileges of a truly great—and Christian—civilization which let its war-wounded sell apples and pencils in the streets of its capitals! . . . Ah, but not this time! No suicides this time! No more of that jumping into the Danube by the hundreds! Of course not! The flotsam, the hurt ones, the apple-sellers, the border-liners, were all "going to be taken care of"! . . . Why, my fellow citizens and constituents, you have only to give me your vote . . . It was to vomit! . . . Vote for whom? For what? Was there the remotest possibility in that amazing country of Bill's of some unborn man, or with luck even some returned soldier, who would find the answer, be able to jolt the world into unity, give it one more chance? . . . Why should there be? What difference was there between their Congress and the House of Commons or any other parliament? . . . No. The aftermath would be historic — a problematical survival of the smartest, and the returned soldiers would learn to drink more whisky and forget . . . and no one would give a damn!

But the problem was not all the figurative Bills who would be shouldered aside in the scramble. It was Bill himself . . . on his way to your house. It was Bill to himself. It was Bill crippled, in his approach to a future which was now permitted him — for, presumably they would have no further use for him in the fighting ranks. But they wouldn't let him out. Oh no! They would keep him on a ball and chain metaphorically doing latrine duty . . . the soul-searing paper jobs around some camp office with its filthy jealousies and shirkings, its suckings-up to senior officers, its slow rot. . . . Every base camp was peopled by derelicts. Your keen man applied at once for the firing line . . . and got it! Since the time of the Greeks and the Romans it had been so. So now, inevitably with Bill . . . The supreme dispensation is that he will have Minchen, as you, by God's infinite mercy, had Muriel! But . . . there will be that look in the eye which was not there before the invasion. There will be moments when he won't hear what you say. There will be those other moments of almost feverish appreciation. . . . How pathetic in retrospect, the sheer marvel of being alive . . . of being let off . . . as though you were born again! And how damnable that you should have to earn it at such a cost! . . . And it was going to be harder for Bill than it had been for you. He had brains, a career already mapped out, while you . . . You were merely a loyal sardine from the Public-School-and-Varsity can! Of course you hadn't begun a career, nor even given it much thought, when the other war interrupted. Like all the rest of your class without special talent you would finally have drifted into something polite with due emoluments, — "something in the City" perhaps, or, with much prodding, would have been called to the Bar in such spare time as you grudgingly made from the more important affairs of life . . . the hounds, August in Scotland, golf at Portrush, salmon in British Columbia! The classic mold! The Pattern of Empire, for which the underdog, in that station of life in which God had seen fit to put him, was so constantly called upon to die, violently, in every other part of the world map! . . . *Et tu, Brute!* H'm! . . . The simple Latin tags we roll off! . . . But you fell in line. You subscribed . . . and you paid your dues! And because all you could find to do was sit on your backside, you've helped to make Bill pay too! You've helped to lose him his chosen career! He will never forget what might have been. You can't give it back to him. Whatever he does in life is going to be a second-best, a makeshift. . . . What are you going to do about it? . . . He is going to be here in your house, probably for the one and only time in his life. They will not return from America. . . . The moment is now . . . if you have anything to offer but vegetables!

REMEMBER Pearl Harbor . . . sez you!

The hell with Pearl Harbor! I'll remember Lichfield!

It don't make no difference why they sent us there.

S'pose I did rub out a coupla guys and s'pose there was a coupla broads mixed up in it. So what? There's a war on, ain't there? And they drafted us, didn't they? And back home if you're flat-footed after a job like that, it's a good meal and the hot-squat and no harm done, see!

But at Lichfield?

It was the job they done on us when they got us there.

And it wasn't the Nips or the Krauts who done it!

It was an American job . . . a U.S. Army job, see, all nice and according to regulations, with the big boys giving the orders and the strong-arms doing their stuff. . . .

Jesus, boy! Maybe you wouldn't squeal with a string round your balls and a six-foot sonuvabitch of a sergeant at the other end having fun!

Bill Mauldin wasn't drawing that stuff for the papers!

You can take Pearl Harbor, and you know what you can do with it!

Me — I'll remember Lichfield!

CHAPTER ELEVEN

THERE WAS A LUMP IN BILL'S THROAT AS THEY MADE THE TURN at the top of the hill.

"That's the spot I'd planned to meet you again!" he said.

"I've sat there a hundred times remembering!" said Minchen.

And then the craggy old Rosinante broke into what passed for a trot after its incredible feat of pulling up the hill.

The turnout was like the ghost of an earlier century. The springs of the four-wheeler drooped on one side. There was no rubber on its wheels. From some long-forgotten cubbyhole the gnarled driver had resuscitated a high hat, all furry, and green in spots. The rusty harness was spliced with bits of string, carefully saddle-soaped. As a final touch, Minchen's bicycle sprawled on the roof, the wheels hanging over each side like the limp untidy legs of a drunk being taken home.

But Bill was staring through the open windows, his hand in Minchen's, and out there, on either side, were once more the unbelievable cottages, the trees, the flowers, the kids still playing hopscotch . . . the same old dog with one eye open . . . everything still . . . and quiet . . . as if he'd never been away. . . .

He turned to Minchen, letting go a deep breath. "Hi!" he said.

Minchen's fingers squirmed in his. "Hullo darling!"

"We're . . . here again!" he said.

"It's been an awful long way!" said Minchen.

Bill didn't answer for a moment. The big Texan, Kamenakis, Salvaggio . . . too long a way for them . . . not many left of the original bunch . . . you could count them on the fingers of . . . of one whole hand! . . . He turned to Minchen. "You're darned right!" he said. "I can hardly see the soldier who blew in here that first day. I guess it must have been my kid brother!"

The edge in his voice was like ragged granite. Minchen was quick. "I remember him perfectly!" she said. "He was a terribly nice boy! I wonder . . . Did he ever tell you about meeting a girl up here?"

It took Bill a moment to smile. It seemed more than that to Minchen.

Bill said, "You should have heard him! He raved about her."

"Really? And what happened? Did they see a lot of each other? Did she fall in love with him?"

"Not only that," said Bill. "She took an awful long chance and married him."

"How wonderful!" said Minchen. "D'you know, darling, I have a feeling that perhaps we might run into them sometime . . . in the next few weeks. Up in the woods perhaps . . . or sitting together on a certain flat stone that's only just big enough for two, a little way down the trail . . ."

Bill laughed. "Where they used to admire the view of each other!"

Now that he could laugh again, Minchen raised the hand that she was holding and rubbed it against her cheek.

They were interrupted from the outside by a loud *Whoa*-ing from under the furry hat. For a marvel the harness didn't break as the old nag set his rump against the weight of the cab and brought it to a successful stop.

For a couple of long breaths Bill didn't move. He sat staring at the cottage . . . the cottage his kid brother had told him about. . . . "God!" he muttered.

Then he eased himself out of the cab and turned to give Minchen a hand. As he did so Muriel and Jack came out of the door and along the flagstones. Minchen saw them and called out, "Hullo Mother! . . . Hullo Dad!"

For an intense flash Bill was back in the Berkshires . . . It was he who had called out . . . bringing Minchen home . . . and they looked so swell, standing there. . . . He turned quickly, eagerly, and then stood still, watching, as Minchen kissed first one and then the other. These people were swell, too . . . and she had been theirs first, before he ever came butting in. . . . They must have taken an awful licking all this time . . . because of Minch. . . . He hadn't thought of it that way before. . . .

"Bill!" said Muriel. She left the group and came to him. Her eyes didn't touch the bandage. "Bill, my dear!" She stood on tip-toe and kissed him.

Bill said, "That was . . . wonderful!" He put his arm around her and kissed her.

Jack Wainwright stepped up to them. "Hullo there, Bill!" he said gravely, his hand out. "Good to see you!"

Bill looked up from his mother-in-law and met the older man's eyes. There was no smile in them. Bill's were equally serious. He gripped the hand. "Thanks . . . for everything!" he said.

Jack nodded. The bridge between the two of them was still there. "I'll help you with your stuff," he said. "Our old friend up there seems to be stuck to his seat. Probably just as well! . . . And that's quite a horse, isn't it?"

Bill gave an exultant laugh. It wasn't the horse or the dry crack. It was everything, the moment, the feeling of it all. . . . And then he too took shelter. "Believe it or not," he said, "it made the hill on its own power!"

"I think it's a marvelous horse!" said Minchen. "I'd like to feed it lumps of sugar." She went round to pat its nose instead. "Incidentally, where on earth is Frankie?"

Muriel said, "I put some food down for him and closed the kitchen door. I thought he'd be getting in everybody's way."

Minchen laughed. "I knew there had to be a reason. . . . Bill, if you'll start lowering the bike, I'll get it out of the way."

"Right!" said Bill.

But Jack Wainwright stepped in front of him. "Damned awkward things, bikes!" he said, and reached up on to the cab roof. "Here, Minch! Take it away!"

Bill's eyebrows went up. He said quickly, "Look . . . I . . ."

Jack Wainwright turned to him. "Delays things to take chances," he said. "But if you insist on getting into this . . ." He reached into the cab and took out Minchen's featherweight suitcase. "Here! Minch and I will handle the kitbag. And, by the way, the cab's mine."

Minchen laughed. "Who's top sergeant now? You'd better take Mother in, Bill, before he bites your head off!"

Muriel touched his elbow. "Yes, come along, Bill! It's a waste of time to argue with those two. I learned that long ago."

Bill's eyes went to the cottage. The door was open . . . of course! There would be flowers in the hallway, and everywhere else they could be put. . . . And there would be again, and always, that quality that he had never been able to define . . . and probably never would . . . impregnated now with what Minch had given him, what they all had given him — what they were giving him this very moment — Minch, who was . . . Minch, and that said everything; and her mother, who just looked at you and took you right straight in; and the Major, who knew it all . . .

He turned to Muriel with a smile. "I guess there are quite a few things I've got to learn!" he said. "And this is the best place I know to make a beginning!"

The beginning was waiting for him in the living room.

It was not in his mind as he walked into the cottage with Mrs. Wainwright. Emotion can distract attention from even an abscessed tooth. . . .

The flaming marigolds caught his eye at once. He nodded at

them — it was almost a salutation — and said to her, "Aren't they marvelous! . . . D'you know, I've always remembered the lupines you had here once."

Muriel gave him a pleased smile. "They were lovely, weren't they? But then, they're all so heavenly. I always feel that without them a house completely changes its character, talks a different language."

"What do you do in the winter?" asked Bill. "At home we buy things in pots and stick 'em around on window ledges. There's one I always liked, called . . . H'mh'm! The darnedest name to remember . . . A pink flower with a hairpin bend, sticking up through shortish leaves . . . The name has something to do with bike races."

Muriel laughed. "That sounds like a crossword puzzle . . . Let me see . . . Pink flower, short leaves, . . ."

"The flowers come white and red too," said Bill, "but the pink ones make you think of flamingos."

"I've got it!" said Muriel. "Cyclamen! . . . Bike races indeed! Bill!"

They both laughed.

Bill put Minch's suitcase on a chair, and his cap beside the marigolds.

"I was waiting for you to do that," said Muriel. "Now I know you're home again! Go and make yourself comfortable, Bill. I'm just going to let Frankie out before Minchen comes in."

"Thanks a lot," said Bill, and, as Muriel went off to the kitchen, his eyes preceded him through the doorway to the remembered room which had bewitched him the first time he ever saw it, and always afterwards. It was going to be like greeting an old friend. . . .

Mercifully he was alone.

He stopped frozen inside the door. It seemed that there was nothing in the room but the big piano. It filled the whole world.

It dragged out from the secret places of his mind all the dark things he had locked there. It was as though the bandages had been torn off and he was left standing staring at the raw stumps where fingers had once been . . . and the taste in his mouth was bitter. The concert platform, career, success . . . Minch and he appearing together like the Iturbis . . . all that had gone into the garbage can when they did the amputation job! Why not a couple of toes, or half a leg, while they were at it? They were welcome to them. But it had to be his fingers! . . . There was no ducking it any more . . . not here! It wasn't only his show now. It was Minchen's. At Weathersford he had made it his own, gone underground with it, on the excuse that neither of them wanted to play that old tin can anyway. . . . But normally both of them would gravitate to a piano as naturally as an apple falls from tree to earth. It was never even closed. Wasn't it one of their means of expression? . . . This one had been faith and hope to Minch. She had prayed on it . . . while he was out there . . . listening. It had made her days go easier, to be able to say things to him on it. . . . Oh God, didn't he know! And although her hands would be itching to get at it as soon as she walked in, she would avoid it like the plague . . . because of him! Minch was the kind who would never play a note again . . . because he couldn't take it!

Outside that room, the dirt road became noisy. The ancient hack turned about, groaning and creaking, and went on its way.

Halfway along the flagstones, each with an end of Bill's kitbag, Minchen and her father had only a few more paces to go. On Minchen's shoulder the yellow cat was riding high, supported by her spare hand, proclaiming his joy loudly to all the world. And Minchen was laughing. . . .

"Oh, Dad!" she said. "Did you ever hear anything like Frankie? He's . . ."

Her laughter was strangled. The piano spoke . . . a series of one-handed chords that clutched at her throat. She dropped the bag and the cat, and dashed inside. . . . The chords had stopped.

"Bill!" she cried.

He turned to her. At the sight of his face she said "Bill!" again, and ran to him.

For a moment they clung to each other. Then Bill said, "I . . . I took the jump, thank God! But I'm scared as hell!"

"Oh Bill, darling! Why did you do it? Why didn't you wait? It's too soon!"

"It was now or never!" said Bill. "We couldn't go on hiding it from each other. And I've . . . been hiding it from myself too. If you hadn't been with me, I . . . But I know now. It's final, absolute. I'm . . . washed up!"

"Bill!"

"There's something else, Minch! . . . It tears me to say it to you . . . Look, quick, before the others come in . . . play something, anything. I've got to find out if . . . if I can listen to you even . . . now that I know I'm . . . through!"

For a moment they remained staring at each other across that thought.

Then Bill gave a savage laugh. "Yes! That's what I do mean! . . . Swell, isn't it?" He pulled out the piano bench. "Go ahead and play! . . . Don't you see, it's for both of us!"

It wasn't easy to reach the bench, even though she steadied herself with a hand on the piano. It was even less easy to see the keyboard. Black notes and white were all mixed up . . . everything was all mixed up . . . one minute you were both so happy, the next you felt as though your heart were breaking. . . .

She sat down, tears spilling on her cheeks. . . . Oh, please! . . . Don't take that away from him too! . . .

On the other side of the room, staring out of the window, his back to her, Bill stood waiting. . . .

Outside on the flagstones, Jack Wainwright had sat down on

the kitbag. He was keeping the cat on his knee, not without difficulty. "They won't be wanting us, old lad!" he said. And while he rubbed the cat persuasively under the chin, his own jaw muscles were tight.

Then, when at last the sound of Minchen's playing came flooding into the open, he nodded to himself, as though in confirmation of something. . . .

"Ah!" he muttered. "Good boy!"

Muriel was nowhere to be seen.

Part Three

"TODAY we seek a moral basis for peace. It cannot be a real peace if it fails to recognize brotherhood. It cannot be a lasting peace if the fruit of it is oppression or starvation, or cruelty, or human life dominated by armed camps. It cannot be a sound peace if small nations must live in fear of powerful neighbors. It cannot be a moral peace if freedom from invasion is sold for tribute. It cannot be an intelligent peace if it denies free passage to that knowledge of those ideals which permit men to find common ground. It cannot be a righteous peace if worship of God is denied."

— Franklin D. Roosevelt

CHAPTER ONE

IN THIRTY DAYS, ACCORDING TO BIBLICAL STATISTICS, THERE COULD have been five other worlds, just like this one.

For the thirty days of November, in the Year of our Lord 1944, a paratrooper found himself spewed up out of the world shambles into the temporary sanctuary of the village of Little Minchen, only because he was no longer of use as an expendable. He could not be sent out, immediately, to kill his fellow man. He had therefore ceased to be an asset — was, in fact, a liability; not only a problem in logistics to the Army, but a burden to the taxpayer, out of whose reluctant pocket would have to come the money for his rehabilitation. (Thirty pieces of silver per finger per month would be about the figure.)

Thirty days off the job is a month's vacation to you. You can lie in bed late, and knock your alarm clock for a loop when it wakes you — if you were fool enough to forget to set it back! And then you can thumb your nose at all the other commuters on the 8:04 and go back to sleep again. . . . Just a touch of nice, healthy sadism, that's all. . . . But a month at Jones Beach or Revere isn't quite the same as a thirty-day stretch on the beaches of Iwo Jima, or other fascinating hops. For one thing, the fireworks are different. But you wouldn't know about that. (You were going to find out, though, that in thirty days Congress, with a recess like a carrot in front of its nose, can hamstring a President, kill an OPA, disband an army of ten million men, sell nine million of them down the river in housing, return her electric iron to the housewife, give proud birth to a stillborn reconversion mouse, and go home to get re-elected — by you — on the strength of having lifted the tired face of the nation.)

In that same brief period, simple arithmetic adding, it will be found that a man can have a mutilated hand dressed eight times: hardly an interference at all in the month graciously handed him to use for his own private purposes, to squander or to hoard, to dance, to sing, to revel. . . .

There was, of course, the small matter of patching up the broken pieces. . . .

"Broken pieces? A puncture or two and a mere couple of fingers . . . with millions of his buddies still in there fighting? . . . Just plain griping!"

Ah . . . sounds like you again — you, the civilian who took a reluctant peek into the foxhole before D-Day and failed to understand. Or else you're a senator "taking the long view," seeing "the overall picture" . . . and putting in a good word for your friends in the matter of war contracts. Or perhaps you've just received your three-hundred-and-sixty-thousand-dollar bonus, so here's to more and better wars!

But Sergeant Bill Thatcher (oh, yes, he'd earned his bonus — a third stripe) was not concerned with griping. He was too busy receiving an education in fields not generally covered by the courses in our better institutions of learning.

The psychology of pain, for instance . . .

Twice a week he had to go down to the army doctor in Friar's Dene and have his wounds dressed. The professional verdict was that both hand and arm were "doing nicely." But to Bill, "doing nicely" meant a continuing awareness of something going on down there that wouldn't let up. It didn't seem to make any difference whether he shifted his position, or wiggled the remaining fingers, or didn't wiggle them, or squeezed the place gently with the other hand, or held the arm close to him, or away from him

. . . there were a couple of rats gnawing at the stumps all the time. He knew enough now to know that gangrene, the thought of which had scared him half to death, was out of the question. That was at least a mental relief. But the steady mystery of pain, with its constant drag, its insistent claim on his inner attention, its provocation of doubts and fears as to the grim possibility of further loppings, despite the doctor's reassurance to the contrary, constituted a brilliant introduction to Part One of the course.

Part Two consisted in methods of behavior resultant upon the mastery of Part One.

It is permissible, recommendable, psychically helpful — in the privacy of the bathroom, say — to resort to prayer as a relief: "Jesus Christ! Won't you let this goddam thing let up!"

There are, however, two schools of thought as to the efficacy of prayer; and, moreover, the problem was not so much one of being alone, as of being with the family.

In all animals, four- or two-legged, there is apparently a common instinct to hide when sick or wounded. There is little difference between the depths of the jungle and the bedroom. Bill Thatcher was denied even the shelter of his bed. Modern therapy, rightly or wrongly, insists that the prone position is harmful. His hiding, therefore, could not be physical. Not for him the harmful pleasure of lying in the secrecy of his bedroom, surrounded by sympathetic but mortuary flowers, tossing, groaning, cursing, as the spirit moved. He had to be out in the open, able only to hide behind the too often difficult mask of cheerfulness, like the grinning lad of antiquity with the fox at his vitals expressing the atavistic pride of the male.

A man, especially one in the middle twenties, lacks the courage to be unmanly — to put his head down on his wife's breast and say: "Hold me tight! I can't take it any more. . . ."

So, with Minchen, awake too in the small hours and suffering sympathetically, it was permissible only to go so far as to say briefly that it was "not so hot." A cigarette completed the manly ritual, the ostrichlike hiding. And, naturally, when Mrs. Wainwright, at breakfast, asked him in all sweetness, "How is it today, Bill?" the only conceivable method of reply was the masculine grin, the push-off, and a dismissing "Oh, coming along fine, thanks!"

Obviously Bill Thatcher would receive high marks.

There were other branch subjects to which his attention was directed.

With pre-invasion and therefore more youthful imagination, he had seen himself coming leaping back, the job well done, eager, alert, urgent to start building for Minchen and himself, to get on with the good life, the rich contributing life that he and she were to lead together back home. . . . And why not? Youth must have visions; and soldiering is only an unpleasant interruption.

He had not suspected the degree of the unpleasantness. It was rendered the more unpleasant by the thought that every day of healing brought him nearer to being sent back to do more soldiering . . . a commanding thought which, during this thirty days, seemed to kill all eagerness and alertness. And not only was the job still being done, not only would he have to go back and help finish it, but he knew now that it was a job that shot any idea of the good life full of holes. . . . You went on seeing it, hearing it, thinking about it, over and over, loathing it, asking yourself questions that got you nowhere, so that while you were out of it you were still in it. . . . And you couldn't unload that stuff on Minch, either! You had to keep it to yourself . . . and the things it did to you . . . and the thought of going back . . .

("Listen, honey! I was just thinking—about the kid. I suppose you're all set for a son and heir! Would you mind frightfully if I did a little praying that it'll be a girl? Damn silly, I know, because women take it in the neck nowadays, too, but — somehow, it isn't quite the same.")

Nothing was. That was the hell of it. The whole thing was . . . out of focus. Before, it had all been so perfect — Minch and he, understanding the same things the same way, swapping laugh for laugh, not at anything special, but because you had to laugh and kid each other about the little things, knowing all the time that you were sharing, and giving to each other, equals, in mind and body and that dream of "someday" for you both. . . . And all you were doing now, for Pete's sake, was hurting her, taking cover, not sharing any more, but going underground. And equal? . . . Thanks a lot! That was out. And the Iturbi stuff, too. . . . She'd have to arrive at that particular "someday" alone . . . while he rooted from the sidelines! He'd root all right! . . . This business of making her play every night . . . looking as though she could see the two fingers lying right there on the keyboard . . . half sick . . . stumbling over them! And that to Minch! Judas Priest! Had he ever expected to be cauterizing either her or himself with music? . . . But it was quicker and cleaner that way for both of them; and, maybe, one day, if ever the damn war stopped, he might be able to get down to putting something on paper. . . . He'd have to find out, anyway. . . . Pastorale? Hell! But something! If not . . .

("Listen, honey! I need air and lots of it. Let's make with the legs, shall we, and climb up and see how those charcoal-burning boys are doing? Or down to Friar's Dene if you'd rather. Your mother said something about groceries. Might be a help if we got 'em for her. . . . Or any old place, so long as you'll come!")

She always came. She was always there, waiting, ready, every time he wanted her, needed her, could come dashing out from himself. . . . If she hadn't been, what in God's name would he be doing? That was a tough one. . . . You couldn't even try and answer it! And that wasn't right either. . . . It was admitting that you were leaning on her . . . using her as a crutch . . . not standing on your own feet, and stepping out side by side with her, owning the world as we did at Oxford! . . . Oxford . . . for better or for worse, eh? She couldn't be having it much worse, right now, with what they'd shipped back to her — an also-ran, a non-starter, a dud!

NOVEMBER 11, 1946 . . . (*the twenty-eighth anniversary of the first Armistice Day*):

"LONDON (UNITED PRESS): *Limbless and other disabled servicemen of both World Wars have joined to organize a new little industry in famed Soho — a revival of hand weaving for the luxury trade. Primitive looms which have not changed much in a hundred years will be used to produce hand-woven and exclusive woolens for luxury trade export to America.*"

God Save the King . . . I mean . . . what?

CHAPTER TWO

IT GOES WITHOUT SAYING THAT, IN HER OWN WAY, MINCHEN WAS taking that course with him.

For Bill, the necessary groundwork had been laid in Sicily, Italy and France. Comparatively, Minchen had no groundwork at all. She was in darkest ignorance. Unlike the privileged women of Europe who had reaped the full benefits of this present-day civilization, Minchen had not been raped, tortured, starved, clubbed, or shot to death; her body tossed into an open trench, or cremated. She hadn't even been bombed, blitzed or doodle-bugged. She lacked the purifying experience of a concentration camp. She had never known the patriotic joy of setting fire to her cottage in the teeth of an advancing army. No one had ever "fraternized" with her. She knew nothing of the pride of "giving" a son, or a husband, to her country. Worse than that, so little did civilization or war concern her, that the possibility of Bill's having to go and fight again was a horror that she tried not to contemplate.

Obviously, therefore, she was greatly handicapped.

You will be the first to argue — you, with your wad of Victory Bonds — that to have sweated, lightly, among her father's vegetables, to have shed a tear or two while her man was doing the normal job of fighting, didn't even constitute "doing her bit!" She hadn't made the slightest "sacrifice!" In your opinion, and of course you are right by all the recognized standards, she ought, instead of selfishly mooning around waiting for Bill to come back and fussing over him now that he was back, to have been devoting herself to doing something really important to the war effort: any full-time employment that would release a man; or, if there weren't anything of the sort in that precious village of hers, she ought to have knitted sweaters all day, or socks, or whatever it is they do knit; or at least she could have organized the women, the farmers' wives, and taught them how to eat less, or how to vote when the war was won, or . . . or hygiene — they must have needed it, in those dirty little cottages with all that Elizabethan stuff. True, she did condescend to play the piano for the boys; but, at that, wouldn't they rather have listened to "Lili Marlene" than to Rachmaninov and Borodin?

So it must again be obvious that during those thirty days all that Minchen could possibly learn were stupidities to any really patriotic wife to whom cocktails and bridge made a perfectly good substitute for a husband.

But to Minchen, since Bill was at least safe, for the moment, and in her keeping, stupidities made for rhapsody.

Upstairs in the bedroom, for instance, Bill's brush and comb hobnobbed with hers again on the bureau; his "undies" had ousted hers from the top right-hand drawer; his jackets and trousers squeezed in with, and crumpled, her frocks in the closet; his boots crowded her shoes; his cigarette ends piled up with hers in the joint ash tray that always seemed to need emptying. . . .

Positively inane; and worse than irritating!

But to her, the room had been a morgue, where loneliness and fear lay on cold slabs in her mind. Now, it was pulsating again, with all his things shouting to her that he was actually back, incredibly alive, with her all the hours of the day . . . and the unbelievable miracle of it was in her eyes which watched over him, and in her brown legs which no longer walked alone, and in her ready hands which she had made his servants, and in her glad body which was the bearer of his child. Life would have been a continual Magnificat . . . but for one or two things.

"I'll do your tie for you now, darling. Here it is!"

She had laced his boots, and buttoned his pants, and squeezed tooth paste on his brush, and cleaned off his razor blade — what an astonishing number of things you couldn't do, with only one hand! And in the doing they had made laughter of it together, and kissed each other . . . and it would all have been fun if, when they took the bandages off, the fingers might have been there. But there would only be . . . gadgets!

"You know, these are really scrumptious ties! Did you buy them in some swagger shop in America, or can they possibly be an army issue? . . . There! You look positively beautiful! . . . I think I'm getting pretty hot as a valet!"

. . . He'd have to live with those gadgets, like Dad with his hand, and they would both be terribly cheerful about them, and admire them, and say how wonderful they were because they could do absolutely anything . . . except one thing . . . damn them! And now you couldn't even put your head on his chest and howl any more because that would let him know that you were . . . sorry for him. Sorry . . . for Bill! It was unthinkable! But you were . . . and not only because of the pain . . . and you couldn't tell him, and you couldn't let him see. He didn't want you to be sorry for him. And of course he was right. And so you had to say one thing when you were thinking a thousand others. . . .

"Well, darling, all ready now? Are you starving? I'm simply famished!"

. . . Oxford hadn't been like that. You simply thought something and said it, and Bill's meeting thought came back straight and swift . . . not from behind something else — pain and the thought that you were a cripple — something that changed the color of it and the flow of it. You had both been your naked selves at Oxford, as free and limpid as two streams meeting on a hillside and making one. There seemed to be signboards everywhere now: DON'T SPEAK . . . DON'T TELL . . . KEEP IT INSIDE . . . BURY

IT. And they'll all be sticking up in front of you this evening when you'll have to play to him again . . . and even though you don't dare look up, you'll see him, poor darling, sitting there frozen, fighting himself! And the hopelessness of it is that you know you're not reaching him, can't reach him! It's too soon. It's simply tearing him now. . . . You can see it! . . . But you must reach him. You must! If it helped him out there, make it help him now. It has become infinitely more important. Make it say all the things he wants to say, and can't. Make it tell him all the things you want to tell him, and can't. . . . It's your job, damn you, to make him hear his pastorale again . . . and those Berkshires! In a sort of way, it would be giving him your hands too. . . .

"I've got to go shopping in Friar's Dene this morning, darling. Coming along? Or would you rather talk to Dad? . . . You're coming! Oh, splendid!"

. . . You couldn't spare a minute of him, not even to Dad, because you couldn't tell when they might . . . take him away again. He would disappear . . . and it would be another D-Day . . . only worse . . . because now you knew. And this time there was the baby! Poor infant! And poor darling Bill . . . not ready. They've robbed him of that. The carillon is only a pitiful little tinkle because Bill can't hear it too. . . . It might almost be somebody else's child. They've cheated him! It was somebody else who sat up on the flat stone. The message never got through. . . . The talks we were to have had! And the exciting plans! And the sort of . . . mutual preparation. Instead of which, there's only a sort of blackout curtain, as though it weren't really happening at all, as though you were going through it alone. . . . Oh well, sooner or later a scab would form over it, and it wouldn't hurt quite as much, and it would be all right, only . . . Bill would never know!

"FOOD Minister John Strachey granted the British people for Christmas extra rations of an extra pound and a half of sugar for everybody, an extra half pound of candy for those under 8 and over 70, and an extra eightpence worth of meat."

"A famous English novelist has just returned to his villa on the French Riviera, taking with him his cook, butler, housekeeper and chauffeur."

"Many wealthy British families are reported to have moved over bag and baggage to Ireland."

"Interviewed in his new island paradise in the Caribbean (15 rooms, 4 baths, swimming pool, and usual offices), Lord Eustace Piddlefoot smiled. 'Really, you know, with British legislation where it is, one can't afford to die any more, can one: much less live over there, if it comes to that! . . . 'Swhy I'm here, if you must know. Y'see, there aren't any taxes here! . . . Of course, I hate the beastly place. So damned uncivilized! I mean, I can't find a butler for love or money! Perfectly frightful, what?' "

CHAPTER THREE

On "dressing" days they bicycled down the hill together, separating at the fountain in the market place, and meeting there again when Bill returned from camp.

On this particular December morning — when the thirty-day course had run its span — they had planned to snatch a bite to eat at the Monk and Paunch and take in the afternoon showing of the movie.

There was no way of telling that the wheels of the army machine had been quietly grinding, that the slack of the ball and chain around Bill's ankle was to be hauled in.

So, at the fountain, they stopped as usual; and Bill said, "Take care of yourself, honey! Be seeing you soon."

And Minchen answered, "Good luck to you, darling! You'll find me here waiting."

Bill rode away, carrying her smile.

The camp was not much more than a couple of miles outside Friar's Dene on a flattish road . . . a matter of minutes only before he would be standing outside the medical hut waiting his turn for them to go to work on him, and biting hard until the major gave that kind of grunt of his and said, "Doing nicely!" It didn't make a damn bit of difference that it was still giving you hell! But he was a good guy, a fatherly old bird, something they had dug up and put into uniform for duration . . . and that photo on his desk had to be his wife. . . . Probably he was bored to death here and spitting mad at not being sent up front.

Wouldn't have a thing to tell the folks back home in Ohio, or wherever. As if they'd want to listen to him anyway! And he couldn't possibly have lasted more than a fortnight in France, at his age! . . .

But there wasn't any queue this morning when Bill braked the machine and parked it against the building. . . . Funny how different the whole place looked now with D-Day and the rest way behind! Seemed to be half the size, and, in an odd way, unimportant, as though the trainees didn't get any real briefings any more. . . . They were getting them in France now.

The last man of the morning queue was being fixed up when Bill entered, saluted the major snappily and nodded to the sergeant.

The major was busy. He had a light strapped to his forehead and was, as far as Bill could observe, peering and poking into the ear of his victim, who didn't seem to appreciate the doctor's efforts, if his squirming meant what Bill knew it did—that he was taking about all he could without making a noise.

The sergeant advanced on Bill. The bandaging had to be taken off.

In an undertone Bill said, "Anything new, Sarge?"

The sergeant shrugged a shoulder, gave him what seemed to be a dirty look and went to work. Presently, with a glance at the major, he muttered out of the side of his mouth. "Lucky stiff, you are!"

"Seems to me I've heard that one," said Bill. "What's cooking? . . . And go a little easy, would you mind? You're not working on a block of wood, though it might just as well be!"

As if he hadn't heard, the sergeant went on with his none too gentle unwinding. Then he said, "The good old U.S.A. is cooking, that's what!"

Bill shook his head. "Sorry. Don't happen to be on the same wave length. Suppose you spill."

"Jees!" muttered the sergeant. "I didn't know they came as dumb as that!"

Bill smiled. "O.K. We can't all be medics!"

The sergeant chose to ignore that one. "Listen, brother! I'm telling you. It's God's country for you, and that means any old dump from Maine to California and I'll take it! And nobody has to tell them what they can do with this so-and-so island of theirs, either!"

For a moment Bill stared at him, feeling all his muscles tighten. Then he gave a smothered laugh. "Call me dumb again! You can get away with it."

The unwinding stopped. There was amazement on the sergeant's face, and, when he spoke again, there was tried patience in his voice. "But I'm saying . . . You're on your way, kid! A nice bucket-seat on a B-26! And by the time you get a hankering to put your lunch, you'll be dodging the skyscrapers and smelling the hot dogs and getting ready to hear real English and — "

Bill grabbed him by the arm. "Listen! Cut out the funny stuff! Is this God's truth?"

And then the major's voice ended the low-toned duologue.

"All right!" he said, pushing away his chair from the man with the ear. "That'll hold you for now. Report back tomorrow morning." He rose, took off the light, turned to see who was the final candidate. "Ah . . . the hand . . . When you're ready with him, Sergeant!"

He washed his hands, then went to his desk and lit a cigarette. Time for a couple of whiffs, all the time in the world for that matter with nothing but dirty ears, hemorrhoids, cigarette throat, venereal . . . intern stuff! Odd what you got for your patriotic glass alley . . . red tape and not even a chance at the stretcher cases!

As Bill Thatcher came to him with the outer bandaging removed, he put the cigarette down and shrugged a philosophic shoulder. "Well," he said, "how's it coming? We'll take a look."

As far as Bill was concerned, the doctor wasn't even there.

But, in actual fact, the doctor went about exposing the wounded areas, touching the arm lightly here and there with the tips of his fingers, examining the hand with close attention. Finally he made the noise that might have been called a grunt. "Good. Doing nicely!" he said. "By the way, do you happen to know the name of the surgeon who operated?"

. . . The B-26's engines were roaring, and all you could see was a vast layer of cloud underneath . . . but Minch was on the next bucket-seat to his . . . and if Mother and Dad couldn't make it to the landing field, pretty soon Minch and he would be hopping a train home . . . and not a pile of rubble like the poor damned Europeans, but the same old house and the elms and the brook . . . and there might be a patch or two of early snow . . . anyway he'd run Minch up through Pownal and Bennington, and up over the . . .

The major glanced up at him. "I asked you a question, sergeant!"

Bill's eyes flicked, came back to earth again. "Sir?"

"Who operated on this hand of yours, do you know?"

. . . They were on their way! Who in hell cared? . . . "No, sir. I don't."

"Well," said the major, "at least you can tell me where it was done."

. . . Done? It was done all right! . . . "Weathersford, sir."

The major nodded. "Ah! That accounts for it. Must have been Bishop of Baltimore. They don't come any better. A handsome job!"

. . . Thanks a lot! Wonder how he'd like to lose half his right hand and then try and operate. . . .

The major continued. "Call it another couple of months, and you'll be about ready to be fitted with . . . er . . . spares, let's say.

And as soon as you get used to them, you'll feel like a new man, Sergeant! All the old pep back again!"

. . . If only to God he'd shut his big mouth! . . . Spares! . . . O.K.! Ask him, you fool! Find out, one way or the other! Maybe, the bucket-seat and the hand tie in. . . . Judas!

"May I ask you something, sir?"

The major was kindly, even if "the old pep" was somewhat unfortunate. He said, "Of course, Sergeant."

Bill glued his eyes to the major's. "Do they send a man back in to fight with . . . spares, sir?"

The major shook his head. "This Army doesn't have to send men like you back in — not with Hitler on the run! No sir! A permanent disability like that means a discharge, eventually. Of course, you may find yourself doing an office job somewhere, but the higher-ups will have to decide that! . . . Incidentally, I've some news for you this morning that ought to make you feel good." He nodded at his patient with a smile. "The orders are to send home all but the serious cases, the ones who can't be moved. They are being flown back on transport planes. So as soon as the lists go through, you can expect to see the U.S.A. again. That won't be hard to take, eh Sergeant?"

If he had expected to see a cheerful grin on Bill Thatcher's face, he must have been surprised.

Bill didn't even hear the second half of what he said, nor did he see his face any more, though he remained staring at him. The word "discharge" had done things to him. . . . It was like stumbling out of the fog into the sun again. . . . You could feel it on your face, and yet not know whether you ought to . . . but you were out there, and without a weapon in your hand . . . ever again . . . because you hadn't got to go back! It wasn't there . . . waiting for you. . . . You hadn't got to go back! . . . The earth was friendly under you and you could stand up on it and there would always be Minch now because you hadn't got to go back

. . . and if you wanted to go down on your knees, the other guys would know what it was all about . . . the big Texan . . . Kamenakis . . . the Italian . . . God, how many of them! . . . You could hear them. "Hiya, kid! What are you going to do about us, now you're out? Going to swallow all the hogwash and forget us? Maybe there isn't something you can do, Wise Guy! Here's wishing you the breaks, bud! G'by now!" . . .

Slowly the doctor's face showed up again, and the four drab walls of the dispensary. . . . Bill shivered suddenly . . . took in a couple of deep breaths. . . . Transport plane . . . bucket seat. That was it! Minch and he were zooming . . . Minch was waiting for him at the fountain . . . Minch? . . . But they'd never let her on an army plane! That would mean . . . The hell with their lousy bucket-seat!

"What about my wife, sir?" Bill's throat sounded dry. "Can I . . . take her with me?"

The major looked at him blankly. "Your wife?"

The blankness was like a door closing in his face. Perhaps if he got a foot wedged in . . . quick . . . "Yes, sir. My wife. She . . . It's impossible for me to leave her behind!"

The major didn't quite laugh. "She'd have to be the Queen of England," he said, "to get a ride in a transport, and only on Ike's personal say-so, at that!"

Bill swallowed. "I know, sir. But . . . she . . . she's going to have a child in March, and I . . ."

The doctor's shoulders went up. "That would be a big help, wouldn't it?"

"But they do fly women, sir!" said Bill. "Red Cross and WACs and actresses!"

This time the major smiled. "The troops must have their cake!" he said.

Bill ignored the crack. "The troops?" he said. "My wife's been playing the piano for the troops every night for a couple of years.

Doesn't that rate her something? Couldn't she go as an entertainer?"

"Listen, Sergeant!" said the major. "The U.S. is crawling with entertainers! It's the place they breed them. Forget it! I know it's tough, but you'd better make up your mind to leave her here. You'll get her over later!"

"Later!" Bill exploded. "When would I ever see her again? . . . You know what they're going to do with me, sir! They're going to poke me off into some base hospital until this mess of mine . . . this handsome job, as you called it . . . becomes usable again, behind a desk! They can do what they like with me then, but right now I . . . I don't see it that way! Can't they leave me here? I'm not keeping any G.I. out of a hospital bed! And that's all I'll be doing back there! . . . I know all right they won't let her fly, but . . . If you could do anything, sir . . . fix it so that I could stay . . . it would mean a hell of a lot to me!"

The major lit himself another cigarette. He motioned to his sergeant to carry on with the bandaging.

Perhaps it was because he himself was only in for duration . . . Perhaps the permanent disability meant something . . . Perhaps his wife's photo touched a chord . . .

He spoke abruptly. "Look, Sergeant! You know as well as I do what you're up against, and you ought to know there's damn little I can do! But I think you've got a case. We'll see if anything can be done. That's all I can say at the moment."

He nodded, turned on his heel, went out.

As the door closed, the sergeant paused in his winding, looked up at Bill. "You don't wanna go?" he said. "Well, I'll be a son of a bitch!"

At the first anniversary celebration given by the officers of Operation "Crossroads," the cake was in the form of an atomic underwater explosion. As guests, the two admirals commanding the operation shared the honor of cutting the cake. There was much laughter, and popping of photographers' bulbs. . . .

At Hiroshima, a Japanese Methodist minister carried water to the dying. He had become a Christian in the United States and, as such, was filled with compassion for the sufferers. He confessed, however, that, as a Japanese, he was "overwhelmed by the shame of being unhurt." And as he passed among the victims bearing water, he bowed to them humbly and said: "Excuse me for having no burden like yours!"

The "Crossroads" officers are all Christians.

CHAPTER FOUR

MINCHEN WAS TIRED. HER BODY ACHED. THE PEDAL OF the bicycle was on the curb. She half-sat on the saddle to rest herself. In the basket on the front were groceries. She had stood in line for some of them.

For the third time she glanced up at the old clock in the Roman tower. . . . What were they doing to him? Had anything gone wrong? Suppose his hand . . . No, that's absurd! I simply won't get panicked! . . . I wonder if I'd better ride out to the camp in case . . . But no. He wouldn't like that, and I might miss him.

Her eyes were like swallows skimming in and out of the traffic on the road to the camp, and then, drawing a blank, soaring to the clock again.

He'll be here in ten seconds now. I know it. I feel it in my bones. . . . Well, perhaps twenty. Certainly in less than a minute! If not, I . . . Oh, don't be a little fool! He's all right . . . How marvelous it is to be able to sit here knowing that in a minute he'll be here, still safe! And before, you never knew from minute to minute! I wish . . . no, I don't really . . . but, after all, in a way I do . . . I wish his hand would never get well — that is, not till the war's over! And I suppose that's perfectly beastly and hateful . . . but I don't care! He's . . . At last! It is Bill!

Ease flowed through her as she watched him coming — steering with one hand, the new bandages snow-white. The fact that her body didn't ache any more made her smile. She didn't wave. He might be tempted to take his one hand off the handlebar in the traffic and wave back. It was just the sort of thing he liked to do — to show that he could do it, bless him!

She sat quiet, waiting; and the look in her eyes was the equivalent of breaking out all the bunting from the highest masthead.

Bill was not the only one who saw her. But she was the only one in the whole market place that he saw. He ducked two carts and went wide round a cow and her calf, coasted while a bus went by, and then squeezed his brake by her machine and dropped off beside her.

"Neat work!" said Minchen. "But tell me, darling. Are you . . . 'doing nicely'?"

It was the first time she had quoted that at him. Had it been two days earlier, he would have wanted to laugh. Not now, though. Maybe later, when it came back to him. . . . He leaned towards her. "Minch! . . . Listen! I'm not going back to France again! They've just told me I'm going to get my discharge!"

Bill had picked out the corner of the hill road at which to meet her on his return from France — and it had turned out to be the railway platform at Weathersford. Neither of them had cared. Now he was standing in the gutter, with his bicycle in between them, and shoppers passing, and buses missing him by inches. And again, neither of them cared.

Not more than one or two passers-by noticed that the girl with the American soldier had tears running down her cheeks. Being women, they barely raised an eyebrow or shrugged a shoulder as they went on their way. It was as though they knew the whole story. . . . "The little fool! Why did she listen to him? It's her own fault!"

Bill took hold. "I know. It hit me something like that, too. It's . . . out of this world! It hasn't really made its way in yet. I'm still trying to get it . . . and of course there are strings to it! . . . But I can't tell you here. Let's beat it over to the Monk and Paunch."

More or less blindly, Minchen followed his lead across the market place and into the yard of the inn.

The oak-paneled dining room was gloomy enough for any woman to mop up her tears unobserved. Minchen was far from being the first to stumble into a seat behind a corner table and do so. And to the old waiter who showed them to the table and stood by for their order it was all part of the day's work.

By the time he had gone, Minchen was coherent again. Under the long tablecloth she found Bill's hand and hung on. "I'm such a fool! Bill . . . darling! Is it true? Do we dare believe it?"

"That's what I've been asking myself!" said Bill.

"You mean we can . . . let go, and not count the days any more?"

"Yes!" said Bill. "We can both breathe again."

Minchen's eyes were like wet stars. "Then it means that we . . . are going to be . . . alive together, and can go on together. . . . Does it, Bill?"

"Yes!" said Bill. "We're both . . . out of it. Maybe we can begin to take down the barbed wire."

Minchen tightened her grip on his hand. "And all this time I've been trying to . . . to get ready. . . . If they'd sent you back there, I . . . I don't know what I'd have done. . . . But you're not going back! You're not going back! Bill . . . oh, Bill!" She gave an excited laugh. "It's as if we'd only been lent to each other, and now . . . at last . . . we belong! . . . Oh, my dear!" She gulped and laughed—but it wasn't a laugh—and was content to look at him.

Bill nodded. "You know, when they told me," he said, "I . . . I had the damnedest feeling . . . that there was something I should have to do about it . . . to pay it back . . . to square it. Of course I know it was just a matter of bull luck that that mortar didn't land a couple of feet more to the right. It got three of my buddies. And here am I, back with you. I don't know the answer. Maybe there isn't one. But I'd hate to believe that you and I . . . and those three . . . have been put through it for nothing. Right now it looks awful like it. . . . I hate to tell you, Minch, but they're still riding us."

All the reckless antennae that Minchen had put out began to curl up in withdrawal from her content. "But how can they, now?" she said.

"I'm still under orders," said Bill. "I'm still just another number. They can do any damn thing they like with me!"

Minchen frowned. "But they can't!" she said. "You're not . . . well yet."

Bill gave a sarcastic laugh. "That's the point! I'm one of those who's well enough to be shifted out of here."

Minchen was ready again. The harness had been so barely off. "Tell me, Bill!" she said quietly.

Bill said, "We're still only lent to each other, Minch! The orders are to clear out all the movable wounded and send them back home to the U.S.A. . . . They've got a bucket-seat on a transport plane reserved for me!"

Minchen leaned into the familiar harness. "When?" she said.

"A week. A fortnight. Who knows?"

Minchen had to swallow. "Isn't there . . . any chance of my going with you?"

"You can believe that I asked!" said Bill. "The major didn't actually laugh in my face, but he might as well have! I even told him that we . . . that you were going to have a child!"

Minchen's eyes flickered. "Did he . . . laugh at that?"

"I should have socked him if he had!" said Bill. "No, there isn't a hope of getting you on a transport. I knew that right along, but I thought I'd try. And then, as soon as I saw it was completely out, I asked him to let me stay. I didn't tell him, but . . . I'd like to be around in March! I did tell him it would mean a hell of a lot to me if he could fix it, and he promised to see what he could do. . . . He could do it all right, too, if I were a buddy of his, but I'm just another sergeant!"

"But at least" — Minchen snatched at the crumb — "it isn't definite that you're going."

"You know the Army! Better put it the other way round!" said Bill. "We'll admit that it's not definite that I'm not going. That leaves us sitting pretty, doesn't it? About the only thing I can do is try to go to work on him." He picked up his fork and began stabbing the tablecloth.

Not so long ago, Minchen had said: "One minute you're so happy, both of you . . . the next, you feel as though your heart would break . . ." How many times would she have to say that? March was not so far away now . . . and Bill knew it and had asked to stay! That was something to hang on to . . . after he had gone. . . .

She watched the violent fork. Then she said, "Bill . . . I've been trying to think. . . . Yesterday we didn't know. Even this morning we didn't. But now . . . if they won't let us have tomorrow, we've got the day after and all the other days. They can't take those away from us! So if you . . . have to go to America, I shall be able to say to myself 'Bill's alive!' And every day I shall know it's true! And I'll go on waiting. . . . You see, I . . . I don't want to stop you from going. It is . . . home! And your father and mother are waiting . . . and for you to be in the Berkshires again would . . . would do things to you! And it mightn't be for so very long . . . and all the time you'd be knowing that I was . . . perfectly all right."

Bill's fork had become still. He looked at her, nodded, and then smiled. "Perfectly all right? . . . D'you remember the night I came into the Recreation Center and sat down on the piano bench beside you? I was bright enough even then to know that you were 'perfectly all right.' And I don't have to be flown three thousand miles to find it out all over again! As far as I'm concerned, the U.S.'ll keep. I've got it all wrapped up in cellophane . . . for you, as a present for the swellest thing you've ever said!"

1914–1918	*WORLD War I.*
	Total Casualties: 70,000,000—dead, wounded, missing, war orphans.
1938–1945	*World War II.*
	Total Casualties: not yet counted; perhaps not countable.
1946	*Luxury liner sails for starving Europe carrying a "screw-thread" commission of American manufacturers to "sell" to the British the idea of standardization of tools, for the sake of "efficiency and economy."*
	The governments of Great Britain and the United States have officially admitted "conversations" (Canada included) for the purpose of standardization of armament, in order that each of the three countries could use the others' weapons in case of war. It was categorically denied that any such agreement would constitute a military alliance against Russia. The idea was merely "efficiency and economy."
1948 (?)	*Standardization of atom bombs.*
1958 (?)	*World War III.*

CHAPTER FIVE

JACK WAINWRIGHT HEARD THEM COMING. HE TURNED OFF THE war news, and was tapping out his pipe against the mantelpiece when they entered the room.

He turned to them. "Hullo, there, fellers! You're back early. Stupid picture?"

"We didn't go, Major," said Bill. "We sat and chewed the rag in the pub."

Jack's eyebrows went up. "Doesn't sound exactly like either of you!" he said. "Slightly frowsty, I should have thought. But then, probably not more so than the picture!" His quick eyes went from one to the other. Was Minchen a little drawn? One didn't sit in an atmosphere of stale beer and sawdust unless there was a good reason.

Minchen straightened him out on it. "Bill will tell you why, Dad," she said. "It's pretty overwhelming one way and another!" And then to Bill, "Look, darling, I'm going out to give Mother a hand."

"Can't I help too?" asked Bill.

"If I need you, I'll yell!" said Minchen. She stood for a moment, not moving, just looking at him. Then she kissed him and went out of the room.

Bill watched her go.

So did her father.

And when she had gone the two men's eyes met.

Jack Wainwright said quietly, "About the only thing that's worth while in this whole bloody world!"

Bill gave a short laugh. "That happens to be the point I was making in the Monk and Paunch. The trouble is that the Army doesn't see it that way. They want us to break it up again!"

Jack looked quickly at Bill, and saw Minchen's face as well. "You mean . . . Good God, you're not telling me that they want you to go out again?"

Bill shook his head. "No, it's not that bad, Major. On the contrary, this . . . thing"—he indicated his left arm—"paid dividends today. It has earned me my discharge. It's what they call a 'permanent disability.' You know the wording!"

But Jack Wainwright's face broke into lines of delight. "Bill! My dear fellow! Your discharge! I can't tell you how glad I am! It's wonderful! Obviously it's the only possible decision, but the damn fools might have sent you back just out of sheer thickheadedness and red tape! I don't mind telling you that that possibility has been bothering me quite a little! However, thank God, for both your sakes, that you're out of it! This cockeyed world needs a lot of people like you and Minch, Bill!"

The laugh he gave was supposed to hide a surge of emotion.

But Bill was neither blind nor deaf. He said, "That's swell of you, Major! Thanks a lot! . . . I know I ought to be damn grateful. I am, I suppose, in a way . . . Sure, I am! . . . But with the rest of them still out there, I . . . I don't know. Somehow it doesn't seem to mean what it ought to."

Jack Wainwright nodded. "Yes," he said, "we all go through that. There are so few things left that mean what they ought to!" He put a match to his pipe and, a moment later, said, through the clouds of smoke, "You and I have got our women."

Bill made no answer. He turned away to the fireplace and kicked one of the logs back on. "Let me tell you the rest of it, Major!" he said. "I'm liable to be shipped back by plane to the U.S.A. at any moment! And they won't let Minch fly with me! . . . Judas! You'd think they drag you through a knothole just for the hell of it! And because you're in a uniform, you can't even talk back to them! All you can say is 'Yes, sir!' and 'No, sir!' How can a lousy sergeant tell an officer that his wife means something to him? How could I tell him that it's only because of Minch that I'm beginning to take hold again? He'd have thought I was nuts! And when I did manage to tell him that she was going to have a child, I might just as well have kept my trap shut! So then I asked him if I couldn't be left here. That didn't seem to me so damn much to ask, but all he would say was that he would see if anything could be done! And I couldn't tell if he meant it or not! . . . A sweet one, isn't it? . . . About one God-damned chance in a million of my being allowed to stay with her!"

He paused to snap a lighter to a cigarette and inhale two vast lungfuls.

Jack Wainwright didn't interrupt. The boy had to get it off his chest. It was imperative.

Bill went on. "You could tell me — but you're the only one who wouldn't — that I'm just griping, that to be sent home to the U.S.A. is a very different story, for both Minchen and me, from being sent back to drop behind the German lines. The doctor nearly did say it — damn him. But there happens to be more to it than that . . . a hell of a lot more! I haven't said anything to Minch, but . . . there's this business of having a child. I mean . . . the moment of its birth. Supposing I were three thousand miles away, and . . . and something happened . . . to her . . ."

He was staring at the red-hot tip of his cigarette, and left it at that.

Jack Wainwright was equally intent on the beeches through the window. His mind and sympathies were too closely linked to the boy to receive personally the full impact of Bill's suggestion. It was as though it came to him in two halves, and the first was Bill's. . . . The boy was right. There was that possibility! Things did happen, even with the best obstetrician . . . last-minute complications, God knows what! . . . And after that hand of his . . . to lose her like that . . . just a victim of red tape . . . "No!" he exclaimed aloud. "No! That would be a refinement . . ."

He swung round from the window, put a hand on the boy's shoulder. "No! . . . Bill, forget that! It's bad thinking! It's not you. It's just part of this inescapable pressure, nightmare stuff, utterly unreal! . . . My dear lad, think for a moment! Minchen is as healthy as an animal, built magnificently, and, according to my wife, who knows these things, everything's going perfectly normally! There's not the remotest likelihood of anything happening! . . . Good God, no! It's . . . it's utterly unthinkable!"

And then, suddenly, as he was giving Bill a reassuring smile, the idea broke in his own mind. . . . Unthinkable? . . . Minch! . . .

He left Bill quickly, began walking. He could feel his good hand slightly sweaty, and cold. He clasped them both behind his back, as though to get rid of them. . . . God Almighty! What had he been thinking of . . . it had never entered his head all this time! It had to be this boy to point it out! . . . Minch . . . Was March to be the end? To bring a child into this stinking world and then . . . out? Had she been saved up for that? Was this to be her offering in this bloody war? How fantastically, willfully, in keeping with the senseless brutal scheme of things! Oh God, why Minch? . . . Why any of them, for that matter? . . . But to go and pick out Minch . . . now . . . at the peak of her loveliness . . . of her fulfillment on this earth . . . at the very moment when she is giving back to that boy everything he has lost . . . that poor lad, worshiping the ground she treads on . . . as I do . . . and Muriel . . . Muriel! . . .

The limping march stopped abruptly. He dropped into his armchair, among all the small everyday paraphernalia — the insignificant clutter that can be, nevertheless, a lubricant — books, each with a marker in it; emaciated wartime copies of *Blackwood's;* a pile of farm journals; the day's paper; a deep metal bowl in which to knock out his pipe; a sheaf of feathers, gathered by Minchen, for cleaners; a footstool, jerkable into position by a reaching toe; a shaded reading lamp at his left elbow; a wooden box filled with pencils, clips, a paper cutter, glasses, magnifying glass . . .

Hardly knowing it, he pulled a feather out of the bundle and began running it in and out of his pipestem . . . At all costs the boy mustn't know! That would merely be adding to the refinement. . . .

He pulled the feather out and dropped it into the wastebasket. Then he said, "You know, Bill, you . . . set me thinking. I have a strong feeling that they may let you stay! That doctor, for instance. He can't be altogether a bastard. He did say he'd see what he could do! If I were you I'd work him for all you're worth. You're going to, of course! . . . Why don't we invite him up here? We could all have a go at him! And when he meets Minch, it might even turn the trick! What do you think?"

Bill snapped round. "I think that would be the cats!" he said.

Jack Wainwright swallowed. "Good!" he said. "Why don't you go out and tell Minch about our plan? After all, she's going to be the *pièce de résistance* of the party! . . . Incidentally, Bill, think this one over: it's going to leave an awful hole in this family the day you and she go off to America!"

THE motor was purring like a contented cat.

A tube led from the exhaust into the tight-shut car.

A "ruptured duck" gleamed in the lapel of the slumped boyish figure. . . .

"Six months old . . . the kid . . . cute little devil!

"And Mary . . . Mary . . ."

Why couldn't they leave you alone? Why did those poor bastards in their straitjackets keep shrieking at you . . . howling, writhing, gibbering . . . and their eyes . . . Jesus, those eyes!

Suppose, one day, the kid . . . Christ, no! . . . But you couldn't tell. You couldn't tell anything any more in this lousy stinking shambles . . .

Some of those G.I.'s had kids too. . . . And they'd make them go on living . . . with that look in their eyes!

"Sorry, Mary . . . oughtn't have asked you to marry me . . . but how could I tell? Didn't know what war was . . . thought you just went out there and did your stuff . . . didn't know it did these things to a guy . . . the wards full of them. . . . Listen to them! . . . Was scared to look at you this morning, Mary. Thought you might see what I was seeing. I couldn't take that. Hell, they can't make you do that to your wife! And they're not going to drag me into one of those wards either. . . .

"Going to be tough for you, Mary . . . sorry . . . but it'll be better all around . . . this way. And I know you'll do your damnedest for the kid. . . . Won't be long . . . now. . . . Lungs feel . . . So long, Mary! . . . So . . ."

The motor purred like a contented cat.

CHAPTER SIX

THAT SAME NIGHT IN THE SMALL HOURS, THE WIND IN THE beeches, steady and gentle, was like a small sea breaking along a sandy shore.

The moon touched the mysterious world with silver and black.

In the cottage there were no lights, but sleep had not come to either bedroom.

In one, two cigarettes were being smoked; and the two voices were close together, almost whispers, but excited.

". . . And what did he say then?"

"Something about its being a refinement. I didn't get that one; and he left it up in the air. Then he began to march up and down the room. You know that iron face of his! Judas, I hate to think what he took in the last war!"

Minchen nodded. "And I don't suppose he'll ever know what he's meant to me in this one!"

"I can make a good guess!" said Bill. "Was I sunk! And he knew it, because after a while he came out of that marching stuff and there was something about him, some change . . . I don't know. It's hard to put your finger on it. It wasn't what he said. It was the way he said it. And after the swell idea of asking the doctor up, he took me over to the map, and you should have heard his stuff on the war! He took it to pieces, sector by sector, and it's on its way out, Minch! He can practically write in the dates! I tell you, before he got through I could almost hear the bells begin to ring!"

"Oh Bill! Just think of it!"

Bill laughed. "I've been thinking about nothing else all evening! It stayed with me. He made me feel like a million dollars! He made me see us getting back there in less than no time at all! . . . I tell you, Minch, we've absolutely got to get them over too — just as soon as we can fix it! I've got a hunch that my Dad and yours would be like a couple of buddies together! And besides, don't forget, honey, it's going to be damn tough on your family the day you walk out of here!"

Minchen shook her head. "The day I walk out of here! . . . It's unimaginable! It's something I don't even know how to think about. . . . Do you realize that the war has already lasted one fifth of my whole life?"

"For Pete's sake!" said Bill. "That's a hot one, isn't it? Hadn't thought of it. . . . Mine too for that matter! . . . Let's hope the peace will see us through the rest of our lives! At least we're going back to a country that hasn't been smashed all to hell! That's something . . . or ought to be! I wonder though . . ."

Minchen waited for him. But, as he didn't finish the thought, she said, "What do you wonder?"

"Oh . . . I don't know," said Bill. "I was just wondering what it's going to be like to get back. I feel a bit like Rip van Winkle! . . . It'll look the same. Maybe it is the same. And that may be the trouble!"

"I don't follow you," said Minchen. "Why on earth wouldn't you be glad if it's the same?"

Bill shook his head. "I'm probably crazy. . . . Maybe your Dad would know what I'm driving at. . . . In one way of course I should be glad — to know that they haven't had to take it like the people over here. But, don't you see, it's that that may have left them completely off the beam. Suppose they don't get what's been going on, and don't give a damn either? See what I mean? Suppose we find it's simply back to peace quick, and the hell with the rest of it? That seems to be what happened last time! . . . I don't know . . . Hope to God I'm all wet!"

Minchen flicked the ash from her cigarette. "Don't let's talk about that tonight! There'll be plenty of time to find that out later. . . . Let's be thoroughly selfish. Let's talk about us . . . There are a million things I want to know about us, now that we're there! Let's begin at the very beginning. . . . Where are we going to live? Boston?"

Bill laughed. "O.K. We're off! . . . Boston, no, not on your life! My idea is that you and I go and park in the Berkshire house and look things over. There's plenty of room for us there. I've never told you the family set-up, have I?"

"It's only one of the million things you haven't told me!"

"You'll be getting them from now on!" said Bill. "Well then, the family has an apartment in Boston, on the Hill, where we all used to dig in for the winter. Mother and the kid sister move up to the Berkshires sometimes in May, and then Dad cuts loose from his law office for week ends. That's how it was up to the war. From their letters, it looks as if they'd been stuck in Boston most of the time since."

"Is it far then between Boston and the Berkshires?"

"About five hours' drive, and the second half of it through country that makes your hair stand on end! I could go on describing it for hours, but it would be a complete waste of time. You have to be there, and feel it, and listen to it, and let it soak into your system. . . . You know something? Little Minchen has a touch of it!"

"It sounds wonderful!" said Minchen. "And what about the house? Did your father build it?"

Bill laughed. "Not quite. It dates back to seventeen hundred and something, and it's built of wood and painted white and sits up on a slope, with enormous elm trees all round, and Mother grows a million flowers, and there's a brook at the end of the garden, and you look out over a range of hills covered with maple and pine, and the sun comes in at all the windows, and all you can hear are the wind and the trees and cows and birds, and cars a long way off . . . and the feeling of it all is so terrific that when you sit down at the piano you know it's all pouring out through your hands as though you were . . ." He broke off short.

Minchen pressed her face against his. "Bill . . . Bill!"

And presently Bill said, "Sorry, honey! I didn't mean to squawk. It sort of got by me . . . Getting home, I suppose!" He laughed — something dry and odd-sounding. Then he said: "It's all right. . . . Look, I was going to tell you . . . There's a clearing up there on the hill, behind the house, quite a way off. You have to walk up a trail — and ruin your stockings, the kid always says — to get to it. But when you're there, you're on top of the world. It looks west down another valley, and across to more hills, and when I was a kid I used to take a blanket up and watch the sunset and pretend I was an Indian. I've always thought that one day I'd like to build there. Originally the idea was a log cabin. . . . What would you say to an old barn — there are plenty of them around — with hand-cut eight-by-sixes, with the planking all sanded down? We could cut huge windows in it and have an enormous fireplace, and a gallery running round . . . It'd be the cat's! How would you like to wake up in the morning with the whole world spread out under you like your own carpet — green all spring and summer, flame-colored in the fall, and clean white when the snow comes . . . and way off in the distance little white church-spires sticking up out of the trees? It's all you can see of the town from up there, but on Sundays the cars are parked thick outside those churches, and on weekdays you drive in to get your meat and groceries and fruit and tobacco and hammers and nails and screws, and to see a movie and eat an ice cream in the drugstore afterwards, and say hullo to everybody up and down Main Street, and ask how Susie's coming along, and whether the cat's had her kittens, and whether Jimmie was plastered or not when he wrecked his car . . . and when you've got all the dirt, you collect your mail from your own box and drive back home. . . . And right now I bet the banks of snow are so high, where the plow has been through, that you can't see over the top of them. . . . Do you think you're going to be able to stand it, Minch?"

Minchen took a deep breath. "My dear," she said, "what a lot you've told me! It's in your blood, isn't it? It's all that it meant to you when you . . ." For a second she hesitated; then she went on steadily. . . . "When you were thinking of your pastorale. Isn't it in your mind now, while you're telling me? Of course it is. I can almost hear it."

There was no answer for a moment.

Minchen found herself holding her breath.

Finally Bill said, "There are other things in my mind now, honey, and one of them is that if I don't go out and earn some money there can't be any old barn! All I was doing up to the war was living on my father's pocketbook. Pretty soft! My scheme was to scratch along giving piano lessons and coaching fellows for their exams in Harmony, and working like hell until I was ready for the platform . . . and then, if I ever managed to make good, I was going to try and write something. But . . . the platform is out, and I don't believe anybody would want to take lessons of a one-handed teacher. I know I wouldn't! And until you've arrived, you can do a nice job of starving while you try and write something. So it puts the whole scheme into the discard. Shall I tell you what I've decided? I'm going to go tearing through law school, and get a job in my father's office! He's always looking for bright young men! And I want that barn for you and me!"

Minchen came up on one elbow and leaned over him. "Damn the barn!" she said. "You're not going to law school! And I won't have you going into your father's office! Bill, don't you understand? I can give lessons! I can teach Harmony too! I can earn something! We can live in one room! I'd rather work and scratch along with you . . . starve with you . . . but you shan't throw your music away! It's what you've always dreamed of, worked for! It's soaked into you. It's you! You've got it in you to write something that they'll want to hear all over the world! And though you can't play it yourself, can't you see yourself conducting it, in Boston, even at the Symphony? Oh, Bill, don't you see? The piano is only a part of it, and you've got so much more. . . . I believe in you. I know you can do it. I know we can do it together. . . . Life wouldn't mean anything if you were stifled in a law office, and I would rather die than have you do it to earn money for me! I'll work like a dog! I'll . . ."

On the landing outside, the sleeping yellow cat lay curled up in a flat ball in the patch of moonlight that fell on the carpet.

And in the other bedroom, across the landing, there was silence.

The physician was unable to heal himself. He didn't even have the satisfaction of knowing that he had helped anybody. He lay on his back staring up at the ceiling, his body motionless — Muriel must not be disturbed: that remained one of the important things — his mind, however, in turmoil.

Perhaps, eventually, it communicated itself; for, suddenly, Muriel became awake, turned her head and looked at her husband.

In a whisper she said, "What is it, dear? . . . Haven't you been to sleep at all?"

Jack Wainwright moved his stiff body, turned towards her. What infinite relief to hear the sound of her voice smashing up the aloneness! . . . "I'm sorry if I woke you, dearest!" he said.

"You didn't . . . but I'm glad I woke," said Muriel. "Is anything the matter?" The light was too dim for her to be able to read his face.

"Not a thing!" said Jack. "I was just . . . revolving things in my mind. You know how it is. But if you really are awake . . .

there's something I meant to take up with you in the morning."

"Better tell me now," said Muriel. "Then you'll get some sleep."

"Well . . . it's about Minch," said Jack. "I was wondering if, by any chance, it had occurred to you that the old doctor in Friar's Dene might be getting past his job?"

Muriel frowned, puzzled. "Past his job? What . . ."

"Oh, I daresay I'm boggling over pin points," said Jack, "but . . . would you agree, for instance, that we were being somewhat casual about Minch . . . and her condition?"

"Not at all," said Muriel. "I feel perfectly happy about her."

"I'm very glad to hear that!" said Jack. "But, the child is due in March, isn't it?"

"Yes," said Muriel.

"That's what I thought," said Jack, "and the idea occurred to me that we might perhaps have her looked over by a first-class man . . . a sort of check-up, you know, that's all . . . just to be quite sure that everything's in apple-pie order . . ."

Muriel missed one breath. "Jack . . . Has Minchen said anything to you? Have you any — special reason for suggesting that?"

Jack said quickly, "Oh my dear, no! Nothing of the sort! . . . This is probably nothing but anxious-father stuff, and I don't want you to think that I'm really worrying, or anything! I thought of it as a mere precaution, that's all. You see, I'd hate to think that we'd left undone anything that we ought to have done. How do you feel yourself? You know so much more about these things than I do."

"Well," said Muriel, "all I can say is that Dr. Merivale has seen her regularly and that what discomfort she's had has been perfectly normal. I don't know of any reason for alarm . . . but, of course, if you'd like me to, I'll talk to Minchen and try to persuade her to see someone else."

Jack let out a deep breath. "You've taken a great load off my mind," he said. "But — I still feel that it would do no harm to suggest that she see someone. You might, perhaps, put it to her that it's for Bill's sake . . ."

"Oh!" said Muriel. "Then it's really Bill who started all this?"

"No, no, no!" said Jack. "Not at all. It wouldn't be fair to say that! He did happen to drop a remark that I caught on the fly, as it were. Any fond husband might have made it . . . and of course I magnified it out of all proportion in my usual stupid fashion! . . . I'll try not to think of it again now that you're going to take hold."

Muriel reached out and patted his hand. "I feel sure that everything's going to be all right!" she said. "You'd better get some sleep now, dear."

"You too!" said Jack. "Sleep tight, my dear."

They lay quiet.

For a long time it was not only Jack who went on hearing the wind in the beeches.

DOUBLE BETRAYAL OF UNITED NATIONS

U.S. NEW DEAL WITH NAZIS

ADMITS DEFEAT ON SCIENCE FRONT: PROMISES CITIZENSHIP TO INVENTORS AND EXPERTS OF V-2 ROCKET

TWO HUNDRED NOW IN PAY OF U.S.

U.S. ORDNANCE DEPT. SAYS: TEN YEARS' RESEARCH, MILLIONS OF DOLLARS ALREADY SAVED

WIVES AND FAMILIES OF NAZIS TO BE BROUGHT OVER BY U.S. GOVERNMENT

You don't believe it? Take a run down to Wright Field and Fort Bliss. You will find there two groups of Nazi scientists who, having sold out their own country, are now happily on the payroll of the United States Army. They are housed, paradoxically enough, in what during the war were hospital buildings, and a National Youth Administration Camp.

The high priests of United States Army air power, in frantic anticipation of World War III, are busily sucking the Nazi brains of everything they know about rockets—admittedly the dominating weapon of "future wars."

A returned G.I. sums it up. He writes: "These scientists worked for and believed in a system that thousands of American boys died fighting to erase forever from this earth. . . . I know that I do not want to be a citizen of the same country as these Nazis."

CHAPTER SEVEN

JACK WAINWRIGHT'S WORKSHOP WAS AT THE END OF THE garden.

It was everything in one — tool shed, greenhouse, carpenter shop, attic, hideaway.

In the winter months, when there was nothing to be done outside except to wait for Mother Earth to have her rest, Jack's morning formula at the right moment after breakfast, having assured himself that tobacco pouch and matches were all present and correct, was a nod to his wife and daughter and a "Well, m'dears! You'll know where to find me!"

No one saw him again till lunch.

The job that he had marked out for himself the following morning was the fixing of an antique chest of drawers. The antiquity was undoubted in regard to the chest, but the dampness of the weather had made the drawers refuse to function. They would neither open nor shut.

But the chest stood unnoticed.

Jack Wainwright had gone to work on himself. He too was apparently jammed halfway, even after Muriel's reassurances.

Breakfast had been an unusually cheerful meal, the two young ones, it seemed, in almost high spirits — enviably so: Minch, particularly, glowing, the picture of health and loveliness and strength.

He repeated the words to himself as he limped up and down . . . health, loveliness, strength . . . what a morbid damned fool you had been to let yourself imagine for one moment that anything could happen . . . that fate had chosen that particular form of punishment. . . . There wasn't any such thing as "fate." That was utter nonsense. . . . Too much brooding about the slaughter. Why, he had had Bill marked down as well! Again, ultra pessimism . . . the same forces at work. He must really stiffen up. After all, wasn't it true that modern surgery and modern anesthetics made childbearing almost a pastime, without pain, almost without effort, totally without danger? Of course. . . . And Muriel was so sure that everything was going to be all right. Had there been the slightest question in her mind, she would have been the first to utter and take steps! He should have thought of that. He should have trusted her. Instead of which—clumsy fool that he was—he had probably communicated his fears to her last night. . . . The very last thing that he had intended! No more intelligence than a horse in a field stampeding at its own shadow! He deserved to be kicked. . . . Minch was all right. She was going to be all right. There wouldn't be any doubt of it if only Muriel would persuade her to have that check-up. After all, they did have a responsibility towards Bill. What would he think of them if the Army insisted on flying him back and there should have to be a cable one day in March to say that . . . Ah, no! Not round the wheel again! She's going to be all right. She . . .

A knock sounded on the door.

Jack Wainwright halted. He stood for a moment while his mind withdrew from Minchen, prepared itself against intrusion.

"Come!" he said loudly.

It was Bill who opened the door.

Standing there, he said tentatively, "Sure I'm not butting in, Major?"

Jack Wainwright waved a hand. "On the contrary!" he said. "You're particularly welcome, my dear boy! Come along in! My . . . ingrowing disposition was beginning to get the better of me. . . . Delighted to see you. . . . It's a little nippy in here, don't you think? How about dropping another stick in the stove?"

"Right!" said Bill. He went over to the stove and put several sticks in it. By the time he came back to the work bench, Jack Wainwright had begun to busy himself on the chest of drawers.

Without glancing up he said, "I take it that Minchen and her mother are still busy upstairs?"

"Yes," said Bill. "And talking a blue streak. . . . Look, Major, I can't hold that chest steady for you, but would it help if I sat on it? A hundred and fifty pounds might keep it firm."

"Why, yes," said Jack. "It might do the trick. Let's try it."

Bill perched sideways on the top of the chest. "How's that?" He bent over, and, in spite of himself began watching the "cork" hand in action.

"Very helpful!" said Jack.

"H'm!" said Bill. "Were you . . . always a left hander, Major?"

There was a fraction of a pause.

Then Jack Wainwright said, "No! Never could do a damn thing with it!"

"I get you!" said Bill. He jerked himself a cigarette and lit it. "In a couple of months they go to work fitting me with . . . spares!"

The older man kept his eyes on the chest. "Couple of months, eh? . . . Bloody business!"

Bill blew out a lungful of smoke. "Makes it sort of final, doesn't it? We were doing a little talking about it last night, Minch and I. . . . The first time since I got back. We'd both been . . . ducking it. I thought, maybe, you ought to know . . ."

Jack Wainwright paused and looked up at him. "Bill, old boy," he said, "it must be alarmingly obvious that anything touching you and Minch is of the profoundest interest to me. . . . Do you mind if I say that at breakfast I had the feeling that in some way you had both . . . what shall I say . . . turned a corner?"

Bill nodded. "That's exactly right, Major!"

"Great work!" said Jack. "Splendid!"

"In a way, we have to thank you for it!" said Bill.

"Good heavens!" said Jack. "I can't imagine . . ."

Bill laughed. "It was your ending the war, added to the fact of the discharge, that got us going. It made us both feel pretty good. I don't know that we didn't go a little haywire! Anyway, we put the uniform in mothballs and made the trip home and started to work again!"

"My dear fellow, how perfectly wonderful!" said Jack.

"It was!" said Bill. "And the thing I wanted to tell is that Minch sold me on making music our job in spite of . . . the hand. I might as well admit that I'd just about given up on it. My thinking only went as far as trying to get into my father's office, but Minch went to town on me! She pumped it into me that, after all, the piano isn't the whole works . . . that you don't have to have two hands to compose or conduct. She's damn right! I'd always seen that end of it as being years ahead, but I've always aimed at it, and Minch believes that I can get there someday. She said she'd stick, and work, while I take a crack at it! . . . What do you think, Major? Does it get your O.K.?"

Jack Wainwright's hands had ceased to be busy. He remained staring down into, and not seeing, the bottom drawer. . . . Soon what was left of world youth would come crawling out, as they had before, beaten and broken, shocked and ravished . . . avid, like this boy, for a few crumbs of life, searching for that which had been destroyed and, not finding it, refusing to believe . . . the scars hardening . . . and becoming bitterly urgent to repay themselves for what they had given in a world that had turned its back on them, discounted them, refused once more to hear any message they might bring back from their foxholes, their maquis, their prison camps, their hospitals. . . .

"Bill, old boy," he said, "if you and Minch have found a way through for yourselves, I thank God! I'd like you to know that I also think you have it in you to succeed. Minch will stick all right while you try. She's that kind. Both of you, it seems to me, have more to give each other than lots of people. And if there's anything else that matters, I'd like to know what it is. . . . All the music in the world is only an expression of it, and every note that you put on paper is going to be because of it, part of it, born of it. . . . You and Minch! Watch it like a hawk, Bill! Don't let them get it away from you when you get back into the damned senseless pathetic mess that will keep us gagging when this war's over!"

He stopped and began groping for his pipe.

Bill nodded, his eyes on the end of his cigarette. "Thanks, Major! I'm glad you feel that way about . . . us. We think we can take care of it. . . . It's the best thing there is. . . . All the same, the other thing won't leave me alone—what you call the mess after the war. Of course I haven't got anywhere with it. It's taken me all my time to try and get myself halfway straightened out, and last night particularly I couldn't help remembering what you said once—that our going back to our piano-playing would be as senseless as your growing vegetables. Remember?"

Jack Wainwright looked at him. "Do I remember? . . . I ask you, Bill, how do you suppose I could ever forget? It's the one article of faith I've got left. . . . 'Faith'! . . . 'Hopelessness' is better, because, good God Almighty, it's about eight wars too soon!"

"That's the point!" said Bill. "I don't see how it lets Minch and me out."

The cork hand waved a dismissal. "It's got nothing to do with Minch and you! You two were a figure of speech. It's got to be all of you . . . or none! And it won't be all of you, because it never has been and never will be! And even if it were all of you, how in God's name could you get near the peace table without machine guns? They don't want you there. You might know too much. You might say things which would jeopardize the system, throw a monkey-wrench into all the stock exchanges, cause crises both national and international, start a movement among all peoples for the dangerous idea, the unwanted idea, of one united world! Hell's bells, that would be treason, wouldn't it? You'd be robbing the politicians not only of their power, but of their dirty little jobs! You'd be showing them all up as half-liars dealing deliberately in half-truths and half-morals. It would be a clean sweep of them all! Can't you see them, pathetic and aghast in their half-honesty, watching their countries going to the dogs because at last 'sovereignty' and 'divine destiny' were being dumped overboard like sacks of rotten potatoes?"

He struck the waiting match and immersed himself in clouds of tobacco smoke. If Bill had been ready to say anything, he didn't get a chance. Jack Wainwright was at boiling point.

"Listen," he said to Bill. "As a helpless pawn in the futile game of world politics, you've seen it, you've lived it, you've missed dying it by a fraction of an inch! And you're going to take out with you a beautiful souvenir that'll last you for life! Do you have to go and ask for another dose? What the hell can you and Minch do, alone, together? Even if you were a born crusader, you couldn't get ten men to rally round you! As soon as they get demobilized, they'll drift away, go home, melt into civilian life again, disappear in the individual struggle! The betting is that you'll never set eyes again on any man you ever fought with, even if he comes from Boston! What's more, you won't want to! You'd find yourselves a million miles apart, almost like strangers! . . . If I thought you stood a dog's chance of doing anything, Bill, I should be urging you to go ahead, because, God knows, until it happens, there will be more and better wars! But there's no one individual in the world who can make us change, and as far as I can see, there's no desire in us to make a change. We're perfect, aren't we? We're man, made in the image of God . . . God help us! And we'll go on contentedly hacking ourselves a bloody path through the ages! Only the weak ones like myself will howl and wail and point out while the happy march goes on! . . . My dear lad, forget it! Why agonize? There's nothing you can do! Thank your God that you've got Minch, that one of the major arts is still open to you, and that you've a hole somewhere into which you can crawl!"

He made an odd gesture and resumed his marching, his hands joining each other behind his back.

For several moments Bill watched him, the thought again in his mind that what they had done to that man in the last war was nobody's business. He was damn nearly out on his two feet, and it was only a queer kind of obstinate guts that kept him going . . . that, and his wife, and Minch. . . . But suppose you did crawl into a hole and you saw everything beginning to go bad, as the Major had . . . wouldn't you rot, sitting and watching, or go crazy, or something? You couldn't sit there and let them run it into the ground. . . .

"You know, Major," he said, "I know it looks awful sour, all over, and I haven't the faintest idea of what I'll find when I get back to the U.S. But I'm not the kind to sit and take it. They've got to do something about it. They can't get by with the 'unknown soldier' stuff this time! That's nothing but hooey! . . . I don't know . . . but I guess I'm just damn fool enough to stick my neck out, and get in there and do some kicking!"

Jack Wainwright stopped, and turned, and looked at him. Was this merely the dissentient voice of youth through the ages . . . that always grew weak and thin with prosperity and children, passed through the stage of acceptance, and was eventually appalled by the revolt of its grandchildren . . . or could there be anything more in it this time?

"Bill," he said, "a man has to work these things out for himself. I'm not pretending to offer you any advice. It may be that this is the moment of change—although personally I cannot believe it. But God knows, it's big enough to constitute a turning-point in the whole scheme of life! If the mark is on your forehead to help clean up the Augean stable, it will manifest itself in due course . . . and if it does, then all I can say is: kick like hell, before it's too late! I wish you luck . . . all of you!"

"DEATH Rays missed the bus for World War II. But after V-J Day, an inventor was told to continue his work in private with Government blessing. . . . The new encouraging factor is probably atomic energy. If a method is developed to concentrate nuclear radiations into a narrow beam, death rays may be available to enliven World War III." (TIME, 1946.)

"In a season of bare-shouldered fashion the big news in the women's underwear field is the strapless wired brassière. This engineering marvel contains a single wire which makes an arch over each breast and a small loop in the center. . . . In the strapless bra the weight of the bust is supported by the wire arches. Some wired bras are made with shoulder straps for use with dresses that cover the shoulders. In this case the wire goes under the breasts and the center loop turns down to permit plunging necklines. But the strapless type is most in demand for the bare-shouldered daytime dresses which are this season's vogue . . . At about $5 apiece the industry expects to sell $10,000,000 worth in one year." (LIFE, 1946.)

CHAPTER EIGHT

"DRESSING DAY" AGAIN — THE NEXT ONE, AND IMPORTANT in that Bill was to invite the doctor up to the cottage.

Minchen put the finishing touches to her husband's tie — the penultimate gesture before going down to breakfast. It was up to Bill to supply the ultimate one. He did so, by slipping an arm round her and kissing her.

They were ready now.

But Bill said, "Would you like to take in the movie after lunch?"

Minchen smiled. . . . The movie? It was sweet of him . . . but how very far away any outside thing was now that every bit of attention she could spare from Bill was turning increasingly on that which was happening within her, claiming her, clamoring to her, coloring her thoughts, her needs, her desires . . . and now, her actions. . . . No more bicycle. No more charcoal-burners up there in the woods. No more Friar's Dene. . . . Just little walks, with him . . . with them both . . . and she'd be able to hang on to Bill's arm. . . .

She shook her head. "I'm afraid you'll have to go down alone today, darling. Coming back up the hill has begun to be a little like climbing Mount Everest!" She laughed, to take the sting out, to make it seem to him a simple thing.

But Bill didn't laugh. Far from it. She had never mentioned her physical condition before. It was a shock to hear her do so, even though she laughed . . . because you knew damn well that even if she felt like the devil she would have laughed and said she felt marvelous. . . . "Minch!" he said, and his lips were dry—"Are you . . . all right?"

At the panic in his eyes, she caught his hand quickly. "I'm absolutely perfect," she said. "I feel as if I'd been in training for this all my life. There's no need to look like that, darling! This moment had to come sometime, you know! And even though I expect to be on my two feet the day the child is born, I'd be a fool to overdo it, that's all! But when you start off this morning, I'm going to walk with you to the end of the village so that I can watch you swoosh down the hill. And if you come straight back after seeing the doctor, you might even find that I was at the corner again, waiting for you!"

"You would be!" said Bill. "But not today! Will you promise me something, Minch?"

She smiled into his eyes. "Anything . . . almost!"

"Then promise me that you won't come out!" said Bill. "Promise me you'll stick around the house where it's warm and where you can . . . be damn careful and take no chances. Will you do that for me?"

"You're a darling to think of it!" said Minchen. "But you don't know anything about it. I need exercise, but not on a bike and not up a mountain!"

Bill nodded. "You're right. I don't know. And I feel like a dog that you should have had to tell me . . . but, Minch . . . you will take care of yourself, won't you?"

Minchen laughed. "I'm going to take care of . . . all three of us! And to begin with, let's go down and eat."

But Bill made no move.

For a moment they stood looking at one another in the mild confusion of the unmade bedroom.

Minchen said, "What is it, darling?"

Bill gave an odd laugh. "It's only that I've decided something. . . . If they pull that transport plane on me this morning, I'll go

AWOL! I'll hide out in the woods or dig a hole under the workshop but, by God, they won't get me!" He reached out and opened the door for her to lead the way down, his face set and tight.

There was something more even than the shadow of the transport plane in his mind, something that he wasn't able to shake off through breakfast, that followed him out of the cottage when he had said good-by to her and mounted the bicycle at the gate and rode off. . . . Was there something prophetic in the fact that he was riding alone, that she was not there beside him, that he couldn't turn his head and see her, her hair blown out in the wind as she bent slightly forward to coast down the hill . . . ?

He wanted to jam on his brakes and turn round and go back. . . . If anything went wrong with her . . . What about this war diet, the continual shortage? What had that done to her? She didn't show anything, but you never could tell. . . . Suppose it had dragged her down so that she couldn't take it when the kid came?

If anything went wrong with her there would be no peace, no music, no Berkshires . . . no Bill Thatcher either! How could there be? Everything you felt and thought was impregnated with Minch, whether you were with her or not. Everything you wanted was for her. Everything you took from her was something that nobody else could give you. Fundamentally there wasn't anybody else. . . . Oh sure, there were lots of people; and you were fond of them, loved them even, but that had nothing to do with it. Minch meant something utterly different. Minch was . . . as much a part of you as that child was of her. You might almost say that there wasn't any you any more — not the kind of you that you were before you married her. And what an unfinished job that "you" was! But you'd become a sort of amalgam, now, two people in one, a one-man team of Minch and you. How could you think for only one of them, or live if

Minch . . . Hell! The Major was right. Unthinkable . . . You'd go completely nuts if you let that get you down.

Without consciousness of it, he had reached the bottom of the hill and slowed up and made the turn. He was coming into Friar's Dene now and there was traffic to call on his attention, the thought of the doctor and the bandaging and the friction of the transport plane to switch his mind at least from the fire to the frying pan.

As he rode through the market place his eyes went to the spot on the sidewalk by the fountain where Minch should have been. . . . Jesus — if anything . . . went wrong! He was still tight-lipped when he rode into camp. His eyes went round it this morning, hating it. It was as though he were not looking at it, but looking back at it, seeing all round it. . . . It was where they put you through it. They didn't need any barbed wire. You couldn't get out anyway. They shanghaied you for duration, and if you tried to make a break you stood to get shot as sure as any convict in the Tombs. . . . And it wasn't duration, because even if you came out whole, it had done something to you. There was always going to be a difference between you and the guy who hadn't been through it. . . . You'd left him behind. He remained an amateur in all his emotions, his viewpoints, his judgments — an enviable amateur without ghosts to pop up and taunt him, without death always in the background of his mind as the point of comparison — and not a nice comfortable civilian death, surrounded by family and church, but a death that pointed a jeering finger at you a hundred times and then came to you all alone and hurt like hell and took a long time . . . or what was even worse the hundred per cent disability that left you rotting on a hospital bed year after year, unable to call it a day, with smirking visitors — full of the best intentions, but, God how dumb, and how crassly impertinent! — coming in to yawp at your bedside and try and amuse you with little therapeutic tricks and then going out again into the lovely crowded streets that you could hear through the windows and would never walk in again. . . . And there was that other kind of death, when you were mustered out unwounded and came back home and couldn't find yourself because of what they had done to you, and you tried to sell apples that nobody would stop and buy, not even the guys with the same ruptured duck in their buttonholes. . . . Why the hell should they? They'd got their own troubles! No, you couldn't remain an amateur once they'd taught you the "yessir" and "nosir," the loneliness, the repression, the waste of life, and then booted you out to learn what it meant to become a hero — that dirty job. . . . And right now back home the older kids from schools and football fields and ball parks were being lined up in streams outside the draft boards, gravely conducted by steak-fed merchants who had never smelled a corpse but whose sense of responsibility was keen — the responsibility of sending those kids out to save their skins, their dough, their jobs. . . . Amateurs, these guys who ran the show? Hell no! It was the kid-soldier who was the amateur, who had always been the goat, the sucker, the cleaner-upper of political latrines. . . .

Christ — if anything went wrong . . .

The medical building confronted him. He almost crashed into it.

. . . And now he must march in there and salute and make it snappy and be told by that so-and-so of a doctor that Sergeant W. B. Thatcher would be ready to board the transport plane in forty-eight hours! . . . He could feel it in his bones. The place smelled of it. . . . Did the army give a damn if Minch lived or died?

He dropped off his bicycle, parked it against the wall of the building, his face screwed up, his muscles braced. . . .

The reek of antiseptics caught him by the throat as he pushed open the door. The man with the ear was there and three or four others. . . . Sure! You always had to wait for everything, even the meat ax! . . . Watch him work! What was the use of inviting that bird up to the cottage? As if the Major and Minch could make a dent! Might as well save his breath . . . He wasn't even a human being! He was Sergeant W. B. Thatcher with eight or nine numerals, — he couldn't ever remember them, — care of Postmaster APO 78, New York — a bunch of numbers on bits of paper. . . .

They'd probably send up a couple of M.P.'s to look for him if he ducked out after they'd told him . . . but it wouldn't be for three days at least, and that would give him time to dig in under the workshop. . . . They wouldn't think of looking there, and if they did, the Major would stand on the trapdoor, smoking his pipe, and hand them a line. . . . It would be like going into the Maquis from your own people! But, by God, he wouldn't come out again until . . . March! They'd taken his fingers, hadn't they? All right, now they could take their damn war and their discharge and their bucket-seat! He was going to stay with Minch. . . .

"*ISN'T it lovely? The drive has been successful beyond our dreams! We've collected* such *a lot of money for the dear boys who have come back without arms and legs! We really feel that this time we shall be able to take care of them, because there are only seventeen thousand . . . Yes, seven*teen *thousand. . . . You remember how shocking it was after the last war? I don't think I shall ever forget seeing them on the streets selling pencils and apples for a living, with nothing but old-fashioned stumps and crutches! Really, it was too awful! But this time it's going to be wonderful for them, simply wonderful! The darling amputees—yes, that's what we call them in* this *war. Such a cute word, isn't it? Well, as I was saying, the darling amputees are going to find* such *changes! No more old horrible blocks of wood and steel and nasty smelly leather thongs! Oh no, my dear! This time all the lovely new things, like plastic, and the metal they make the kitchen things of . . . aluminum, that's right! But it's wonderful what can be done with plastic, perfectly fascinating things that of course I don't understand a bit, called 'suction sockets' and 'elbow locks,' and—what is the delightful word?—oh yes, 'rotators,' and cables, and things; and it's all going to weigh at* least *half a pound less than* any *other artificial arms and legs* ever *made before! So you can just see how* lucky *they are!*"

CHAPTER NINE

It was at the door of the cottage that Minchen had said good-by to Bill that morning, in spite of her own desire to walk with him as far as their corner. But he had wanted her not to. So she waved and called out "Good luck to you, darling! You'll be back in an hour . . . won't you?" And he had nodded, frowning, and ridden away. . . .

It was too bad she couldn't go too, but . . . she'd promised to take care of all three of them.

For a moment or two she stood there drumming on the doorpost, as though she were following him all the way down the hill, wondering about the worried look on his face.

But it was chilly, standing there, even with a sweater. So she closed the door and went back into the living room where the wood fire was an invitation to sit in front of it. But, instead, she chose the piano bench and opened the lid of the keyboard. . . . He'd be back in an hour.

Her father was out in the workshop, her mother upstairs. Minchen began to play . . . "*Au Clair de la Lune*" melted softly into old "*Frère Jacques*" and then became a small Humpty Dumpty who tiptoed into Peter and such a little Wolf and then crept through nursery rhymes into a *berceuse* . . . fairy music, almost like an echo, because its ears were so tiny and so delicate . . . and mustn't hear ugly things like anger and hate and war . . . only the beautiful clean vibrations of love and music to stay in its ears forever. . . . At least she could give it those while it was growing and getting ready . . . swathe it round with all her thoughts of Bill, bathe it in sound with the tips of her fingers. . . . It might remember, when it was born; and, like a sea shell, its ear might carry a special rhythm . . . and someday . . . perhaps that restless tiny body curled up in her might outdistance both Bill and herself . . . that rhythm might belong to the world. . . .

Her eyes came up from the keyboard and went to the clock on the mantelpiece. He had already been gone an hour! That meant he'd be here any minute now. . . . She smiled, as she went on playing. . . . He hadn't actually said that he was "ready"—he probably never would say it—but his face this morning had told more than he knew! He was completely aware of what was going on, and twice he had even mentioned it—the first time when he hoped it would be a girl, and the other time when he had said in the Monk and Paunch that he "wanted to be around" in March. And this morning he didn't even want her to go out! That was why this morning he was going to invite the doctor up to the cottage, so that Dad could put in a word, so that she could add her mite to the concentrated effort to dissuade him from sending Bill in the transport. . . . The transport? Where was Bill? Her hands left the notes. . . . He was a quarter of an hour late already. That couldn't possibly mean . . .

She was standing now, leaning on the piano.

. . . Oh no. That was ridiculous. She was making a fool of herself. They wouldn't whisk him off to America at a minute's notice . . . Why, all his clothes were upstairs. At least they'd have to give him time to pack! . . . Time to pack. . . .

Her hand came up over her mouth. The knuckles of her other hand grew white against the piano edge.

. . . That extraordinary look in his face up in the bedroom . . . and when he had ridden away . . . Did he know then that . . . that today . . . and he had burst out savagely and said "By God, they won't get me!" . . . On D-Day he had just vanished! And today she had simply let him go . . . without thinking, without realizing . . . She had just taken it for granted that he would be back in an hour! Had they . . . got him?

The clock had gone another fifteen minutes.

. . . If only the damn thing would stop, or go backwards . . . to breakfast time!

She couldn't stand still any more. She felt physically sick. She began walking, her hands clasping and unclasping—her father's daughter—a bitter taste in her mouth.

And presently, because motion is an antidote, a minor friction, she made her way back from panic, tried to cheat herself with a hundred reasons for his not having come—a lot of men ahead of him at the hospital, the doctor not on time, a puncture going down the hill, a half hour used up in finding someone to mend it and getting the tire blown up again, a sudden decision to get his hair cut while he was down in Friar's Dene—all the simple homely reasons that invariably fall short of their mark and fail to convince, and leave one still shaking with nerves.

More walking . . . and then, fighting away from the picture in her mind of a far-off dot in the sky that was a transport plane, she tried calling herself names, insisting to herself that it was nothing but morbid imagination, perhaps because of her condition—that there weren't any transport planes in Friar's Dene, that no army in the world would do a thing like that without orders having to go through, without preparation, without some notice, so that you could . . . get yourselves ready. . . . Didn't they know how frightful it had been for Bill? Didn't they care whether he had a chance or not? Couldn't they get it through their thick heads that if they dragged him off and sent him back alone, it would be the cruelest thing in the world? That doctor would understand. He wouldn't let them . . . She must get to him . . . tell him . . . if only it wasn't already too late. . . .

She came hurrying out into the hallway, grabbed her overcoat and flung it round her shoulders, wrenched open the front door and was on her way. . . .

"ATOM bomb? What's all the squawking about? Was Guadalcanal a Sunday School picnic? Or Tarawa, or Iwo? First all the ship's guns blasted them. Then the planes dropped their eggs, and then we went to work and roasted the little bastards to a crisp with flame-throwers, didn't we? And what was left we ran over with bulldozers, or heaved dynamite at them, and finished off the wounded ones with grenades. But it all took time, see, and a hell of a lot of dead G.I.'s. And then some guy flies over alone and mops up a hundred thousand of them with one bomb . . . so what? Kind of neat, ain't it? And saved a whole bunch of Yanks from being planted! . . . But the squawk . . . Jees! You'd think it was something new they'd invented instead of just another way of bumping them off! There's only one thing new about it, bud! And it's why they're all hollering. They know that in the next war it's going to get them, see—all the big boys who do their fighting behind an office desk, all the lousy senators who dish out the war contracts, all the sons of bitches who start a war and keep it going! That's what they're thinking of. It puts the squeeze on them, don't it? It could put them right out of business, just like it did the Nips! And that would be just too bad, wouldn't it? . . . Listen, sucker, who do you think 'civilization' is, us G.I.'s who did the job, or the guys with the desks and the dough and the loud mouths?"

CHAPTER TEN

THE STRONG BROWN LEGS THAT HAD CARRIED MINCHEN UP AND down hill like a feather all through the summer refused to give her the turn of speed that she wanted this morning. Moreover breathing was not so easy. And the distance to camp was some two and a half miles.

None of these points had been in her mind when she came out of the cottage. She was intent only on doing battle for Bill. But within a hundred paces of the gate the conquest of self was forced upon her, the misery of driving a once-agile body that liked to be driven, and was now incapable of its task. She found herself reduced to a maddening crawl. And every time she had to stop to get her breath, she could have cried with rage. It seemed to her that time was of the essence. Planes didn't wait. . . .

She drove herself to keep on going by telling herself that once she got down to the main road at the bottom of the hill, there would be traffic—a bus, or a farm wagon, or a milkman's cart, or an army truck, or something on wheels, to give her a lift . . . and it would hardly take any persuasion to get the driver to take her all the way to camp, once she explained how urgent it was, how desperately important. All she need tell the man was that she was a soldier's wife. He'd understand!

Soldier's wife! What did you know when you married a soldier? You thought you had argued it all out, that you knew exactly what you were in for, but nothing that you had ever imagined came anywhere near what it really meant. You never knew where he had gone, what he was up against, what it was doing to him, whether he would ever come back. . . . You couldn't tell what it was going to do to you, until you'd married him. You couldn't tell that you were going to die ten times a day, only to find yourself crawling back to a numb half-life with the hours, and days, dragging along filled with damned crowding stupid things that had to be done with the bit of your mind that was not there, reaching and groping . . . and failing. Oh no, you didn't know that! You only found it out afterwards, when he'd gone off, had disappeared, was "somewhere in France," and all you knew about him was that you loved him, and that the best part of you was with him. . . . The rest of you was just a shell, empty, waiting, trying to pray. . . . And when he did come back, he wasn't yours. You only had a bit of him, strained, hungry, distracted. . . . They had all the rest! And they lent him to you, like a toy on the end of a string! Anytime they wanted it, all they had to do was to give it a jerk. They had jerked Bill back from their honeymoon . . . jerked him away for D-Day. They wanted to jerk him away now, even though he couldn't fight any more! Even though the toy was broken! They wouldn't let you keep it, mend it, help it to run properly again. They were jealous of you. They wanted it. They wouldn't let it go, because they might find another use for it, wring the last ounce out of it. . . . And if it was broken completely, they sent you a telegram . . . and that was that. They could take another toy from their crowded shelf. You couldn't. . . . And what did it matter, to them? You weren't even supposed to scream, or smash things, or want to die. You were supposed to be glad and proud. You had "given" him — which was their way of camouflaging the fact that they had taken him! And you were supposed to accept that and bring up his child in the way it should go — ready and willing to do it all over again! . . . Like an octopus . . . greedy, horrible! . . . And now that you were going to have his child in March, what did they care if you had it alone, without him? They didn't even care what would happen to him! Didn't they know that it wasn't only his hand that had to be healed? Didn't they know that it was Bill himself — the Bill who was on his way to getting back to himself, or what was left of him; the Bill who was beginning to find out the new self that had been grafted on to him? He wasn't ready yet. If they took him away now, they would rob him of the one thing that was vital, the spiritual value of being with his wife, and child, of beginning to know the reality of being a husband and a father. . . .

Somehow or other she must tell the doctor that. Somehow she must make him see — if he was so blind that he couldn't see already — that at this special moment in their lives, she was as necessary to Bill as he was to her. What kind of married life was it when their whole relationship was based more on their being separated than on their being together? Were they always to be ghosts to each other, each one trying to build up an ideal of the other from an enforced distance? Were their entire lives to be spent writing letters, exchanging photos, waiting, eating their hearts out . . . perhaps even changing towards each other? Had the doctor thought of that, or was it something else that didn't matter? If they flew Bill off to America now, how long would it be before he would even see his child? . . . They couldn't! They mustn't! There must be some way . . .

She was halfway along the village now. The corner had never been so far off. Each time she stopped and hung on to a fence, her breath coming in jerks, the thought of the transport plane was a torment, enraging her, driving her on, so that each cottage passed became a triumph, each bend in the road a campaign won.

The one thought she shied away from, fought against, refused to let herself phrase, was that Bill was already on the plane. But though she succeeded in denying it utterance, it pressed at the outskirts of her mind like an icy wind trying to get in. She knew that if she yielded to it, she would have nothing to go on with. And she was going on, with everything she had, for Bill, for the child, for herself. . . .

The time before, when she had invaded that camp, they had laughed at her, told her there was a war on . . . but that was before Bill was wounded, and she had really known all along that she didn't stand the remotest chance . . . although she had taken it, hoping against hope. . . . Today they could laugh at her if they wanted to, but they couldn't laugh at Bill's bandaged arm, and they wouldn't dare look at his hand! And they wouldn't dare to tell her that there was a war on if Bill were there. . . . And he was there! And she'd fight, argue, beg, anything . . . go down on her knees . . .

The corner came in sight.

It did something to Minchen. It came to her like a renewal of faith. It was "their" corner . . . where as a girl she had met Bill's "kid brother," where she made the great discovery that she loved him, where she had waited to meet him each evening after they were married, where she had so often sat alone after he had gone, sick with fear, learning the lesson of remembrance. It was the corner where Bill had planned to meet her when he came back from France. . . . Perhaps he would be coming up the hill now, on the other side of the woods. . . . Perhaps he'd reach the corner at the same minute she did! That would make it unforgettable forever!

She kept her eyes on it as she went along. It was a friendly rope, pulling her, helping her. She began talking to herself under her breath. "He'll be there! I feel it! I believe it's planned for him to be there! I said to him that I would meet him at the corner . . . and that was this very morning, before breakfast . . . and he didn't want me to come . . . and now he's behind the trees, walking hard . . . and it's so steep. . . . I'll go a little slower. I don't want to get there before he does!"

Her pace became a crawl. . . . It was better. It would give her enough breath to be able to greet him. . . .

But she got there before he did. Their corner remained empty.

And when she could see down the hill, there was no one on the whole length of it.

And presently the hill itself became blurred and out of shape, so that Minchen couldn't see it any more . . . and didn't want to.

Her hand came up to her throat. "You fool!" she said—and then, with a choky sarcastic laugh, "You ought to have known! There is a war on!"

She turned her back on their corner. This time it had failed her. She clenched her hands and started down the relentless hill.

On their bicycles they could do it in about a minute flat. How long it would take her this morning was pure speculation, but at least the law of gravity was on her side, and at the bottom, about the size of beetles, army trucks pursued their innocent passage and, from time to time, a jeep ran by like a gazelle. . . . She wouldn't need even to hook a thumb! Any one of the homesick youngsters driving would give Minchen a grinning lift, with just one look at her and the hell with regulations!

As she came steadily down, they grew, not only in size, but in importance and the thought of speed.

And then, out from behind the woods, there appeared a jeep which paused, panting, at the foot of the hill, and leaped forward again after disgorging a man in uniform whose left arm gleamed with fresh white bandaging. . . .

Minchen stopped walking. She stood, rocking on her legs, staring down at him as he turned from the disappearing jeep, started up the hill . . . saw her, waved, broke into a jogging run.

Her body remained tense. "They shan't fool me now!" she said aloud. "I won't believe . . . Why a jeep? Why did they keep him so long? . . . Have they sent him to pack his clothes? Is he going to tell me . . ." She caught her lip with her teeth to stop herself.

Bill's speed and hers were very different, even though he had to hug his left arm close to his side in order to run, even though it soon became impossible to continue running up that hill, and he dropped to a hard-breathing walk.

And when he drew near enough for her to be able to see his face, she still couldn't tell . . .

He called out to her as he came. "Minch! . . . My God, what are you doing way down here?"

She dismissed the question. It didn't matter about her. But it did about Bill. She waited until he came, and stopped in front of her, breathing hard. Then, rigid as a board, she said, "You'd better tell me at once . . . are you . . . going today?"

Her question explained everything to him — her being there, the hard wound-up look in her eyes, the scary tenseness of her anticipation . . . as though she were facing a firing squad . . . He said quickly, urgently, "No! I'm staying! They've let me off!"

It was almost as though God had tapped Minchen on the shoulder and said, "It's all right, my dear! You can come out now."

It took time to reach her — it came from behind so much. But it came, and at the touch all her defense works crumbled.

Bill saw her eyes melt and her mouth begin to pucker like a child's. "Minch!" he said, and caught her in his arm; and tired body and battered mind found sanctuary.

And while the storm shook her, she clung to him — it was allowed for still a little while — her face hard against his satisfying shoulder . . . and the things he said filled up what had been an empty world. Age-old things, humdrum things, miraculous always between a man and a woman.

There was no one to see them, no one to laugh at their tears, no one to raise a sophisticated eyebrow when finally her head came up and they kissed each other.

And when at last they started off, back up the long steep oddly symbolic hill, they made unconsciously an all too familiar picture — a soldier, one useless bandaged arm hanging, the other supporting a drooping comrade out of the firing line.

PLASTIC and wood, plastic and wood,
Give them a toy to keep them good!
Pandas and Teddies are out of date,
And none of them want a crayon and slate!
A tank, a bomber, a twelve-inch gun,
Plastic soldiers by the ton!
Battle wagons and jumping jeeps
That knock the soldiers down in heaps!
Good clean fun . . . and then off to bed!

"*Give me the children!*" *Hitler said.*

CHAPTER ELEVEN

"IF I WERE YOU, I'D GIVE MYSELF ANOTHER DAY IN BED, MINCH, MY dear!" said Dr. Merivale. "You'll be as good as gold again by then. Furthermore, I should say that we can expect you down at the hospital any time after the last of February. I'll be up to see you again before then, just in case you forget it!" He cracked a smile at his own joke. "Now no more wild goose chases, understand!"

Minchen smiled up at him. "You couldn't make it the last of May, could you? Or June?"

"What on earth are you talking about?" snapped the old doctor. "Haven't you had enough?"

"I was thinking of Bill," said Minchen.

"H'm! . . . What about Bill?"

Minchen's hands moved on the bedcovers. "Well, you see . . . they're only going to let him stay till the baby's born."

Dr. Merivale's eyebrows went up. "Ah! I do see!" He snapped his bag shut. "You're lucky he's not in the firing line with the rest of them! Half a loaf's a pretty generous ration these days. You know it better than I do, my dear! I'll have a word with him on my way out. . . . Be a good girl and stay where you are till tomorrow. G'by!"

Muriel and Jack Wainwright were hovering at the foot of the stairs—she pretending to arrange leaves in a vase, he with a hand on the door as though he were just coming in or going out.

Dr. Merivale nodded at them in complete comprehension. "Nothing to fuss about!" he said. "Relax! If only all my patients were like Minch! Perfect waste of time to come up here! But see that she stays in bed all day tomorrow. Where's the boy?"

Jack Wainwright said, "Thanks, Doc! . . . You'll find the boy laying for you at the gate."

"Good-by, Doctor!" said Muriel. "We're awfully grateful to you for coming."

The old man patted her shoulder. "Wish I could come more often. Never get a minute for friends these days. 'By, my dear! 'By Jack!" He jerked his thumb up the stairs. "Grand job! Wonderful girl!" He crammed on his hat and went abruptly out.

Bill was smoking a red-hot cigarette at the gate. At the sight of the doctor he threw it away.

Dr. Merivale marched up to him. "So!" he said. "You're all hot and bothered like the rest of the family, eh?" He smiled.

"She all right, Doctor?" Bill searched the old man's eyes.

But Dr. Merivale was equally intent on discovering what manner of man Bill was. He nodded to himself as though he had come to a conclusion. "Flourishing!" he said.

"Thank God!" said Bill.

"Correct!" said the old man. "Go on doing it! You've got several good reasons . . . among them Minch! What kind of useless hell is under all that bandaging?"

Bill ignored the question. "Look Doctor," he said, "I wanted to ask you . . . about March. Is there any danger of . . . I mean nothing is likely to go wrong at the last minute, is it?"

The old country doctor's eyes remained steady. "Young man," he said, "you must have found out in France that in the last analysis most things are in the hands of God, however much we may fool ourselves to the contrary. When it comes to delivering a baby, don't let anyone tell you that a woman can't have a hard time. She can, even if most of them come out of it, with luck and good doctoring. As far as Minchen is concerned, I see no reason why she can't expect a perfectly normal delivery. I know how you feel, but I don't believe you have to worry too much. Incidentally

I'll guarantee not to go to sleep on the job! You see . . . I happen to be rather fond of Minch, myself!"

He nodded, stumped out of the gate and climbed into the waiting carriage.

Bill remained staring after him. . . . So that was that! Queer old bird, and dressed for the part, black bag and all. But you liked him, and he gave you something even if he did drag in that "last analysis" business . . . which left you just about where you were before!

He went frowning back along the flags and into the cottage and upstairs two at a time.

"Hi!" he said at the door of their bedroom.

Minchen was waiting for him. "You've been asking the doctor about me, haven't you?"

Bill made a stab at a laugh. "How d'you possibly guess?" He sat on the edge of the bed. "I'm all pepped up! He says you're flourishing!"

Minchen nodded. " 'Course I am!" Her eyes were on his. "Did he tell you anything about . . . March?"

For a second that "last analysis" got between Bill and her. He didn't want her to know it. She had to be on the top of the world, and kept there. So he said quickly, "Did he! Why, honey, it's going to be a cinch! You've no idea how simple he thinks it's going to be! To hear him talk, you'd say that having a child was about as easy as cleaning your teeth. Absolutely nothing to it . . . just a routine!"

Minchen smiled. "But unfortunately, Bill darling, you didn't believe a word of it, did you?"

It was like a pin pricking his toy balloon.

Bill moved uneasily. "Why, of course I did! Why shouldn't I? . . . He's quite a character, isn't he? And besides, he's crazy about you! He thinks you're . . ."

Minchen touched his hand, stopping him. "I know, my dear!

You don't have to go pretending. I know I should be worrying my head off about you if the positions were reversed, but will you believe me if I tell you something about it? You see, I happen to know that there's no reason to worry. And it'll spoil it all if you can't believe me and be as happy about it as I am. Shall I tell you how I know?"

"I wish to God you would!" said Bill.

"All right," said Minchen, "I will." She gave the pillow under her head a tug and settled comfortably. "It's inside information . . . very secret, just for you and me! You see, the extraordinary thing is that the child has been with me all day and every day for a longer time than you have! And we've been through the most amazing things together, terrific things, all the important things that have ever happened to me . . . first of all you; and you in France; and your being wounded; and meeting you at Weathersford; and then your coming home, and your . . . your hand; and all the appalling uncertainty of your having to go to France again; and then the magnificent news of your discharge; and right up to yesterday when I saw you actually on the plane, and you weren't and came back. . . . Do you see what I mean? Not many women have had such things crowded at them, so how can we be just an ordinary mother and child? We've established an extraordinary past together before it's even born! And every time I played while you were out there, it was—listening, hearing, at least feeling the vibrations. I don't suppose there has ever been quite such a relationship before between a woman and her unborn child. And after all that, can you possibly imagine its trying to hurt me when it's born? I simply don't believe it! It seems to me even more ridiculous than if someone said you were going to hurt me! I absolutely know that it's going to be born without the slightest difficulty! It's almost as though the baby had told me, had given me its promise, that it would behave like an angel! It's . . . a message, an understanding between us! And I'm so perfectly serene about it all, that I want you to be. . . . It's a nuisance to have all the fuss of going down to the hospital, that's all. It would be so much simpler to have it quietly here, in this room, our room, but I do see that it would make an awful lot of trouble for everybody else, so I suppose I'd better forget it and go down. And presumably, they'll only keep me for a couple of days or so, and then, my dear, you can come and get us in the funny old cab and we'll come driving up again, feeling pretty cocky . . . all three of us, Bill! . . . I promise you!"

Bill's fist was clenched and his mouth set tight. . . . To hear her say these things . . . for him! Was there anybody in the world more infinitely wonderful. . . . She was promising him at the moment of her having to face it . . . and all the time there was that "last analysis." . . . He had promised her once! He'd said that they weren't going to touch him . . . he was immune . . . he was coming back as he had gone out . . . he knew it, believed it just as profoundly as she did now. . . .

He took her hand and bent over it. . . . God, you heard what she said. Give her a break, won't you please? . . . Bill kissed the palm of her hand and closed the fingers down on it and put the hand down on the bed. "I'll be there, Minch!" he said. "And believe me, if there are any birds of paradise around, I'll have 'em all singing for you inside that cab!"

UNESCO: "It is in the minds of men that the defense of peace must be constructed."

South Africa refuses to give up German Southwest Africa.
The United States insists on keeping the Japanese islands.
Greece demands more weapons from England.
Reign of terror in Jerusalem.
Order to cease fire at last given in Dutch East Indies.
Burma in rivers of blood wins independence from Great Britain.
France sends more regiments to Indo-China.
Vatican in crusade against Communism.
Arabs on verge of "holy war."
Moslems and Hindus tear India apart.
Yugoslavs engaged in frontier war with Greece.
Chinese Communists have over a million troops in the field.
Russia puts pressure on Turkey for Dardanelles; demands military bases in Spitsbergen.
Great Britain foists King back on Greek throne, using tanks and bombers.

In whose minds?

CHAPTER TWELVE

THE PLAN THEY MADE CALLED FOR ARMFULS OF HOLLY AND mistletoe for Christmas, the looting of the Monk and Paunch by Bill, the throwing of a party that would crowd the previous four uncelebrated Christmases all into one. It was going to be Minchen's Christmas.

But when the day came there was neither holly nor party. The war had taken a turn. There was a thing called the Bulge, and it was nine days old and already fifty miles wide and fifty deep . . . and among the minor items of it was a certain field outside Malmédy where the deep snow decently covered the indecent bodies of massacred unarmed Americans. They had found the peace on earth that comes to men of good will.

And however far away Bill Thatcher had managed to get because of Minchen, because of his permanent disability and discharge, the impact of the Bulge glued him, in spite of himself, to the radio with the Major.

It was not like the attrition of every day, bad enough of course, but which could leave a returned man shrugging a shoulder and saying "It's the other fellow's job." This was disaster. This was every man's job who called himself a man; and there was a sense of guilt, ridiculous, but in a curious way atavistic, at being on the side lines. Even the useless hand served as an excuse only momentarily. After Malmédy, he ought to be out there, doing something, anything. . . .

Thus the male in him.

But there was Minch . . . and the little time left that she had to go, and that "last analysis" which refused to leave his mind in spite of her own serenity.

And through it all Jack Wainwright not only moved the markers on his map, but made the march back with them, as he had in the flesh in that other break-through in his own war, when the line had ceased to exist, and day and night had become one; and the human body, beyond the limits of endurance, was, save only in the matter of obedience, completely dissociated from the grooved mind that desperately drove it. Fear was by-passed. Death attained the unimportant. There was only timeless time, emotionless, feelingless . . . This time they were doing it in the snow, slithering on frozen roads, unable to light fires, hands and feet numb, everywhere grayness and half-light and being always pushed back. . . . Last time the enemy had only been stopped by their own inability to keep up with the speed of their advance. This time . . . what? Could they be stopped by the snow, or was their mechanization too perfect? . . . Mistletoe, holly, Happy Christmas . . . Why not gather joyously round a hand-picked corpse, nine days old, and you could raise your glass — if you hadn't gagged on your turkey and plum pudding — and drink to the boys in Bastogne and say: "Stick to it, fellows! We've all got our eyes on you while we keep the home fires burning!" . . . Blah! They'd let 'em sell pencils in the streets again this time when they came back, armless, legless . . . heroes! . . .

Somebody came into the room. He turned from the map, and from his thoughts.

It was Bill — who had not showed up at breakfast, who looked now preoccupied.

Bill said, " 'Morning, Major!" and then, as though with an effort to leave his own thoughts, "Anything new?" He went over and took a look at the markings. "Judas! . . . Are we ever going to hold 'em?"

Jack Wainwright said, "It may add another year to this stinking war, unless we can pinch them off from the north and the south. . . ." He laughed. "We! Did you hear that? Easy to sit here and be Eisenhower!"

"Must be hell on wheels out there!" said Bill. "It's no picnic to sweat it out here either, one way and another."

Jack Wainwright raised a sarcastic eyebrow. "H'm! I noticed that you forgot to wish me a happy Christmas!" He laughed again. "We seem to lack the right kind of armor, you and I, Bill! The wrong school or something. . . . Have you happened to notice, for instance, that the stock market has been going up since the beginning of the break-through?"

Bill looked at him, startled. "Up? You don't mean that, do you?"

"You've only got to look at the papers," said Jack Wainwright. "A longer war means more profits. You'll see the market tumble to its knees at the first hint of victory. Of course, intellectually, peace is a good idea, but in this world one has to be practical."

"God!" said Bill. "But . . . the boys in Bastogne! It makes suckers out of them!"

"Wrong school again!" said Jack Wainwright. "My dear chap, Bastogne is merely good publicity. The break-through is worth millions! A few soldiers more or less . . . What the hell? Don't be so crude! . . . Let's forget it, on this merry Christmas . . . Tell me, your empty chair at breakfast . . . I hope it doesn't mean that Minch . . ." He left it intentionally in the air.

" 'Fraid it does," said Bill. "She had a godawful time last night! When I came down she had only just begun to feel human again. . . . Mrs. Wainwright's in with her now, thank God!"

"Good!" said Jack. "That'll help."

Bill had been standing in the same place for at least two minutes. He began moving restlessly, touching things as he passed. "Makes you feel like a lug," he said. "There isn't a damn thing you can do while she has to go through it. . . . Don't you think we ought to have that doctor up again, Major?"

Jack Wainwright reached for a pipe cleaner. There wasn't room for the two of them to move up and down. . . . He said, "You may be right, Bill. We'll ask Muriel when she comes down. She'll know!"

It was said with complete conviction, but Bill found small comfort in it. . . . Minchen trying to smile between spasms that drained her face white and left him shaking . . . and so utterly helpless! And she'd refused to let him call her mother. "It'll go soon . . . I'll be all right if I can hang on to your hand . . ." And she'd hung on, like the big Texan the night they'd dropped him behind the piece of wall in the orchard . . . "The bastards have got me! Gimme a hand, Wise Guy!" . . . and after a while he'd let go! It was almost as though he'd been in the bedroom while Minch was going through it . . . and suppose Minch had let go too . . . pushed to the point where she couldn't take it any more . . .

Bill Thatcher turned abruptly to Jack Wainwright—unconsciously reaching for a metaphorical hand himself. "I wish you'd tell me something, Major! Do you know how much more of this Minch may have to stand?"

It was the question that Jack Wainwright had been asking himself.

But he said at once, and with emphasis, "My dear boy, she may not have another go like that for days and days! Possibly not at all! . . . I haven't altogether forgotten the unpleasant moments that I went through before she herself was born. But they were apparently quite unnecessary! Muriel only laughed at me, afterwards! . . . If I can offer anything, I'd say, Take it easy. Don't let it get you. I know it's hell, but you mustn't forget that it won't help Minch to know that you are agonizing."

Bill nodded. "I'd thought of that, but last night drove me nearly nuts! . . . Judas! It's a damn sight easier to go through it yourself than have to watch someone you . . ." He broke off, began moving up and down again, gave a quick apologetic laugh. "God, you've no idea how I envy you, Major! You've made yourself invent a million jobs out in the workshop! Right now, I . . ."

His eyes went to the piano, but he bit the sentence off, switched it violently. . . . "Right now, I'm about as useless as a sick headache!"

Jack Wainwright had seen the direction of Bill's glance. He felt it like a blow in the stomach. He knew what Bill might have said, what he was forever denied. Minch had taught him that, during those long months after D-Day when the piano had been her confessional! The boy should be sitting there now, playing . . . playing . . . And all he could do was to walk up and down, tearing himself . . . but with the guts to say nothing at a moment when he would have been justified in saying anything!

Bill spoke again. "You know, Major, I used to wonder . . . A lot of the guys out there were all set up about becoming fathers . . . being the father of a son, that was the big idea. But their wives didn't seem to matter a damn! What the hell was biting them? Male vanity? . . . I suppose so. But doggone it, I don't seem to have it! 'Far as I'm concerned, they can go take a jump in the lake with it . . . the son too! Am I crazy, or what?"

Jack Wainwright shook his head. "You're right, Bill, of course! The answer probably is that most of us are not one-woman men . . . but I have a strong suspicion that you and I are penalized that way!" He laughed. "I'll make a confession to you, Bill. When Minchen was born, I told Muriel that it was a crime to have brought her into this stinking world. I meant it . . . but today I've changed my mind. It seems to me that you and she have already done something to improve it. I . . ." He stopped.

Upstairs the bedroom door closed and there were footsteps.

In their minds both men were with Muriel, stair by stair as she came down . . .

She was smiling when she reached the door.

"Bill, my dear," she said cheerfully, "Minchen would like to see you! She's quite comfortable now, but I shouldn't be surprised if she wanted to drop off to sleep in a few minutes so don't stay long!"

Bill let out a breath. "Right!" he said, and made for the stairs.

When he had gone, Jack Wainwright took his wife by the shoulder. "And now, tell me," he said, "what do you really think? Have we got to send for the doctor? Is she . . ."

Muriel patted her husband's arm, smiled into his eyes. "I'm not so sure that you're not even worse than Bill!" she said. "Of course Minchen had a very nasty time—don't we all?—but I can assure you that the doctor would be bored to death if he had to listen to that! . . . Couldn't you possibly find something for you both to do in the workshop? . . . Anything to take you out of the house!"

Jack Wainwright looked into his wife's eyes. They were quite sure of themselves. . . . He nodded. "Very well, my dear," he said. "But don't forget that we are both relying on you . . . more than you know! Tell the boy to join me out there when he comes down."

"WE, the peoples of the United Nations,

"Determined to save succeeding generations from the scourge of war, which twice in our lifetime has brought untold sorrow to mankind, and

"To reaffirm faith in fundamental human rights, in the dignity and worth of the human person, in the equal rights of men and women and of nations large and small, and

"To establish conditions under which justice and respect for the obligations arising from treaties and other sources of international law can be maintained, and

"To promote social progress and better standards of life in larger freedom, and for these ends

"To practice tolerance and live together in peace with one another as good neighbors, and

"To unite our strength to maintain international peace and security, and

"To insure, by the acceptance of principles and the institution of methods, that armed forces shall not be used, save in the common interest, and

"To employ international machinery for the promotion of the economic and social advancement of all people, have resolved to combine our efforts to accomplish these aims.

"Accordingly, our respective governments, through representatives assembled in the city of San Francisco, who have exhibited their full powers found to be in good and due form, have agreed to the present Charter of the United Nations and do hereby establish an international organization to be known as the United Nations."

—June, 1945

CHAPTER THIRTEEN

THE FIRST OF FEBRUARY . . . JUST ANOTHER DAY . . . AND then, like a jagged fever chart, the third, the seventh, the ninth . . .

The workshop had become a sort of Staff Headquarters, with Bill acting as runner from the front line — not in relation to the Bulge: that was taking care of itself, had become secondary.

At Bill's entry, the Major would cock an eye at him, sometimes with a spoken question, apparently of the most casual: "Well?" or "All right?" Bill's answers were in kind: "Okay!" or, frowningly, "Not so hot right now," and, once or twice, simply "Jees! . . ." At which there was silence.

Jerky stuff, but it was a moot point as to which of the two men needed the other more.

Up in the bedroom, where Minchen took cover in her discomfort, and to which Bill, uneasy and restless, came tapping at all moments, she said to him once, "What do you do out there with Dad?"

"Do?" Bill considered for a moment. Then he said, "Frankly, I don't know! He seems to be working away all the time, and I . . . I don't seem to do anything. I'm there, that's all. 'Course we smoke and chew the rag and . . ."

Minchen laughed. "Don't tell me you ever get a chance to say anything!"

"Don't kid yourself!" said Bill. "He lets me sound off all right."

"What about?"

Bill shrugged a shoulder. "Darned if I know. I don't believe either he or I could answer that one. Guess we're both of us just making the air vibrate! Sounds cockeyed, doesn't it? But you can take it from me there's a reason! And I can tell it you in one word — you! You're the whole works, honey. You'd be scared stiff if you only knew how important you'd become!"

Minchen shook her head. "No! You're wrong. I believe I do know."

Bill looked into her eyes. "I guess you do, Minch. It's a long way from Oxford! They know how to sock the kid stuff out of you, don't they? We're old all right. We've learned too much, too fast. And that's O.K. too! It has saved us a lot of flapping around, not knowing what it was all about. . . . Do I have to tell you that you're the woman to end all women as far as I'm concerned?" He smiled. "Listen, honey! All I want is for you to keep that promise of yours. Remember?"

"I will!" said Minchen. "I promise you again!"

So went the eleventh, the fourteenth, the twentieth . . . like telegraph posts flashing past the windows of an express . . . an uneasy journey, however cheerful on the surface, reluctant thoughts pressing up, but not allowed to take shape nor find utterance . . . each doing his best to help the other by disguising his own inner fear . . . an increasing tension permeating the cottage, and the workshop.

It broke one morning, shortly after dawn. In a blur of agony and panic and rage, Bill found himself trying to hold Minch, to help Minch, to take it away from Minch, as she writhed in the first of her labor pains . . . and after an incredible period when it seemed to him that she must die at any moment, her mother appeared and took over, and Bill, shaking and nauseated, tried to get into his clothes. There was the cab to be fetched, the doctor to be told. . . . Those were his orders, quite calmly from her mother . . . the pain would soon go, she said. Soon go . . . Christ! She was twisting like that on the bed . . . while all you could do was fumble with these lousy buttons . . . Soon go! Yeah! As soon as he could get the cab Minch would go and they'd kick him the hell out while they shot her full of dope and went to work on her . . . to do what? How in Christ's name did they get a baby? Suppose they had to cut? Minch wouldn't know. She'd be out. She'd be taking it alone while they did the deciding . . . they'd decided for him all right! . . . and, as that old guy with the black bag had said, in the last analysis it was in the hands of God . . . which meant that he wouldn't come clean, didn't know. . . . "In the last analysis" . . . Surely God couldn't pull a dirty trick on Minch! She'd taken enough already, been through it ever since D-Day, and without a squawk. . . . But that didn't mean a thing, not after what you'd seen out there . . . He could pull dirty tricks all right . . . good guys crawling along the same hedge with you one minute and blasted to hell the next; kids all bloody on the cobbles in village streets; and women . . . Jesus, some of those women! Either God had quit for duration or it never was in his hands! It was all a bunch of hooey! And anyway he had never heard of Minch . . . She didn't count. She was nobody. She was just his wife. She was just little Minch, the only thing that counted in this whole goddam stinking lousy world. . . . It was up to those doctors to bring her through . . . if only to Christ they knew their job. . . . To hell with being handed a howling brat this side up with care, if . . . Oh God, she's got to come through! . . .

Somehow the essential buttons were forced into their proper holes—enough of them at least to keep the clothes on his body . . . and all he could see was Minchen, her eyes staring, her head turning from side to side on a crumpled pillow . . . and then he was twisting the doorknob, the cat at his heels talking to him and running out with him as he stumbled across the grass to the bicycle shed.

Action is an anodyne. A job to be done, if it takes mind as well as body, can pull a man back from the edge of the pit. But merely to pedal a bicycle, ring a doctor's doorbell, jerk a cabdriver away from his breakfast, hardly qualified either as action or job. They couldn't penetrate Bill's mind. They weren't enough to dull the picture of Minchen in torture that he carried with him down the hill, would carry with him for the rest of his life. He was unaware of the white frost that covered the silent fields, of the cawing of rooks in the high trees, of the wind that beat on his face and made his one hand ice-cold on the handlebar, of the barely stirring streets of Friar's Dene, shop shutters still up, only a hesitant trickle of smoke from the chimneys revealing awareness of the new day. . . . There was only Minch . . . and ether . . . and hands in rubber gloves. . . .

The doctor's bell — once a carillon — made him catch his breath. He hated the woman who answered the door . . . hardened, icy. The doctor was already out, at the hospital; a childbirth: very well, she would phone him there, leave word for him; oh yes, he'd get it . . .

Bill flung on to his bicycle again. . . . The old bitch didn't give a damn. . . . Routine . . . feeding them into the hopper . . . Thank Christ the doctor was crazy about Minch . . . she wouldn't be just another female to go through it. . . .

"Yes, sir! Be up there in a jiffy, sir!" The old cabby wiped his mouth with the back of his hand. His cheek bulged with a lump of breakfast. His eyes were popping. "Bless my 'eart and soul, I'd do anything for Miss Minchen! And don't you take on, sir! She's built right. She won't 'ave no trouble!"

"You're a great guy," said Bill, "but get going, won't you!"

The bicycle again . . . Minch! Minch, are you . . . making it? . . . Built right, she won't 'ave no trouble . . . there might be something there. They could tell about their horses and cattle, these hillbillies. Why not their women? Maybe through the centuries they'd learned a hell of a lot more about it than the lousy doctors! Nice job they did on Jack Hunter's wife . . . let her bleed to death after they got the baby out! Jees, that's a hell of thing to remember right now. . . . But it's a thought! Suppose Minch . . . oh God! Anyway I'll take damn good care to tell that old bird at the hospital that if he needs to give her a transfusion he can have all the blood I've got. . . . These stinking bicycles . . . takes a year to get anywhere! Why in hell didn't I pinch a jeep, anything with cylinders? . . . And that prehistoric cab! Has he even got started yet? . . .

The hill brought the bicycle to a standstill. Bill Thatcher dropped off, began the trudge up, breathing hard. . . . The corner was up there at the top. What a lift she always gave you when you saw her standing there! She made you forget everything else. You just wanted to be with her, to stay with her. . . . She was . . . a need, a part of you, a completion. You didn't have to . . . go on looking any more, wondering, unsatisfied. When you saw her, you knew you'd found the answer. She was . . . repose . . . peace . . . so that you could go on from there, taking her with you . . . no, it wasn't taking her with you, but going together, body and mind. There would never be antagonism or contempt or separation . . . that damned senseless urge to prove that you were always right and she was wrong! Boy, had you seen that! But with Minch? Ah no! She wasn't that kind! You didn't have to try and prove anything to Minch . . . nor she to you. You just looked each other in the eye and that's all there was to it. You knew . . . both of you . . . just as Mother and Dad have always known, or the Major and Mrs. Wainwright . . .

He reached the corner, completely breathless, turned round and looked back down the hill. At the bottom, like a large black beetle, unduly hurrying, was the cab.

"Good guy!" muttered Bill aloud. "He's on the job!" And, watching, he laughed. The old man was bent forward, urging on his angular horse. "If only the nag can take it!"

He mounted the bicycle again. It was at least a relief to know that Minch wouldn't be kept waiting long. . . . Kept waiting long? Extraordinary thought coupled with the vision of those rubber gloves! But now that the moment of ordeal had come, anything — almost — was preferable to another go such as he had tried to help her through. That had seemed to him beyond human endurance, and now, as he rode through the village, the cab coming up behind him, he found himself facing the thought that he had urged upon himself at Weathersford: "If they've got to do a job, let 'em get it over with, and quick!" Minch's face had showed that she too understood that now! Just one other little piece of acquired knowledge that they shared!

He dismounted at the cottage gate, leaned the machine against the fence, stared up at the untelling bedroom window. . . . Would they have to carry her down? How was she going to stand the ride in the cab? Was there any chance that they'd let him go down with her? Or would there be a damned football interference, with the family closing in on Minch so that he wouldn't be alone with her, wouldn't be able to tell her all the things that he had to tell her before . . .

The yellow cat was rubbing at his ankles. For a moment he looked down at it as though he didn't see it. Then suddenly he bent and scooped it up. It began to purr loudly against his chest, and knead his jacket with its paws. Presently Bill rubbed the top of its head with his chin. "Have you been up with her?" he said. "Are you trying to tell me something good . . . or are you just another cat?" And then, at the other end of the village, he caught the *clip-clop* of the old horse beginning to trot again after having rounded the corner. His eyes went up to the bedroom window once more. The moment seemed to have come. . . . He let the cat spill down . . . his stomach shrinking to the size of an apple . . . and suddenly, to his amazement, there stood Minch in the doorway, on her two feet as she had said she was going to be . . .

but ready for the cab . . . ready for the ether and those rubber gloves . . .

The taste of salt was in his mouth. He forced his legs to obey and went to her. "Minch!" he said.

Minchen wasn't breathing very well and she was holding on to the door, but at the sight of what was in Bill's eyes she held out a hand to him, smiled reassuringly. "It's all right, Bill darling!" she said, quickly. "It's all right! . . . And I want you to ride down in the cab with me. You will, won't you?"

Bill swallowed. She knew. She always knew . . . There'd be a chance to try and say things. . . . "Sure you wouldn't rather . . . have your mother?"

Minchen shook her head. "Mother's going to bike down."

Bill breathed again. "That's . . . swell of her! You and I . . ."

There were *Whoa's* outside the gate, and the cab turning round, and Mrs. Wainwright came out behind Minchen; and from the side of the house the Major limped swiftly to the gate and held it open. His smile seemed glued to his face.

Bill held on to Minchen's hand as he walked down the flags with her, his jaw muscles tight.

Jack Wainwright said, "I'm staying here. You don't want a mob . . . Bless you, my dear, and . . . good luck! . . . I'll be down to see you tomorrow, when you're . . . when you're feeling like a queen!"

Minchen released her hand from Bill's, slid an arm round her father's neck and kissed him. "Tomorrow . . . That's right, Dad!" she said. "It'll be wonderful, won't it?"

Jack Wainwright turned to Bill. "You can do something for me!" he said. "You might bring me the good news as soon as you get it. Would you do that?"

The good news . . . the good news . . . Bill looked at him. That grin . . . after all those hours in the workshop! You could hear it creak! . . . Bill nodded. "I'll do that!"

"Good! Take it easy . . . both of you!" Jack Wainwright turned and walked away from them.

"So long, Dad!" said Minchen.

He didn't answer.

Bill pulled the cab door open, savagely. Then he turned and helped Minchen to get in, got in beside her; and as the horse lurched forward its feet were like the poundings of his own heart. They'd be there before they knew it, and then Minch would have to be left alone in that hospital room. . . .

He found her hand. "Everything . . . O.K., honey?"

For a moment Minchen didn't answer. Her hand moved in his. Then she said, "Tell me something, Bill. Were you . . . frightened . . . just a little, on D-Day?"

Bill moistened his lips. Minch wasn't . . . frightened . . . was she? Oh, please . . . no! . . . He laughed. "Just a little? I was scared stiff . . . but it . . . came out all right. I thought afterwards what a fool I was . . ."

Minchen laughed too, in the same way. "Then . . . if I said I was . . . a little nervous, you wouldn't think I was . . . altogether an idiot, would you?"

Bill tightened his grip on her hand, for the moment so overwhelmed that he was unable to offer anything. It was no longer the comparatively simple matter of hiding his own devastating scaredness that kept him dry-mouthed, twitching with nerves, the well-remembered smell of ether at the edge of his nostrils. . . . Somehow he must pull himself together and try and help Minch, kid her out of it, get off the kind of wisecracks that had helped in the dawn before you started moving forward in the fog. . . .

Minchen went right on. "I've never been inside a hospital in all my life and this morning, after you'd gone, I . . . I felt pretty awful. Of course I know that Dr. Merivale will be there, but I . . . I can't help wondering . . ."

Bill found his voice and broke in. "Listen, honey! You've got it all wrong!" he said. "You don't have to do any wondering. They'll have you laughing at yourself two minutes after you get in there. It's just the feeling of going, that's all. I used to be scared to death at the idea of being sent to hospital, but I'm telling you it's the one place I didn't want to leave! You'll see. You won't want to budge. It's the lap of luxury, everybody doing everything for you. I'll have to come and drag you out! And then for the next three weeks — that's usually about the time it lasts — all I shall be hearing from you is 'How perfectly sweet Dr. Ump was!' . . . I tell you frankly, until you've worked that doctor stuff out of your system, life's going to be hell on wheels!" . . . He saw her mouth curl with the ghost of a smile. But it didn't reach her eyes. Why should it with a bunch of drool like that? It wasn't good enough to bring her back from what she was seeing. . . . She was way off. . . . She probably hadn't even heard it. . . . You never did. All the gags were only a nervous noise anyway. . . . You were always alone when you took it. . . . O.K. . . . But not Minch! Not now! . . .

He let go her hand and put his arm round her shoulders and pulled her to him, kissed her, pressed his face against hers. "Minch . . . Minch!"

This time she heard him . . . and came back, at least part of the way. A shiver ran through her body. "Yes, hold me, Bill! I'm . . . I'm cold . . . shaking all over . . . as if I'd never be warm again. It's awfully silly, but I can't help it."

"God!" said Bill. "Don't I know! It's this waiting . . . But you'll be all right when you get there. They'll sock you into bed quick, with hot-water bottles and . . . everything, and old Merivale will be flapping around like a wet hen. You know how crazy he is about you, honey! He's going to be right on the tips of his toes, and you can take it easy and forget all about it, and, before you know, everything will be . . . jake!" Jake! . . . If only to

God you could believe that drip yourself! Merivale with his helpless "last analysis" . . . "Shall I tell you something, honey? It sounded pretty good to me when I heard it this morning, and it confirms everything you've ever said. It was the old cabby still chewing his chow, and he said 'Miss Minchen ain't got to worry! She's built right!' . . . It puts you right in with the sheep and horses and cows!" . . . He laughed, to see if it wouldn't make her smile. . . . "But at that, these country birds know their stuff! Doesn't it make you feel good to know that you're passed by an expert—built right? Why, you'll be going in there and showing them how it's done! You'll be Exhibit A! They'll be publishing photographs of you in all the medical journals—maybe even the farm journals—as the perfect type! You'll be . . ." He choked on it. . . . Such utter drool! If some guy had filled the air with that stuff just before the take-off, he'd have got somebody's boot in his rear end. . . . She seemed suddenly awfully limp . . . and her eyes were half-closed . . . Jees . . . "Minch! . . . Minch, are you . . ."

Minchen pressed her head into his coat. "I'll be . . . all right in a minute. Are we . . . almost there? . . . I . . ."

Bill tightened his aching arm round her. "Minch! . . . Oh Christ! . . . Yes. It's just ahead of us . . . a couple of minutes . . . Can you . . . hang on? You've got to! You must! Do you hear me! Hang on I tell you! Minch! . . . Minch!"

A couple of minutes, or a couple of years while he held her, urged her, commanded her?

And then at last the cab stopped.

Dr. Merivale's smiling face appeared at the door . . . Smiling! Bill gasped, "She's . . ."

But from that moment he didn't count.

A stretcher appeared . . . Minchen was on it, being carried up the steps . . . disappearing inside . . . and Merivale was saying "Easy! Easy! She's all right! There's plenty of time!" He caught

Bill by the arm as he moved to leap up the steps. "Now listen to me, Sergeant Thatcher! I'm giving you orders! Go into town and get yourself a stiff drink, and take your time about it . . . and then come back here . . . and wait! Understand?"

. . . Minch had gone!

The doctor clapped Bill on the shoulder, went up the steps, followed into the hospital.

Minch had gone. . . .

From his box seat the old cabby called down. "It's too early to buy yourself that drink, sir, but if you'd let me drive you to my 'ouse . . ."

. . . Minch had gone! Oh sure, penicillin and sulfa and plasma and ether and every other doggone thing, but they chopped you at the drop of a hat, didn't they? They liked to chop! And they'd got her scared at the very end . . . scared . . .

He groped suddenly with his one good hand and grabbed at the wheel of the cab, retched, and was very sick. . . . Then he began to walk. He didn't know where. It didn't matter. All he could see was Minch . . . on a stretcher.

The old cabby scratched his head and spat. Then he jerked his reins. At this accustomed signal, the horse leaned into the harness and acquired motion, following Bill. But a walk wasn't fast enough. The driver jerked again and said, "Giddup now! Giddup, d'you 'ear?"

. . . There was always a chance for walking cases, but once you were down on a stretcher it wasn't so good. You knew damn well that most of 'em never made it, never even got to a place like Weathersford . . . where they did the final job on you. . . . They'd be undressing her . . . ready to sock the dope in her. Thank God for the dope anyway! She wouldn't have to go on being torn to pieces. . . .

" 'Ow about 'oppin' in, sir? It's only a minute to the 'ouse, and it ain't no manner o'good you takin' it that 'ard!" The lumbering cab was alongside and the old man leaned like a tilted barrel as he talked down. "Y'know, sir, wot the doctor sez was right. I've got a drop of something that'll take proper 'old! And I don't mind saying as 'ow I could do with one meself I could!"

The voice was like a large fly buzzing around his ears . . . and for God's sake what was that damned horse keeping pace with him for? Why couldn't they get the hell away and leave him alone . . . Alone? Minch, I . . .

"I always sez it's worse for the man than wot it is for the woman. She's busy doin' the work, but a man ain't got nothin' to take 'is mind orf of it like, barrin' a drop or two, and I know Miss Minchen wouldn't be the one to grudge you that!"

Perhaps it was the name Minchen that made its way through to Bill. He stopped. The old man promptly leaned back on his reins and the cab stopped too. "You still here?" said Bill. "What do you want?"

The round face split in a broad smile. "Ah! I fancied you wasn't 'earin'. Wot I was tryin' to tell you was that Miss Minchen and I are old friends in a manner o' speakin', and I wouldn't want 'er to 'old it aginst me that I 'adn't done my best for you while she was 'ard at it! I know wot it is, sir! I've 'ad six of 'em meself. Three boys and three girls. The two oldest boys was bumped orf in the last war and two of the girls was blitzed in this one. It's the way it goes, ain't it? But come on now, sir. You 'op in, and when we've 'ad a drop to pull you together, we'll go back to the 'orspital in time to get the good news about Miss Minchen! And it's goin' to be good, you take my word for it! I sez this morning and I sez it again, she's built right!" He nodded several times in complete agreement with himself.

. . . The good news! The Major had said that too, but he was bluffing, or trying to. You knew damn well he didn't believe it. And right now he must be tearing the workshop apart . . . waiting . . . waiting! The Army taught you that all right, but, Jees, it didn't help now. This was waiting for somebody else. It didn't matter what in hell became of you if Minch . . . But she was built right . . . built right the old guy said. . . .

He opened the door of the cab. "O.K.!" he said. "Let's go!" He got in and sat down. It was almost as if she were in his arm again . . . almost . . . but she had gone, and there was only the fragrance she had left behind in it. . . .

He sat hunched down in a corner staring blindly out.

It was barely a minute before the cab rounded a corner and drew up at a neat cottage behind which was a ramshackle stable patched here and there with old gasoline cans.

The stop made Bill look at it. Hadn't he seen this before? . . . Why, yes, on his bike . . . and it was this morning, when Minch . . .

" 'Ere we are, sir!" More like a barrel than ever, the old man stood there holding the door open. "The old woman will be out doin' the marketin', and by the time she comes back we'll both be feelin' better. So let 'er come, I sez!" He gave a fat chuckle.

Bill got out.

The cabby made a lip noise to his horse. It continued alone with the cab to the stable door and stood there with its head drooping. Then Bill was led into a small living room with velvet-seated chairs and lace curtains. The walls were covered with colored magazine pictures of race horses, four-in-hands, the Derby, the Grand National, all fastened up with thumbtacks. And in the middle of one group was a faded photo of a jockey weighing-in. The old man's past was a long way behind him.

He pulled out a bunch of keys and unlocked a sideboard, with a smile at Bill. "A man's got to be boss in 'is own 'ouse!" He laughed and took out a bottle of whisky and two glasses. "It's 'ard to come by these days," he said, "but I wasn't born yesterday, and wot I sez, if Winnie 'as to smoke all them cigars to win the war, 'ow can the likes o' you and me be expected to give all the bloody sweat and tears without a spot from time to time? 'Tain't 'uman!" He poured out two three-finger "spots" and held one out to Bill. " 'Ere, sir! Lower that one down the 'atch! And 'ere's to Miss Minchen's first!"

Bill took the glass. "No!" he said. "Just . . . Minchen . . ." He didn't drink. He stood staring into the tumbler. It seemed to contain nothing but glaring lights and gauzed faces and rubber gloves gathered round an operating table . . . until the whisky began to ripple in his shaking hand. Then he raised the glass to his lips and drank it down as though it were water. "For God's sake," he said, "how long a job is it? How long will she have to be on the table?"

The cabdriver swallowed his mouthful, put his glass down, sucked his mustache, wiped it with the back of his hand. " 'Tain't no good you askin' me that, sir. Times 'ave changed since I was doin' my bit with the wimmen. Now take my oldest, 'im as got 'is at Wipers in the third battalion of the Royal 'Ampshires, and when they marched out only six of 'em left in the whole bleedin' battalion! Take 'im, as I sez. 'E was nigh on twelve hours a'comin', and 'ow the wife come through without any of these Annie's thetics that they give 'em nowadays is a proper mystery! But was she discouraged? Not 'er!" He tilted the bottle over Bill's glass, not bothering to measure this time, not for a man who could drink like that! "The rest of 'em come as easy as lambs in March, no trouble at all, just a few hours from the time she got started like! There was Mary now, 'er as went into service in London, and 'ad four 'erself, and was blitzed as I told you. Well, Mary, she . . ."

. . . Twelve hours? Surely to Christ . . . But that must have been all of fifty years ago. . . . No, he didn't know. None of them knew. It came right back to that futile "last analysis," that confession of damned ignorance. If a woman lived, it was the doctor's skill. . . . Oh yeah! And if she died . . . Just a bunch of guinea pigs, all of them. . . .

Between the table and the door there was an eight-foot walk more or less. For Bill it was a bare three paces each way. He was going up and down it, savagely, closing his ears to the well-meaning rumble of reminiscence. Almost brutally he cut in. "Listen! You might know this one. How about this guy Merivale? Is he halfway a doctor or just another box of pills like most of them in the Army?"

The old man broke off what he was saying and shook his head. His stubby fingers were loading a pipe, the dottle of the previous smoke lying carefully in the heel of one hand. "Ah no, sir! Nothing like that! Dr. Merivale's as good as they come. 'E's kep' up with the times, 'e 'as! They can brag all they want about them London doctors, but I'd put a tidy sum on 'im to beat 'em all! Listen to this one, just as a sample. There was Tom 'Iggins's boy, years back it was, and 'im only a little nipper at the time, when 'e got tossed orf the 'aying machine into the blades. Everybody said as 'ow 'e'd 'ave to lose both 'is legs. Even the Major, and 'im putting up a 'undred pounds for the boy! Likely as not, them busy fellers in London would 'a taken one look and snipped 'em orf. But not Dr. Merivale! 'E sez them legs meant the boy's whole future and 'e went to work. 'E was right, up to Dunkerque that is! The boy got there, but 'e never come back to no future! And then there was Lizzie Turnbull when she got put in the family way, and 'er under age and all . . ."

Bill's march hadn't stopped. And now he was dragging on a cigarette . . . Well, if his own people backed him against London maybe Merivale did know something . . . and the fact that he was crazy about Minch added up too. At least he'd be in there trying, on the tips of his toes . . . And Minch had been so sure right along. She knew it was going to be all right. She had promised . . . and then this guy insists that she's built right, whatever the hell that means! And maybe even her scare only lasted while she was in the cab. . . . She can't be scared now . . . or can she, with the crowd of them working on her? And they might tell her that they'd got to cut! And my God I forgot all about the transfusions! I've got to get back there! She . . .

"Look!" he said. "I . . . I forgot something. They might need me right away. . . . Thanks a lot! You've been damn swell! 'Be seeing you . . ."

His getaway was so quick that the old man was still in the middle of a sentence of protest when Bill was out of the room and into the street.

The cab horse, its legs crossed like a ballet dancer's at rest, inclined one ear in his direction, as though the sound of feet indicated more work.

But Bill was hurrying. . . . There had been just that one thing he could do for Minch, and he had flopped! The lug! The so-and-so! And just about now she might be needing all the blood he could give her! Suppose they were outside looking for him . . . and Minch . . .

He broke into a run.

But the hospital steps were empty when he arrived there.

Nevertheless he went through the door like a rocket, expecting anything. . . .

The only live person around was a female receptionist sitting tranquilly at a large desk. Still on the run, he made for her.

With apparent reluctance her head came up from the papers at which she was working. "Yes?" she said. "Is there anything . . . ?"

"Yes! Has Dr. Merivale sent down for me?"

The female raised an eyebrow. "Really, I . . . Why should he? Does he know who you are?"

It was like a douche of cold water in the face. Bill gasped. "Listen, you . . ." Then he caught himself, but his voice was saw-edged. "My name's Willard Thatcher and at the moment my wife is having a child under the professional care of Dr. Merivale. Thatcher, I said. T-H-A-T-C-H-E-R. Get it?"

The becapped female tossed her head. "Thank you so much

for spelling it!" she said. "The pronunciation was a little . . . strange. The . . . er . . . waiting room is over there." She pointed with a languid pencil. "You will be informed as soon as she leaves the delivery room." She went back to her papers.

Behind his back, Bill's one hand was clenched. It wasn't that she was simply another hospital attendant — they were all carved out of blocks of ice, utterly without bowels — but this one hated his guts . . . It would have been a pleasure to tell her, handsomely, that he returned the compliment . . . and that would help Minch a lot! . . .

He swallowed his rage, took another breath. "Look," he said, "I'm . . . sorry! I asked for it. I guess I was . . . rude. I apologize . . . Couldn't we get off on the right foot together?"

This time the faintest curl of the lip indicated that she knew she had put him in his place. V for Victory! But she enjoyed rubbing it in. "Oh . . . quite all right," she said. "One does have to meet all kinds of people at this desk!"

"O.K.!" said Bill. "You win. But would you do something for me . . . that is . . . would it be too much trouble for you to send a message to Dr. Merivale? I meant to tell him this morning when my wife was brought in here, but I didn't have a chance. Things were sort of jumbled. . . . It's that if he needs to give her a blood transfusion, he'll find me down here all ready. . . . It would be swell of you if you would do that!"

The new approach worked. She was evidently incapable of perceiving sarcasm. She thawed sufficiently to say, "Very well, Mr. Thatcher. Or shouldn't I say Sergeant Thatcher? . . . I'll see that the doctor receives your message at the proper time!"

"Thanks!" said Bill. "It means a hell of a lot to me. I . . ."

What did she care? He turned, and crossed the shiny parquet floor in the direction given by the female pencil, and, with a cold feeling in his stomach, pushed open the waiting-room door . . .

The room was empty. Visiting hours were in the afternoon.

But to Bill it was full. . . . It reeked of a million hours of wait-

The girl's eyes didn't flinch. "Good heavens!" she said. "You really are in a dither, aren't you? But I give you my solemn word that she's just as comfortable as she can be at the moment, and that in a few days she ought to be as right as rain! . . . Now do you feel better?"

Better! . . . He gave a queer laugh. What a word now that there was Minchen again! She put it all back in its place . . . everything there was! It was worth going on now. . . . You could try. . . . You could do your damnedest . . . with Minch, for Minch . . . and she was waiting for him . . .

"Come on!" he said. "Let's go!"

. . . There were stairs and corridors and rubber-wheeled trays rolling and the smell that you always got . . . but Minch was all right! The job was all over! . . . The job . . . and it wasn't a girl! This kid had said it was a boy! . . . Judas . . . a boy! . . . Well, anyway, another Thatcher at Dartmouth . . . and then Minch and I will be told what he wants to do . . . and we'll both take it, and like it . . . only, will we have to see to it, by God, that he keeps the use of both his hands . . . and legs and . . .

"This is her room," said the nurse, stopping. "Just a moment and I'll see if . . ." She opened the door and disappeared.

Bill kept his eyes on the door. . . . *She's going to be as right as rain* . . . as right as . . .

He had only said it four times when the girl came out and nodded. "You can go in!" she said.

It was like leaving one world behind and going into another. . . . Her hair was black on the pillow . . . once more . . . and even if her eyes were closed she was . . . waiting for him.

In a voice that didn't seem to work Bill said, "Hi!"

It was a long way off, but Minchen heard it. Her eyes opened. . . . He was there . . . close to her. "Hullo . . . darling!"

That was all she said. The rest was in her eyes. . . .

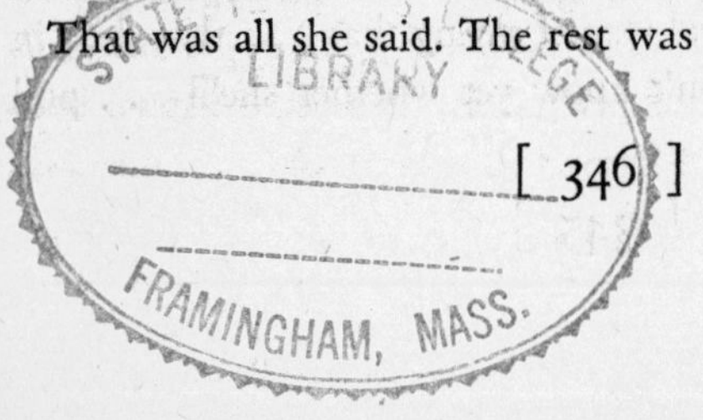